A BAD WAY TO START THE DAY

There was a sharp knock on the door.

"Save your knuckles, I'm coming."

When I pulled open the door, I was eyeball-to-eyeball with a rent-a-cop decked out in a black silk uniform. He was leprosy-pale and his eyes were two piss holes in a snowbank. On his hip was the biggest frump I'd ever seen.

"You Swain?" he asked, and there was a definite feeling of frenzy behind his voice.

"You want an answer, cowboy? Okay. Hit the streets." I swung the door closed in his face. I didn't get three steps before I heard the world coming to an end behind me. I swung around and my front door was gone, blown to toothpicks.

He stepped through the blown-out place, never taking those eyes off me. "Swain," he rasped. "ARE YOU SWAIN?"

"Yeah," I shrugged. "I guess you win the Kewpie doll."

He sighed, deeply, gratefully, then raised his frump to the level of my head. Without another word, he clicked the hammer back . . .

Bantam Books by Mike McQuay

MATHEW SWAIN: HOT TIME IN OLD TOWN
MATHEW SWAIN: WHEN TROUBLE BECKONS

MATHEW SWAIN

WHEN TROUBLE BECKONS

Mike McQuay

BANTAM BOOKS
TORONTO · NEW YORK · LONDON · SYDNEY

MATHEW SWAIN: WHEN TROUBLE BECKONS

A Bantam Book / November 1981

ISBN   0-553-20041-0

Published simultaneously in the United States and Canada

Bantam Books are published by Bantam Books, Inc. Its trademark,
consisting of the words "Bantam Books" and the portrayal of a
rooster, is Registered in U.S. Patent and Trademark Office and in
other countries. Marca Registrada. Bantam Books, Inc., 666 Fifth
Avenue, New York, New York 10103.

PRINTED IN THE UNITED STATES OF AMERICA

0 9 8 7 6 5 4 3 2 1

*This entire series is dedicated
to the memory of Raymond Chandler,
who understood.*

1

No matter what the hell we think, life works on its own level. We can charge around like gooney birds, pulling out our hair and wanting things to be just the way we like them to be. But it doesn't matter. Life just rolls along like a turbine in a waterfall, spinning out its cycle, charging its engines the only way it knows how, making chumps out of every one of us. They call it justice, and somewhere in there I'm sure that's exactly what it is. Funny thing, justice. Funny like a kick in the balls, or like the long shot coming in on the only time in your life that you've ever bet with the odds. It's funny like being tickled to death is funny. When you try and separate it all out, program it all into the proper relays, the rights and the wrongs, it sneaks up behind you and starts tickling. People go—and have gone—crazy trying to work it all out. And being crazy, I'm told, is a counterproductive way of dealing with reality. As for me—I'm not ticklish.

I go with the flow.

So, I sat at my real wood desk, still feeling my head bruise from the Grover thing, and buttoned down the best part of a fiver of my old friend Black Jack. Things were slow as a muddy racetrack, and I felt like I had to keep moving my legs so I wouldn't grow roots.

My eyes drifted to my backward name through the frosted glass of my walk-up office door. People who cared to come all the way up to my cubbyhole would find the place in the universe that was rented monthly by one "Mathew Swain, Confidential Investigations," but to me inside, I was looking at the door of niawS wehtaM. And judging by the size of his office, he was doing one hell of a lot better than I was.

Turning from wehtaM's door, I looked out a window so thick with dust that I could have grown tomatoes on it. The

1

smog cover was low that day, which meant humidity, which meant sweat, which meant more booze to replenish lost fluids.

Just like yesterday.

Just like the day before.

I really needed to work. I needed to work like pigeons need to sit on the roof of the federal building.

I drank from a chipped glass and watched the dying city. In the chess game of life, the place had lost its queen and was simply playing out the remaining moves to checkmate. It stank on the outside, and it stank on the inside. An occasional meat machine would dip, red- and white-crossed efficiency, out of the smog bank and swoop vulturelike to the decaying streets below to acid-bubble away some poor unfortunate who was inconsiderate enough to die on the cracked, concrete bankruptcy. I toasted each one as it went down, my never-ending wake for an unstoppable parade.

Cheers.

My vis buzzed, and I almost didn't answer it. The only people who focused me anymore were bill collectors or Foley from Continental Insurance wondering why I never finished with his life policy follow-ups. I never finished them because I never started them. It was a logical progression.

Swiveling my spring-creaking chair back around to the business end of my desk, I reached out and juiced the wall screen into fuzzy focus. The eternal optimist. What greeted me was blond hair and devil eyes and lips that pouted like a four-year-old's with a broken toy. It was Ginny Teal, late of Planet Earth, temporarily recuperating from sins past in her orbiting summer home. She was a rich girl, and rich girls did things like that.

"Business?" she asked when her form took solid hold.

"Drowning in it," I replied, and held my shot glass up to camera range. "You can talk in front of my friend, though. He's real understanding."

Ginny smiled, but it wasn't a real smile. "I thought you were coming up to see me," she said, reminding me of a hasty promise I had made two weeks before when I'd put her on the shuttle.

I wanted to go to the moon just about as bad as a jeweler wants to appraise rhinestones. "Yeah," I said, sipping my whisky like a country gentleman. "I guess I've been . . . tied up."

2

"Well, why don't you get untied," she replied, and her voice was flat, lifeless. This wasn't Ginny at all. I couldn't quite put my finger on it. She was there, yet she wasn't there. "I'm going to hold you to your promise."

I got up and moved away from the desk, my vis cam following my actions like a mongoose with a cobra. I turned to face the cam's angry red eye. "I'll tell you the truth, lover. I just don't have the cash." That was true enough, but I've found in this world that people are usually able to do just what they want to do.

She licked dry lips. Her eyes were afraid, darting. "I've booked you a flight this afternoon. Already paid for."

Ginny knew that I didn't work that way. Something was wrong here. I returned to the desk and poured myself a stiff one. "Are you okay?" I asked.

"Sure, street person," she answered. "I'm fine. Just a bit . . . lonely."

I creaked back into my chair and tried to picture Ginny lonely. Couldn't. Staring hard at her projection, I said, "Spoke to my mother last week. She sends you her best."

She seemed to relax then, like a spring uncoiling. Her smile was more relief than happiness. "Well, tell her hello for me."

That iced it. My mother had been dead for as many years as I had been alive and Ginny knew it. Something *was* wrong. Something was as wrong as it could be. I wiped a wet palm across my one-piece and sighed. "You know, I haven't had a vacation in years. Do they drink up in outer space?"

"At my place they do," she said, and almost looked like her old self. "You'll come?"

"Only if you ask me."

"I'm asking."

"I'm coming. What time is my flight?"

"Four," she replied, and held up three fingers, her eyes drifting down to them.

I tried to think of something else to say, something that would somehow clear it all up, but Ginny was obviously afraid to talk over the airwaves; and whatever her problem was, I didn't want to make it worse.

I also held up three fingers. "Four sounds great," I said. "Stock the liquor cabinet, chill some ice, and I'll be there before it freezes."

3

She took a deep breath, let it out. "Thanks, Matt," she said. "I'll see you in a few days." Her eyes were glazing over again, as if maybe she had to go back to whatever deep cave she had just crawled out of. I didn't like it.

"Bye bye, gorgeous."

"Hurry," she said, and blanked immediately. The way she said that one word chilled me like a freon highball. I just sat there, my neck hairs prickling, staring at an empty wall. The call had caught me off guard. Trouble is something you look for wrapped in all packages except familiar ones.

Leaning over the desk, I spoke to the vis. "Time?"

12:03 flashed on the screen. I'd have to hurry to make a three o'clock flight. Screwing Black Jack's head back on, I stood up and moved to the door. Opening the thing, I looked back once before heading into wehtaM's domain. The office rent would be due in a few days, but what the hell. I was about to practice upward mobility in its purest sense, and if they wanted their money, they'd just have to find me.

I tried to consign Ginny's call to the back burners of my mind. She seemed to be in real trouble, and I was days away from helping her in an alien atmosphere with absolutely no information to go on. It almost made me want to work on the Continental Insurance stuff.

I left the hot office and went out into the hot world. The steps down were steep, and dirty handprints covered the walls on both sides because there wasn't any banister. A space jockey lay sprawled on the steps near the street-side door, his heavy-lidded gaze totally involved in the dirty walls. You could always tell when it was near the first of the month; the drug welfare rations were doled out then, and everyone in the decay moved in slow motion for a week or two.

After some coaxing and a few well-placed kicks, Mr. Lethargy drew up his legs, and I moved out into the smoglight. My bullet sat, unharmed, by the crumbling curb, and I thanked my lucky stars and the drug handouts for the third straight day without vandalism.

Hatching the door, I grunted into the bullet and keyed the magnetic whine. Feeling the thing rise up off the broken street, I hummed it homeward. I lived in the decay—partly from choice, partly from circumstance. Most of my work was here, and a person needs to be close to his work. It wasn't as simple as that, though. I didn't trust the nice end of town.

The people there could do you in with a smile. I liked to see where the knife was coming from.

It was hot, so most everyone was off the pitted streets. The fun would start later, after the sun kissed the city goodnight. I hummed at a decent clip along Tremaine, stopping only long enough to draw what little cash I had out of the steel-cocooned drive-up bank on Harvey. As I rode, the sepulchured concrete tombstones sprouted all around me, fifty stories high, and the sky pressed low, suffocating. It was a mammoth terrarium with cement flowers, and I was a June bug getting ready to fly.

And fly I would. All was not kosher in outer space, and I was supposed to come straighten it out. Great. And the postcards had always looked so appealing. I figured that I could be about as useful in orbit as a one-legged runner in the Boston Marathon, but I gave up trying to figure things long ago.

I just flow, remember?

I lived in a converted basement, no more than a K from the office. My building had the name ETERNITY etched in cement above the big front door, but it lied. ETERNITY was past ready for the old tenement's graveyard, which spoke volumes about the human animal's ability to appreciate absolutes. But I didn't mind. The price was right; the location was good; the roof didn't leak; and sometimes, when the gods were willing, I even had hot water. Well, semi-hot.

Hand-printing through my door, I caught Matilda in the garbage can, rooting around.

"What do you think you're doing, black cat?"

She sprang from the can and charged around the kitchen like a tornado on a leash for a minute, then, unexpectedly disappeared under the couch. Shaking my head at the bits of torn garbage on the floor, I moved into the room. In a flash, Matilda was out from under the sofa, jumping at my foot as if it were the biggest mouse in the history of mice. She rolled on her back, going at it with her claws.

"Don't you ever give it a rest?" I asked her, trying to shuffle past.

She looked up at me with those black-dotted yellow eyes, blinked once, and sank her teeth into the meat of my leg.

"Damn it!" I tried to shake her loose, but she thought I was finally playing the game and held on happily for dear

5

life. "Shoo." I kicked out again and she lost her hold, slipping across the floor. With that, she ducked back quickly under the couch before I could retaliate.

"Some gratitude," I muttered, and liked it so much I said it louder. "Some gratitude!"

Brick support-pillars ran in double rows along the length of my flat. I moved past them, back to what I called my bedroom, but what is actually the back part of my living room/kitchen/den. I did have a free-standing closet back there, and from the top of it, I got down my cardboard and leatherette suitcase. It wasn't much, but then again, I didn't need much. I hadn't traveled out of the city in years.

"I'm going to fix you good," I called to the still-hiding cat. "You know my Aunt Gertrude? Yeah, that's where you're going for a while." I opened the case onto my bed and started rooting through the drawers of my dresser. I got out a lot of socks and underwear, and began stuffing them in the case. Somehow, it seemed like I'd need a lot of socks and underwear up in space. Then again, maybe I just wasn't thinking straight.

"Do you remember Tunky?" I called. "That gray and white tom that lives with my Aunt Gertrude?" Turning around to look back through the rooms, I could see her little head barely peeking out from under. "Mean son of a bitch. You're going to have to earn your place over there. Some gratitude," I said again.

Going to the closet, I pulled out every clean one-piece in there, plus a couple of dress waistcoats that weren't frayed too badly, and an extra pair of calf boots. But I had put so much underwear in the suitcase that I didn't have room for any real clothes. So I pulled some out to get the other stuff in. All the while, my mind kept flashing to the faraway look in Ginny's eyes. I wouldn't forget that look. It would follow me around like a cheap-booze hangover.

I had just finished packing when there was a sharp knock on the door. I stopped and looked at it for a minute. My rent was paid up and my friends didn't come to this end of town. There was another knock.

"Save your knuckles, I'm coming." I snapped the suitcase closed and moved to the door. When I pulled it open, I was standing eyeball to eyeball with a Fancy Dan with permit. He was decked out in a black silk uniform with big brass buttons and patent leather doodads all over. His face was all bone, with sagging skin like maybe he was melting. He was leprosy-pale and his eyes were two piss holes in a snowbank. On his hip he wore the biggest frump I'd ever seen; it hung almost all the way down to his knees.

"You Swain?" he asked, and there was a note of urgency in his tone. There was something about him that I couldn't quite touch.

I hate rent cops like turkeys hate Thanksgiving. "Who wants to know?"

"Just answer the question," he said, and there was a definite feeling of frenzy behind his voice. A lack of control.

I didn't have time to be messing with a crazy Dan. "You want an answer, cowboy? Okay. Hit the streets." I swung the door closed in his face and turned to walk back into the living room. I didn't get three steps before I heard the world coming to an end behind me.

I swung around and my front door was gone, blown to toothpicks by the Dan's frump. He stood there, gun still drawn, on the other side of the large, char-blackened, still smoking hole that used to keep punks like him out.

"You Swain?" he asked again. And I knew what had bothered me about him. His eyes had the same look that I'd seen in Ginny's.

Raising my hands, I stepped back a pace or two. "Since you put it that way, come on in and make yourself at home."

He stepped through the blown-out place, never taking those eyes from me. His mouth worked furiously, chewing air. His hollow eyes were caving back into a mind that was a bottomless pit. "Swain," he rasped, and his voice dripped sheer terror. "ARE YOU SWAIN?"

"Yeah," I shrugged. "I guess you win the kewpie doll."

He sighed deeply, gratefully, and the tension seemed to ooze out of him like lube out of a grease gun. He took a satisfied, easy breath, then raised his frump to the level of my head. Without another word, he clicked back the hammer on the boxy thing.

It was then that Matilda decided she was ready for round two of our earlier skirmish. She raced out from under the couch and pounced on the Dan's leg the way she'd done with me. He jumped, screaming. I went for his arm, hitting him as

7

the frump went off with a whoosh. We twisted wildly, and the charge sent Matilda's couch to never-never land. Off-balance, we crashed to the floor amidst a blizzard of foam rubber and naugahyde.

The gun skittered away from us, and Matilda playfully gave chase, batting at it with her front paws. I came down on top of the guy, bashing his face with a good forty-pound weight advantage. Even at that, it took a hell of a long time to whip the fight out of him. But when it went, it went all at once. Like turning off a light bulb.

He slumped beneath me, blubbering through a bloody face. His head moved back and forth, eyes distant and life-less. He was mumbling to himself, indistinct, disjointed words.

"What do you want, cowboy?" I screamed into his face, as I straddled his chest.

"Beckon," he said, mouth sputtering red, body jerking spasmodically.

I sighed. "God, a fruitcake." I took his face in my hands and tried to connect up with those eyes. I may as well have been trying to get in touch with a glacier. "Come on," I said, grabbing him by the ears. "Talk to me."

"Beckon," he said again.

"Never mind beckon. Who sent you here? You sure as hell didn't think of it all by yourself." There was nothing there, a blank slate. I let his head drop back to the floor and climbed off him. Maybe he was in shock. I sloshed through ankle-deep sofa stuffing to the tap and drew a glass of water to splash on him.

Walking back, I scooted Matilda off his frump. Picking the thing up, I put the safety back on. "Nasty things," I told him. "You shouldn't be playing . . ."

He was putting something in his mouth. I ran to him and tried to get a finger in his throat, but he was already gagging, his sunken eyes bulging. I stood there, helpless, watching his life leak away. Seconds later he was dead. Stone dead.

Looking down, I stared at him dumbly. An hour before, I couldn't have paid anybody to buzz my vis, and now people were in here killing themselves over me. What a waste.

"Damn you," I said. "Damn you for dying."

Things were getting desperately out of focus here. I needed that punk and I needed him alive. Alive he was answers; dead he was just another question in a world full of questions.

"Time," I said, and the tension inside of me came out in my voice.

My tiny living-room vis bleeped out 1:15. I wished that I had the time to find out more about the Dan, but it just wasn't in the cards. Bending down, I quickly went through his pockets, but wasn't surprised when I found nothing but lint.

Grabbing him under his shoulders, I dragged him back out through the open place, then up the stairwell to street level. The super was going to charge me plenty for fixing that door, but it couldn't be helped. There were several people out on the streets, but in my neighborhood, minding one's own business is a virtue much prized.

I no sooner got him out there than a meat machine keyed in on his drop in body temperature, and drifted out of the clouds to take him away. The thing floated down, its bulbous underbelly half on the street, half on the curb. The black-garbed attendants hurried over with their stainless steel pallet. This was the bad end of town. There would be no police investigation here. No one could afford them.

They loaded the dead hulk onto the pallet and hefted him up. The attendant facing me nodded quickly, then winked. I smiled an automatic smile in return, the kind of smile you put on for the vis.

They carried him to the back of the machine, hooked a flanged edge of the stretcher onto the back of the acid pit, then raised the other end. My assailant slid quickly down the slick surface and disappeared into the all-consuming maw of bubble-crackling evaporation. A dead end with the emphasis on the dead.

Beckon, he had said to me. *Beckon*.

Beckon.

2

I left Matilda and my bullet at Aunt Gertrude's, and took a heli-bus to the spaceport. We floated lazily, at bird level, above the decay, and I watched it all unwind beneath me like a rotting table of food in an old Dutch painting. All things being equal, it wasn't much of a city, I guess. Just a failing shot at civilization marring the symmetry of the Texas landscape. But it was *my* city. I'd miss it.

Thoughts of that dead punk kept pushing into my head. I couldn't get away from him. I kept seeing his face and the fear that stuffed it full. That face gnawed at me like a dermestid beetle on a dead cow. Thinking about it, I felt as if killing me was probably the single most important thing in the punk's life and, unable to accomplish it, he had to die himself. Who could hate me that bad? Who could hate anyone that bad? I didn't want to connect the punk up with Ginny, but my brain wouldn't stop doing that either. Logically it could all have just been coincidence. Yeah. Logically, things that are heavier than air shouldn't be able to fly either.

The ride was over before I knew it. We floated down to the yellow bull's-eye helipad on the port grounds. Climbing down the short ramp, I could see our tri-engined gouger waiting malevolently in the launch bay to whisk me away in the face of logic. It had a rusty, fused metallic color, and bright white vapor snorted continuously from bleed-off valves at the base of the nose. It looked old the way an elephant looks old. This horrible cry-baby whine squeezed from its innards from time to time, calling to me like a hound dog calls to a treed coon.

After we unloaded, the bus up and floated over to the ship to load our baggage into the hold. A moving sidewalk was taking my fellow rocket rangers from the pad to the

10

terminal fifty meters away, but I opted to walk and get my last taste of stale air.

The terminal was a tangle of confusion. It was filled to distraction with people unable to get what they wanted when they wanted it. Professional Spacers mostly, they looked like they were all coming from or going to the aluminum and titanium mines on the moon. Space pros were a strange breed. Like three-time losers, they enjoyed the confinement. They dressed bad, talked bad, drank bad, doped bad, and loved trouble in small places. It takes a certain type of person to hate, and then revel in the proximity of hatred. Spacers died young, and rarely from natural causes.

It looked as if all systems in the terminal had once been automated, but given the ravages of time, certain of those functions had broken down beyond repair or simply proved to be worthless. So, the running of the mechanical functions of the place was a strange combination of humans and machines working at seemingly cross purposes to one another. The science of synoetics tells us that the combination of a human with machine parts can equal a whole greater than the sum of its parts. Don't believe it.

The sound in there was heavy as Jovian pig iron, and there was an all-pervading odor of burning circuitry. The air coolers had all broken down, but so many angry arms were waving all around that there was actually quite a pleasant breeze drifting through the room.

Large readout boards located at ceiling level juiced a continual barrage of comings and goings, plus hiring and firings on the mine sights. When openings were posted for miners, everyone in the terminal rushed to the reservation counters and tried to hire on, getting a ticket at the same time. Hirings were confirmed immediately from the mining sites by satellite hookup, and the worker would take his ticket and wait for his flight. Unfortunately, things changed quickly on the lunar surface, what with crumbling shafts, or air leaks, or wildcat strikes, or new trade regs, or multi-national border wars; and companies that were hiring one minute were firing the next. As I lined up at the counter to get my ticket, I heard the guy in front of me say that he had lost three jobs already that day and was trying to hire in to number four. He didn't seem to mind, so I figured that I shouldn't either. I lit a cig and waited my turn.

11

It was two-thirty before I got up to the counter. I'd burned both a pack of cigs and the best part of my already shaky disposition just waiting. A woman in her mid-twenties was working reservations in my line. She wore a cheap burlap toga that was ripped and disheveled from countless run-ins with countless spacer paws. Her green lipstick and matching eye tone were smeared all over her peaches-and-cream face, and she had a small cut under her right eye. A black machine was protectively clutched under her right arm. It blinked and giggled and every once in a while, in a hard Southern drawl, it would say, "Feed me, Florie. Feed me."

A freshly cut red rose sat forlornly in a plastic vase on the shiny steel counter. I leaned up close to smell it. As I did, the woman jumped back, petrified. She hugged the box to her bosom.

"Florie?" the box said. "Florie?"

"Black line," she said through clenched teeth.

I looked at her. "What?"

"Black line. Behind the black line." She was nearly hysterical.

I glanced around. The guy behind me was glaring and pointing down near my feet. A thin black line was painted across the floor in front of the counter. I was standing on it.

"Florie?"

"Sorry," I said, and stepped back a pace. "I didn't know."

"Florie?"

"It's all right," the woman told the box. She sighed audibly and stepped back up to the counter.

"Feed me, Florie. Feed me."

Florie looked at her machine for a few seconds, turning it this way and that in her hands. Then she began banging it viciously. It put up a horrible squawk for a time, then groaned. "Thanks," it said.

"What's wrong with your friend?" I asked her. The thing began coughing the way I do when I've had too many fags in too short a time.

Florie shrugged. "Short in his power train. Got to tap him just right to get the juice going good. Say, what do you want anyway?"

"Name's Swain. I've got a reservation."

12

"Could you spell your last name please?" the box asked me officiously.

"I was talking to the young lady," I told it.

"Florie . . ."

Florie looked impatient. "Max wants you to spell your last name," she said. "And sir, no smoking is allowed in the terminal area."

I took the fag from between my lips and dropped it on the black line. "Swain," I said. "S-W-A-I-N. There, do I win the spelling bee?"

Max coughed. "Do you have a reservation?"

I looked at the woman. "I already told you that."

She wagged a hand in front of her face and pointed to the box.

I leaned over the counter, being careful not to step over the black line. Florie held Max up near my face. "I have a reservation," I whispered.

"In what name?" Max asked me.

I looked at Florie. Her face was sand on the beach. "Swain," I said.

"Spell that please."

I looked at Florie again, and understood why she was in such bad shape. She was tensed, ready to spring at even the thought of a punch being thrown. I took a deep breath. "S-W-A-I-N."

Max bleeped a few times, then said, "Florie, come here."

Florie bent down hesitantly, with her face near Max's speaker grill. Her eyes kept drifting fearfully in my direction. She stood up straight and stepped back a pace. "Max says that you have no reservation. He says that you had a reservation, but that it's been canceled."

I couldn't keep the anger back much longer; it was trying to bubble out, like milk burning in a pan. I didn't have time for this. "Who canceled it?"

We both looked at Max. He was whining. Florie bent her head down again and flinched when he talked to her. She straightened. "You were canceled by satellite control from Freefall City."

"And who might that be?"

"Anyone who has access to their transmission equipment," Florie answered, ready to duck.

13

I put my hands on the counter. "What we're going to do here is reserve me all over again. All right?"

Florie hesitated, then said, "Maybe if we rechecked the source . . ."

"FLORIE!" the machine said angrily.

She snapped to attention. "I'm sorry, sir. Your reservation has been canceled. There's no more room on the flight. Next." She tensed, waiting for me to grab at her.

Instead, I reached out and snatched Max from her hand. Her eyes grew wide in horror.

"Florie!" the thing called. "Get the law."

"Don't," I warned, and grabbed the vase with the rose off the counter top. Tipping it threateningly close to Max's control circuits, I brought the vase water right up to the lip.

"Florie!"

"Another word, small change, and I dump the water from this thing all over you." Florie's look of fear slowly melted into something else, something a lot more pleasant.

The machine gulped audibly. "What do you want?" it choked out.

"I want my reservation back," I replied.

"Okay. Okay." It bleeped and flashed for a few seconds. "It's done."

"Don't I get a ticket?"

"Florie," Max said. "Get the gentleman a ticket."

"With pleasure," Florie smiled, and began typing beneath the counter. She clacked for a minute, then happily ripped the ticket out of the machine and handed it to me. "Here you are, sir. And have a pleasant flight."

I took the ticket and returned Max to her. "Here's your box, miss. I hope I didn't break it."

As soon as Max was back in Florie's grasp, he started up again. "Get the law, Florie. Get the law."

She winked at me. "I can't seem to see any, Max. They must all be on coffee break."

"Find them!"

"You know I can't leave my post." She inclined her head toward her left shoulder. I followed the motion and my eyes grabbed the doorway that said: TO ALL FLIGHTS. I nodded and moved away from the counter.

"Sound the alarm," Max was saying.

14

"Must be shorted," she answered. "I can't seem to get it working. Next."

Pushing through the crowds, I ducked into the loading tunnel. Someone was going to some trouble to keep me away from Freefall City. And now I had three long days to wonder why.

3

The trip up was awful. Going to the moon is probably a lot like picnicking in a wind tunnel—a new experience, but you're anxious to get to the apple pie so you can go home. I was already worried about Ginny, and the claustrophobic atmosphere of the gouger just made it worse. On top of that, they didn't allow cigs, and the only kind of booze they had was champagne. Champagne, for God's sake. Those bubbles gave me so much gas that I kept floating out of my seat.

We came down in a place called Lunar Depot One, but everyone called it Loonie One. It was a huge complex, consisting of a series of domes formed of clear tetrahedral segments. Looking up, I could see black night and bright white and blue-white stars shining like mirrors in the sun. The moon was nongovernmental, a corporate playground for whatever mining companies had the resources to get up there and the military power to hold their claims. Each mining company had its own army to defend it, and holdings apparently changed hands through skirmishes more often than a hooker changes her pants.

They gave us heavy shoe weights when we got off the ship, and those took some getting used to. Trying to walk in them was like sloshing through knee-deep yellow mud. Everything was slideways, so a lot of cumbersome maneuvering was unnecessary. I was directed down a long tunnel that pulsed neon blue along its length in spider-web patterns before terminating at the baggage claim area. I was I.D.'d and hand-printed for my bag, and then turned loose on my own.

I wanted Ginny to be there to meet me. I wanted her to say that everything was all right and let's go have a drink and laugh about it. But that didn't happen. She wasn't there, and I was sloshing through yellow mud after having spent three

16

days in a flying can floating out of my seat with champagne gas. I had a bookmaker friend once who said that no matter how bad things got, you could always take heart in the fact that they could be worse. I hoped he was wrong.

Grabbing my suitcase, I slid down another tunnel, exiting in the main bubble. The place was jammed with Spacers, many in uniform. They represented a lot of different countries, and languages bounced in and out of earshot like hailstones on a tin roof. They pushed their way in groups through the chamber. The air crackled with the sound of an electrical storm, for Spacers yelled and warbled at the peak of their form like inmates in the monkey house. They pressed in around me like a fleshy vise, and I nearly drowned in the smells of ozone and sweat.

Occasional fights broke out between different groups, but they all subsided quickly, owing to the high-riding defensive platforms that stood at regular intervals all around the bubble. These were all manned by white-garbed andies that turned multi-barreled air guns on any altercation that lasted for over a minute or so. The guns fired trank gas that anesthetized the room by quadrants. The folks who ran Loonie One had no desire to mess up their business by hurting any of the customers, so they used the gas. But, just to make it memorable, they put a kicker in the juice that left the drugged parties with the grandaddy of all hangovers when they woke hours later. Like putting alcohol on a cut, the gas did a humanitarian service but left a sting.

I still kept hoping that Ginny would show up. I wandered around for a while, taking it all in and giving her a chance to get me off the hook, but eventually I came to decide that I was going to have to get myself over to Freefall City.

Loonie One was beginning to get to me. There were too many mercenaries moving around. They all wore gray exoskeletons that could pressurize for vacuum, and each had a red circle tattooed in the middle of his forehead. They all carried big, ugly laser rifles strapped to their backs, and the lunar equivalent of a frump hung down from their belts. They were multilingual and worked for anyone who could stuff enough scratch into the money pouches strapped to their thighs. They were all punks. Fancy Dans in spacesuits.

I had to change my money if I was going to get along up

there. I walked around until I found a small alcove with a horseshoe ring of tellers. Above each barred cage was a sign that said CURRENCY EXCHANGE in twenty-seven different languages. The going currency up there was plastic, the scarcest and most valuable commodity they could think of. I gave them my long green and they gave me various sizes and colors of plastic in return, along with a small pouch to carry them in.

Moving out of the alcove, I took the slideway to the goods-and-services bubble. There were stores and bars and restaurants displaying fake food samples in glassed-in cases in front. They were all long and narrow and crammed side by side along the moving walk. All of them were full, packed solid, with long lines waiting to get in. Judging by the crowds swarming the bars, I wished I had the liquor franchise up there. People on Loonie One had to drink a lot. With no smoking allowed in the terminal, all those nice folks had to have something to do with their hands. I was getting a little cig-crazy myself.

Finally, I found what I had been looking for. On a bare wall across from the shops, a whole line of people stood talking or watching tiny vis screens set in the wall itself. They were bored and fidgety and watched the passing parade like a pickpocket watching a rich boy. This had to be the cab stand. A man sat at a small desk at the head of the line. I jumped off the slide and approached the desk.

He didn't look up at me until I got close. He was busy cutting a wart off his thumb with a razor blade. He had a face that was nearly triangular with the big part on the bottom, as if everything had drained from his head and settled in his chin. His features were set in a classic pose of studious indifference, like the Sphinx eternally keeping watch over the shifting sands of Egypt. As soon as I got up to him, he began talking in a monotone. The language or languages made no sense to me, and I tried to tell him so, but he just kept blabbing away. This went on for a time until he suddenly very plainly said, ''What language do you speak?''

''English,'' I said quickly. ''I didn't know what the . . .''

''Hey, English!'' he yelled, cutting me off.

A woman four spaces down the line slid off a metal stool and came over to me. She had short copper-colored hair, and was small without appearing small. She had a face that told me she had been all the way down the road and back, but somehow, on her, it was appealing. She was chewing snuff and carried a small tin can around that she would stop and spit into from time to time. Her faded tan one-piece had a tiny brown stain lacing its front.

"So, you need a lift?" she asked, giving me the once over. She had cat eyes, one gray and one green. I couldn't peg her accent, which was usually the sign of someone who had spent a great deal of time moving around.

"I need to get to Freefall City," I told her.

She turned up her nose. "What the hell do you want to go out there for?"

"Heard the surfing's good," I answered. "Can you take me?"

She spit into her cup. "Cost you three blues," she said.

Not knowing how much three blues was worth, the price sounded just dandy. "You've got yourself a fare."

She held out her hand. "Let's see the color of your plastic first."

Unclasping my pouch, I sifted through its innards until I fished out three triangular blue chips. I counted them into her hand. She spit into her can and counted them again. Then she lost them in her pocket. "Freefall City it is," she said. "Follow me, good-looking. And carry your own bag."

We went through a door set behind the line of cabbies, stepping into a barely lit hallway of cement and metal beams. The hall was narrow, and cold as a tax man's heart. I felt as if I had walked into the meat locker at the Chicago stockyards.

We had to walk single file on the metal grates in the floor, our weighters clanging with every step. She spoke to me over her shoulder. "We don't get too many out to Freefall anymore," she said. "You surprised me."

We were passing a series of round wheel-lock doors marked with consecutive numbers. "Why's that?"

"They raise the young ones to stay, I guess," she returned. "And they don't take too well to outsiders. Got their own ways of getting along."

"What do they do?"

I could hear her spit plop into the can. "Beltel owns the

place, has for about a century. It's the best gravity pocket in the whole damned orbit. They build and repair communications satellites and do a lot of manufacturing for some of the other cities. Here we are.''

She had stopped in front of number 17. I came up beside her just as she was getting the wheel unscrewed. It groaned loudly as she pulled it open. The thing was damp and rusty, as were the walls. The door opened to a clear tube. The cabbie hopped up and started crawling through the tube—that's how small the space was.

As I watched her fanny wiggle along the tube, her face turned to me. "My name's Porchy Rogers," she said. "How about you?"

"Swain," I answered and hopped up myself, pushing my suitcase in front of me.

"Just follow me," she called.

"Yeah, I wouldn't want to get lost."

We crawled through the clear tunnel, suddenly away from the buildings, into the lunar landscape. It was bleak, but almost compelling in its stark contrasts of light and dark. I had been in worse places. The tube hissed loudly in my ears. Other tubes fanned out on both sides of me. Those, like mine, terminated in round metal spheres that sprouted porcupinelike protrusions all around. The spheres were dark-toned and heavily riveted.

Porchy Rogers stopped ahead of me. She unwheeled another door. This one was connected to her sphere. The door pushed inward, and she tumbled through the opening. I could feel my knees starting to stiffen as I hurried to get through the door. Pushing my bag through, I fell in on top of it, sliding rudely to the floor.

"That first step's a killer," she said, and didn't even flinch.

I lugged myself to my feet, arching my back to loosen it up. Inside, the place was about as large as a good-sized bathroom. It was straight steel, cold and unornamented, like a round paddy wagon.

She closed and locked the door. The only light in the ball was a red one that showed when the oxy flow was operational. After wheeling the door shut, she went to a small control panel and flipped some switches. White cabin lights came up and the air hiss got louder, and I got a little better look around. There was a worn, flowered carpet on the floor that looked as if it had been old when the world was young. Four used bullet-seats were bolted to the floor. One of the seats had controls wrapping around it in a semicircle. There were several windows of porthole size and shape placed around the sphere, but most of them were so dirty that it was impossible to see through. Food wrappers, plates and cups, and other bits of garbage lay on the floors and bulkheads. They were wedged between things to keep them from floating. Pictures of naked weight lifters with oil-slicked bodies were tacked onto the walls and ceilings. The place needed a woman's touch.

"Are you bonded?" I asked her.

"Only my whisky," she returned and spat into her cup.

"Whisky?"

She turned to me and smiled like a Fancy Dan with a new gun. "Would you . . . yeah, you would." She began rooting through a metal tool box that was set into the floor, coming out with a bottle of Black Jack. She handed it across to me. The bottle had a nipple on the end, just like a baby bottle. I put it to my lips and milked the thing, and I'm proud to say that zero gravity didn't affect the quality even a little bit.

I handed it back. "No charge," Porchy said, and took a big pull herself. "You're a man after my own heart."

I took the bottle back and had another drink. "People of distinction always manage to search each other out." I was happy to know that pioneer life retained at least a modicum of the genteel pleasures.

Porchy put the bottle back in her tool kit and strapped herself into the control seat. "Park it anywhere," she said, wiping a drop of brown juice off her lower lip. I took the seat next to her. "I like you," she smiled, letting her eyes frisk me again. "You remind me of my ex."

"Divorced?" I asked.

Her eyes softened just a touch, sagging like bread dough. "No," she answered softly. "Dead."

"Tough luck," I replied, and moved on because I could see that she wanted to move on. "What's the chances of getting a smoke?" I asked.

She winked and started flipping toggles on her control board. The sphere began vibrating, a low whine filling the cabin. She juiced a small vis on her board and a set of numbers started reading across the screen. She punched another button and a sucking sound joined the whine. "You can smoke now if you want to."

Gratefully pulling a fag out of the pocket of my waist-coat, I stuck it in my mouth. "What's that sound?" I asked.

"I opened a hole to the outside, so you wouldn't smoke up the place."

"You mean we're leaking air?"

"Don't worry about it."

I shrugged and lit the cig, watching the smoke scoot at an angle and quickly disappear through the hull.

Porchy pulled a blue baseball cap out from under her seat and stuck it solidly on her red hair. She hooked earphones and throat mike over that. She spoke to the mike. "Control Charlie, this is Shuttle 17, over."

"Shuttle 17, this is Control Charlie. Over." The voice had a metallic ping to it that could get real distracting.

"Request undocking and flight space permission," she said casually, while her hands danced across the board, running preflight.

"Permission granted. Request terminal coordinates."

She reached next to the control panel and took up a tattered black book that was attached by a small chain to the floor. The book was bloated and mildewed. She opened it and flipped through the worn pages. Finding her place, she quickly ran a blue-nailed finger down the page, pausing midway. "Terminal coordinates: 2Q2-1719."

"Repeat coordinates please."

She hunched down closer to the book. "2Q2-1719."

"Permission denied to those coordinates."

"Are you saying no?" She gave me a sidelong glance.

"Permission denied to those coordinates."

"Request reason for denial."

"To file a complaint or request, grievance form 47D must be filed in triplicate for a period of thirty Earth days in the office of the air controller. A copy of this form may be obtained . . ."

"Never mind," she said, and shut down communications. She looked at me. "You heard it," she said.

"Is there anything you can do?"

"What are you asking me?"

I took my plastic pouch and dropped it in her lap. "It's all I've got," I said. "But it's yours if you can get me to Freefall."

She hefted the pouch, then gave it back to me. "Listen, good-looking. They don't make enough of this stuff to buy my ass," she said, then looked at me, those eyes sagging again. "You really want to get there bad, don't you?"

"Yeah."

She was looking at me, but I could tell that she was thinking about someone else. Her face pulled against itself for a while, then she just shook her head.

"I guess you just found yourself a sucker," she said and rejuiced communications. "Control Charlie, this is Shuttle 17. Request permission for direct flight path to coordinates 8P-517."

"Purpose of flight?"

"Sightseeing."

"Permission granted for flight, but landing permission must be granted by ground control at coordinates."

"Roger, Control. Out."

"Thanks," I said. "You're okay."

"I'm a fool, and you know it," she replied, and unplugged her headset. Reaching out, she pounded the undocking lever with a closed fist. There was the sound of a hydraulic swoosh, a rocket thrust, and I saw the ground leaving us through the porthole. It tilted crazily off at a gray, pitted angle, then it was upside down. Porchy punched our coordinates into her computer, flipped to auto, then sank back heavily into her seat. Rocket thrusts blurted from several different locations, then we were back in proper perspective to the ground. I finished my smoker, ground it out in my hand, and stuck it in my pocket for lack of an ashtray. It made me feel better when Porchy shut down the sucking sound.

"Where are we going?"

"Well, eventually we're going to Freefall, but we're going to have to go through the back door."

"The back door," I repeated.

"I hope you don't scare easily."

23

I wanted to ask her about it, but decided that maybe I didn't want to know. As we floated across the surface at skyscraper height, I stared out the window at the mining sites that scarred the surface like thorns on a rose bush. There was activity all over the surface—moving machines, pumping diggers, and ugly bulbous freighters that fed off the lunar bowels like metal ticks. This went on for a time, until the light gave way to a line of total darkness. We were losing the sun.

"Dark side," Porchy said. "We'll be there soon."

After that, ground operations could only be seen as camp lights, shining brightly in the unatmosphered night. It began to get cold in the cabin, and Porchy turned up the heat. "Darksiders are crazy," she said, and drew in her eyebrows. "Confinement and darkness, not many can handle it." She shivered. "Even the pros hate them."

Up ahead, we could see a series of unrelated flashes brightening the perpetual night. As we got closer, tiny laser streamers could be seen zipping pink-hot lines through the cold, bleak landscape.

"Battle," Porchy said. "It looks like someone is going after Marseilles, a big Frenchy company."

"Who?" I asked, as I watched buildings explode in brilliant flashes that lasted only an instant before the vacuum sucked up all their air.

"Germans, maybe. I don't know."

"Does this happen often?"

"All the time."

"Who's going to win?"

She chuckled low, and gave us a little height to avoid the carnage that was now directly below us. "I don't know who will win," she said. "But the Frenchies will lose. They always lose."

We left the battle behind us, and floated in silence for a time. All at once, she sat up straight and cut off the auto pilot. "Here's where it starts getting rough," she said.

A huge mine was coming up rapidly in front of us. It was vast, far larger than any of the others we had seen. Its lights stretched out, defining a vast plain like a field of stars ready for harvesting. "Western Mining," she said. "The oldest and still the biggest."

She hit the port and forward thrusters and turned us sharply. "Western does all of the mining for Freefall. We're going to hitch a ride with some titanium."

"What?"

"Just watch."

We were coming up on a large, well-lit area. A round building sat in the area of orange light. It was painted red and tilted at a slight angle. Train tracks led up to the building from all around, and then tracked backwards into the night.

"Gas gun," she told me, and as I got closer, I could see what she meant. The thing was shooting ore out of its open end at an incredible rate of speed, snorting large chunks into the darkness. "Compressed hydrogen shoots the metals out of here and they catch them at Freefall. If we handle it just right, we can travel the ore path and avoid the radar."

"Is that good?"

"This is the frontier, Swain," she replied. "Vehicles found in unauthorized air space are shot down on sight."

"Wonderful." I took a deep breath and thought about my friend the bookmaker.

"Ready?" she asked, as we closed in.

"No," I answered. But she took us in anyway. We swooped in close to the gun, then she goosed her reverse thrusters for all they were worth. No sooner had we cleared the lip of the gun than we were caught in a tooth-cracking turbulence. We started vibrating like a fat man with a jackhammer.

"Hold on!" she hollered over the sound of my body shaking to pieces. But I had already figured that out for myself. Porchy's hat came off her head and hung in the air of the cabin, her hair dancing a samba around her head. Loose plastic and cigs went around my head like visions of sugar plums, and the naked weight lifters came off the walls and gyrated through the cabin.

Then the rocks.

Mammoth and frightening, they raced silently past our portholes, blocking out everything for a few seconds, only to leave us quietly behind.

"Is this safe?" I yelled.

"Hell no!" she returned, hands shaking wildly on the thrusters.

25

"Don't tell me that!" I hollered back.

"What?"

"Lie to me!"

"It's perfectly safe," she returned, and then ruined it all with a wink.

4

We rode the rocks for nearly an hour, the trip getting easier the farther we went. We stayed on the ore trail until making visual contact with the huge collection net that hung in the sky like the king of the wind socks.

"We're close enough for local traffic now," Porchy said when contact was made, and it was with obvious relief that she took us out of the fast lane.

"That wasn't too bad," I said proudly, then realized that my hands were cramp-locked onto the chair arms. "Is Freefall near here?"

She pointed to a small cluster of stars out the front port. "There it is," she said.

"That doesn't look like much," I told her, and fished one of my cigs out of the air.

"It will," she responded. "Where exactly do you want to go?"

I stuck the smoker into my mouth and chewed on it. "It's a private home. She calls it Miss Lily."

Porchy looked at me and almost smiled. "Rich girl, huh?"

"Yeah."

"Friend of yours?"

"Sometimes."

The city was no more than bright pinpoints of light for a long time. Distances in space are impossible to judge, so I had no idea how far we actually were from the place. The light became brighter the closer we got, then divided itself off into a sequence of light rings.

"What's that?"

Porchy was busy laying city grids onto her vis, looking for Ginny's place. She answered without looking up. "The city gets its light from the sun," she said, as if she had said it a thousand times before. "They do it by orbiting reflecting mirrors between the sun and the wheels. What you're seeing is the reflection around the edges of the mirrors. It bounces light onto the wheels where other mirrors reflect it back and forth before letting it into the habitations, so that they can get the light without getting the cosmic radiation." She spat loudly. "I found your friend's house."

I looked down at her city grid, and saw a flashing pinpoint of green light in the corner. She jacked the thrusters until we had bull's-eyed the flash into the center of the vis.

It was a while before the city came into clear view. It was a strange sensation moving up on Freefall, like flying into the innards of a cosmic watch. There were spoked wheels of various sizes rotating slowly. The outer circumference of the wheels was nonrotating, a dirty gray and black band made of moon rubble that acted as radiation shields for the various wheels. The reflecting mirrors orbited at an angle to the wheels, like open-mouthed clams, and their reflection was too brilliant to stare at directly.

There were hundreds of satellites within the city proper. Most were wheels, many were balls or tubelike affairs or even corkscrew ships. Most of them clustered around the Beltel wheel, which was the matrix of the city. It was startling in its size—something that I was unable to appreciate until we were close up—and it housed the Beltel headquarters and homes for all but its upper management employees. All of the agriculture was done on the main wheel, called Papa Bear by the inhabitants, as was the raising of animals. Papa Bear was the focus and lifeblood of Freefall City.

The city looked used, like an old bullet or a worn-out coat. The radiation shields had a lot to do with that; they made the wheels look like dirty snowballs. But it was deeper than that. There was a trail of garbage and refuse that tagged along after the city like a process server on a child-support case. The trail was miles long and wide and contained enough scrap metal and other junk to fill the Grand Canyon. I bet *that* never showed up in the postcards.

We kept closing in for what seemed like forever. It was like we were right there, and yet the place never got any closer. Then, suddenly, we were in it. Mammoth rotating wheels turned the clockworks and clicked out some uniformity in a place that had no natural rules. I felt like a virus invading a body, skipping erratically amidst the eternal machinations. There was something else, too. From the first moment we entered the city, I knew that I didn't belong there. In a sense, I *was* a virus, infecting a foreign body with my own particular brand of malaise.

There were other ships moving through the city. They drifted indolently, casually, occasionally showing signs of life by spurting short bursts from their thrusters. Porchy, more frenetic than the market could bear, charged in and out of their congestion, punching her thrusters like a boxer with a body bag.

The area around Papa Bear was the most crowded. Once we moved through that, the wheels thinned out to private dwellings, the snob hill of the ether.

As we moved past these silent temples, I couldn't help being struck by the loneliness of it all. Rich people hiding out from poor people, forced into hiding because they don't have the guts to face life anymore.

"There." Porchy was pointing through the front porthole at a small torus off by itself. She said it was Ginny's place, but I sincerely hoped that she was wrong. The wheel was churning with activity, and it wasn't the kind I liked.

Several ships that looked almost like bullets were docking and buzzing the place like mosquitoes at mating time. They were sleek and white and had large gold stars painted on the sides. Cops. Even in a vacuum I could smell them. They stunk up the place like rotten mangoes.

"Looks like your rich girl is having some problems," Porchy said, and her face was twisted with distaste.

"You sure that's her place?"

"Afraid so." She reached over into her tool kit and pulled the bottle back out again. "If we're going to deal with cops," she said, "I'd better get lubricated." She took a long pull on the bottle and handed it in my direction.

I waved it aside. "Not right now," I said. My body was tensing. The whole business had started out bad and was getting worse by the minute.

We came up on the wheel and circled it for a time before finding an open dock. Porchy kissed up to the thing and engaged the clamps. I moved right to the door and began unwheeling it.

"You want to take it easy in there," she warned, and

her tone was harsh. "The cops here don't take well to strangers butting into their business."

"I'll keep that in mind," I answered, knowing full well that I wouldn't. The door swung open to a short connecting tunnel that was lit to a green haze. I hopped up.

"You want me to wait for a while?" she asked, taking another pull on the bottle. "Just in case."

I nodded, still chewing on my cig. "Thanks," I said. "Don't mention it."

I crawled through the space. There was another wheel-lock at its terminus. Unlatching it, I climbed into a warmly lit hallway. The wheel's rotation gave the place Earth-type gravity, so I got those weights off my shoes and started moving. The hall was carpeted in deep-pile earthen brown, and the light seemed to come from diffusing panels in the ceiling, the mirror-reflecting Porchy had told me about earlier. It seemed that the hall was always inclining upward because of the curve, but no matter how much I walked, I never could get up that hill. There were doors set into the wall opposite the docking bays that led into bedrooms and sitting rooms. I could hear the sounds of activity as I walked, but hadn't reached it yet. I came to a large hole in the ceiling with ladder rungs leading upward. One of the wheel spokes. I kept going, hearing the voices closer in the distance.

"That's about far enough," came a voice from behind me. From the sound of the man, I really wasn't very anxious to see the face that connected to that voice. A second later it all became academic as a beefy hand grabbed me by the shoulder and spun me around.

I found myself staring into the maw of death. The man smelled of it. It dripped from his face in long slender shards and soaked into his clothes, giving them a putrefying stench. His face was lean, angular, and blanched white as the Dan's who killed himself in my apartment. His eyes were small dark dots floating in a white endemic sea. His hair was short and brown, nondescript. Thin lips mouthed silent epithets, as if he were reciting to himself. He wore a black kevlar uniform with a small gold star embroidered on the right sleeve. He was shaved and tidy, and blank as the faces on Mount Rushmore. In his fist he held a deadly looking black tube, and he was just itching to use it.

I shrugged and took the cig out of my mouth. "Got a light?"

"Shut up!" he screamed, and slammed me against the wall. I started for him and the gun came up in my face. He was breathing quickly, shallowly. "You're an Earther," he said, and smiled wide, a smile that was really something else. "I got me an Earther. Hands behind your head."

My mama always taught me to respect people who carried guns and had I.Q.'s that were lower than their shoe sizes. I did what he told me, but when he walked up close to pat me down, I realized that punks have to be taught object lessons if they ever expect to learn anything. I just pretended that his shin was a soccer ball and that I wanted to kick it all the way downfield. I whacked him good, and when he doubled over, I introduced his chin to my knee. He must have decided to take a nap after all that education, and crumbled to the floor like one of Paul Bunyon's trees. Leaning down, I picked up his funny-looking gun and moved toward the commotion.

I wasn't prepared for what I found.

The hallway widened to a large, sunken living room. The place was crawling with cops dressed just like my star pupil back down the hall, plus a couple of plainclothes done up in long black coats and gold ascots.

I walked right into the middle of it. "Your friend lost this," I said, dropping the gun onto the floor so they wouldn't get the wrong idea.

Faces turned to me. They were all pale—deathly pale. One of the plainclothes moved toward me. "What are you?" he asked.

I started to answer him when I saw her. It was Ginny. She sat motionless and distant in a fat, stuffed chair, her arms draped formally on the arms as if she were posing for a picture. She was naked, her clothes ripped to shreds, scattered all over the room. At her feet lay the body of a man, face down. There was no doubt that he was dead; the whole back of his head was caved in. Some of the cops were running prelims around the room. Many were simply standing, looking at Ginny. Some were reaching out. Touching.

"I asked you a question," the plainclothes said, but I heard him off in a part of my brain that didn't relate to things very well. I started across the room to cover Ginny.

31

The plainclothes got in my way and I shoved him, and then they were all over me, all hands and sewer breath. I think I said something, but it was in a language that hasn't been used since men had tails and ate lizard eggs. I struggled, but they had me good. And then that plainclothes was in my face. "What are you, what classification?"

"Cover her," I managed, and it was as if my guts were coming up my throat. "For the love of God, the least you can do is cover her!" I kept forcing myself against the punks who held my arms, and they kept hurting me.

"I don't have to do anything," the man said. "But you, you're hampering a murder investigation. You have to do plenty. And right now you're going to talk to me. What are you?"

"Cover her!"

The cop nodded to his buddies. They twisted my arms, and the pain got serious all the way from elbows to shoulders. My knees decided to take a vacation about then, and I slid to the floor. "Son of a bitch," I strained through waves of pain.

"You going to talk to me now?" Plainclothes asked.

"Yesss," I hissed.

He nodded again, and the pressure eased up. They pulled me roughly to my feet.

"Your name?"

"Swain," I said. With that, the pressure eased to nothing and I took my shot. Forcing my arms outward, I threw the punks away from me and started swinging at faces and guts. I think they were surprised at the opposition, because I was able to deck three of them, including the chatty plainclothes. My path freed up and I moved toward Ginny, taking off my waistcoat to drape around her.

I called her name, but she didn't respond. It was frightening, as if her mind had taken the shuttle back to Earth and left her body unattended. I was just about to get my coat around her when I heard a whoosh, followed by a sharp pain in my rib cage. Jerking, I looked at the place. A small steel dart was poking me. I pulled it out and turned to finish what I started.

All at once, there was a horrible stiffness in my muscles. They tightened and knotted like a rubber band being twisted, twisted. I started to cramp badly, my whole body. I managed to turn once toward the punks; the plainclothes held his dart

32

gun stiff-armed in front of him, ready to sting me again. I would have told him that it wasn't necessary, but my mouth didn't work either. I went to the floor, paralyzed. I couldn't move anything; even my eyes were locked open. I was almost glad that my mouth didn't work, for I would have been screaming. Screaming with the knot-cramping pain, screaming with the fear of total paralysis. I lay there on the carpet, frozen in posture like a statue knocked from its pedestal.

The plainclothes walked up to me, spitting loudly in my face. Everyone laughed. They were having a marvelous time—a real party. They were punks and they enjoyed suffering more than anything else in the world. I lay there and tried to kill them all with my mind. I wanted to burn my hatred out through the bottled air and sear them like a napalm rifle and watch them burn black with liquid gelignite, charring them to the nothingness that they were.

But I couldn't.

One of the punks went up behind Ginny's chair and, leaning over, began fondling her breasts from behind. I kept willing myself to rise. Drool was running out of my mouth, wetting my cheek.

Plainclothes got down on the floor with me. "My name's Beemer," he said. "Captain Beemer, Beltel Security. Does it hurt real bad? How about the breathing . . . can you get the old lungs to work. Bet you can't swallow, though."

I drank in Beemer. I wanted to remember him, desperately wanted to remember him. He was a good-sized man, but looked clumsy in clothes that didn't fit him well. He was ghostly pale like the rest of them, but a crop of the darkest ebony hair and moustache made him look almost transparent. His hair was slicked straight back, wet and shiny, and his eyes stared intently, obsessively. They all seemed to wear dark make-up around their eyes to accentuate the hollow appearance. With Beemer, the make-up made you think you were staring into twin manholes. He was lean and hard, with pockmarks on his cheeks and nose. And I didn't need to ask him to know that he was bad news.

"Friend of yours?" he asked, nodding in Ginny's direction. Several other punks had taken the first one's lead and were clustered around the chair, probing her with sweaty hands.

They worked on her for a while, taunting, playing it for

my benefit. Just when I thought I'd go crazy with it all, I heard a voice from outside my limited range of vision.

"Stop that!" It was a female voice. A small, middle-aged woman walked into my line of sight. She marched right up to the punks around Ginny and began to roughly pull them away from her. "Don't you animals have any sense of decency at all?"

Beemer turned to look at her. "She's just an Earther," he said.

"So's your boss," she shot back, and stared defiantly at him.

Cursing softly, Beemer stood up. "I'm sorry, Irene. I guess we just got a little carried away."

The woman was busy pulling a green pastel slipcover off one of the sofas. "Henry's going to hear about this," she said, draping the cover around Ginny. She bent down and stared deeply into Ginny's eyes, then passed a hand in front of her face several times. She wore a doctor's pouch on a shoulder harness. Reaching into the thing, she extracted an air hypo and pumped it once on Ginny's arm. Her body loosened up immediately and she slumped over, asleep, in the chair. The woman clucked down in her throat and moved in my direction. "And what have you done to this poor man?"

"He resisted arrest," Beemer told her. "It's not your concern."

She waved him aside. "I don't want to hear about it." She leaned down and spoke to me. "You have to excuse them," she said. "The only Earth women they ever see are prostitutes. I'm going to give you something to help you sleep for a while." She searched through her bag for a few seconds. "Don't worry about the dart. The effects wear off in a few hours."

I was beginning to feel better already.

5

I slept.

I slept and dreamed of dungeons and thumbscrews and iron maidens and big wooden racks with crank handles and creaking chains. And when I finally awoke, I was swimming in a pool of my own sweat, and my body felt as if it had made a double-gainer from the high board into an empty pool.

I floated into consciousness slowly, reluctantly. Then I remembered Ginny, and bolted upright like I had just stuck my finger into the light socket. A searing pain charged up my neck and blurred my vision for a minute, but it soon subsided and I looked around.

I was in a white room, a room so white it was almost blue. It was like lying in a bale of cotton. I was sitting on a stainless steel table covered with a white cloth. There was some furniture around. White, metal stuff that had tiny cushions on the seats, paying scant lip service to comfort. White tables and cabinets held various pieces of medical gear that just begged for someone to guess what they were for.

Climbing off the table, I stood on shaky legs. My tan one-piece was drenched dark and heavy, and smelled as if it had just floated out of a septic tank. My hair was wet and plastered, and I hurt in every joint. But I was alive and walking, and for that I was grateful.

There was a white door set in a white wall. I shuffled weakly over to it and pushed it open. I found myself in a room as green as the other had been white. Even the light was green. It was a spinach soufflé of a room. I looked down at my hands; they were the color of baby limas.

"Hello?" I called, and my voice was hoarse. "Room service."

The entire wall to my left juiced into a vis. I was looking

at a monstrously inflated image of the face of the woman who had helped us out at Ginny's place.

"Welcome back, Mr. Swain," she said, smiling cheerfully. "Nice to see you on your feet again."

"Nice isn't the word," I returned. "Thanks." I took a breath and my lungs hurt. "Where's Ginny?"

The woman's wrinkle eroding face grew somber. "She's here with me."

"Where?"

"There's a door to your right," she answered. "It leads to a hallway. Follow the hall until you reach a door marked 'Psytronics'."

I thanked her and moved through the doorway. The hall had bare aluminum floors and walls, and it curved upward, just like the ones at Miss Lily. People were droning through the halls, all with those same zombie pasty-faces the cops had. They all gave me a wide berth, then would turn and stare at me over their shoulders after passing me. I figured that if they were going to treat me like a leper, I might as well get a tin cup and collect some alms. There were a great many doors all along the hall, all marked with words you would expect to see in a clinic; so I assumed that was exactly where I was.

Finally I arrived at Psytronics. I opened the door, and the woman was smiling up at me from a shiny desk/console. I nodded, but my eyes drifted to take in the rest of the room. There were several empty beds in there, and one that wasn't empty. I moved to it.

Ginny floated on a stasis field, the kind of place they put people who are going to stay down for a long time to avoid getting bed sores. She was dressed in a hospital gown, starched and proper. Her face was tensed and her eyes, opened wide and moving slightly, stared intently at the ceiling. It was as if some bloody battle were going on inside of her head, a battle that only she could fight. Her hair fanned around her head, a golden halo undulating easily, like rippling water around a moored rowboat.

I watched her lonely, struggling form and felt sorrow that quickly melted away, exposing a foundation of anger beneath, like the bitterly lasting taste of an orange rind.

A hand lay gently on my forearm. I looked down at it and saw that my fists were clenched. "I'm sorry," the woman said softly.

I turned and looked down at her face, a real face, an Earth face. She was fading roses, the first frost of autumn. Her eyes were steady brown, wide and loving. Liquid. Her hair was gray fighting with black, and she wore it loose, down around her shoulders, the way most middle-aged women don't wear it. She went without make-up, proudly facing her appointment with Father Time. She was small and the least bit overweight. Some would call her dumpy, but I found her appealing, like a candy machine in a drug center. Her voice was deep and comfortable, and when she said she was sorry, I couldn't help believing it.

"What's wrong with her?" I asked.

"I've been a doctor for thirty-three years," she replied, her eyes drifting down to Ginny, "and all I can tell you is that something happened to her mind."

"Her mind—how?"

She took me by the arm and led me away from the stasis. "Come out of here. We'll talk."

I went with her, my head turning back for another look at Ginny. She led me out of the room, back into the hall. "How are you feeling?" she asked as we walked. Being with her seemed to give me some kind of legitimacy. The ghosties in the halls nodded and even spoke to us as we walked.

"I'll live . . ." I said. "Irene, isn't it?"

She threw up her hands and stopped walking. "Excuse me," she said, and shook my hand. "Irene Jacobi."

"Swain," I returned.

"I know."

We started walking again. "Did you get the number of the truck that hit me?"

"Curarine," she told me. "Distilled from curare. It works on the motor nerves."

"I'll attest to that."

She looked up at me, eyes intent. "You were fortunate Captain Beemer didn't have a kill stinger in the gun, or you'd be dead right now."

"Yeah, some people have all the luck."

She took me into an apartment. We went through a sitting room that would have made my Aunt Gertrude feel comfortable, then into a small dining area off the kitchen. It was all closed in; I suppose you could call it cozy. There was a window over the kitchen sink with lace curtains. It looked out over rolling farmland with wood fences and a barn. A thunderstorm had come up and was pouring rain as a line of cows moved quickly into the barn. I sat down at an aluminum table and watched the holorain roll its thunder out the fake window and tried to convince myself that I had gotten my sopping clothes in the downpour. It didn't work.

Irene moved around the kitchen area opening metal cabinets that were painted to look like wood. "I don't bring the Freefallers in here," she said. "They wouldn't understand. Coffee?"

"You wouldn't happen to have anything stronger?" I asked.

"No, I'm sorry, I . . ."

"Coffee's fine."

I watched her moving around the small room, the sounds of muffled thunder in the distance. She wasn't going to talk to me until she was good and ready, so I just sat there waiting in the pretend country-kitchen, wondering why someone who obviously hated the space life so much would bother to come up at all. Her homey atmosphere made me fidgety. It was as phony as a decoy duck and I could never convince myself otherwise.

She hummed to herself as she worked, sliding the cups under the mike rod. She wore a simple, dignified shift the color of the sky without smog. When the rod did its work, she came and set two steaming metal mugs on the table with a clang.

"They don't allow stimulants here," she said. "So this isn't real coffee. It's wheat that I caffeinated myself." She took a sip. "Being a doctor definitely has its advantages."

I tasted it; it wasn't the worst by any means. "Where are we?"

"Hmmm." She raised her eyebrows while she drank. She was one of those people apparently unaffected by heat, because I could barely get near my cup.

She set her cup down. "This is Freefall General. I'm Chief of Staff here. We had you vaced over after your run-in with Beemer. But I know that's not what you want to talk about." She lowered her eyes to her cup and ran an unpolished nail around its rim.

"I'm hedging with you because I don't know what to tell you about your friend."

"We can start with everything you know."

She nodded, pouting a lower lip. I'd bet she broke some hearts in her day. "Security received an anonymous call to go to her wheel. They found her just the way she was when you arrived. I brought her in here and had every kind of neurological test run on her that I could think of. There's no damage— no physical damage—to her brain at all. It's a perfectly healthy brain."

"But," I helped.

"But," she repeated. "Look at this."

Getting up from the table, she juiced a tiny console attached to her breakfast bar. A vis appeared where the rainy day had been. It was a picture of Ginny. The cam moved in close on her face.

"This is the first thing that I noticed," Irene said. "Look at the eyes."

I did. They were the first thing that I had noticed, too. Her eyes were moving, blinking rapidly.

"A lot of activity in there," she said in a matter-of-fact doctor's manner. "Her brain is just popping. Now this." The vis showed a graph full of moving static lines. The lines were harsh, like an angry five-year-old's scribble. Irene's voice went low. "EEG. There's more activity of a violent nature in that lady's head than I've ever seen before."

"So?"

"So it's not a coma in the usual sense." She switched back her country day and returned to the table, sitting down heavily. "It's more like a withdrawal. Her brain is closing in on itself, retreating further and further inward. Her pulse rate is up, she's feverish and getting worse. The adrenaline is pumping through her system just as fast as she can manufacture it."

"What's all that mean?" I asked, afraid to hear the answer.

"It means that she's wearing her body out even though she's not moving."

"Why?"

"It's fright, Mr. Swain. Plain and simple. Your friend is slowly dying of fright. Something has scared her so bad that she's running from it consciously, subconsciously, and physically."

I was up on my feet, looking hard at the woman. "Did you say, dying?"

She showed me empty palms. "No human being can take the kind of punishment she's enduring without burning herself up in short order. Her body chemistry will begin to break down, and her fever will eventually start eroding her brain."

I started pacing, trying to figure it all out. "There must be something you can do."

She leaned against the table. "We've tried central nervous system depressants in nearly dangerous amounts to slow down the activity, but they've had absolutely no effect. We even hooked her up to an alpha ring and tried to stimulate some of her pleasure centers. We can't seem to reach her on any conscious level at all."

"How long can she stay this way?"

"With intravenous feeding and constant care, I'd give her about a week at the outside. Maybe less. Maybe a lot less."

I banged my fist against the table, tipping it, almost knocking it over. "There must be something!"

"It's gunslinger medicine," she answered, eyeing me fearfully. "The brain is a complicated organism. Without knowing the cause of her psychosis, we have no real way to treat the effects of it. Shots in the dark. If I spend too much time treating the wrong thing, I'll never have the chance of finding the right thing."

"What about another opinion?"

"I've already sent my data over the satellite to Johns Hopkins and the Brigham Young Psi Center in Utah. So far I've had no response."

I was down in her face. "Well check them!"

"They're moving as quickly as they can," she said, her lips straining to wrinkles as she tried to control herself.

I straightened. "Don't mind me. You're doing your best. I just feel so useless."

"So do I," she replied. "Believe me, we're doing everything that can be done. If we only knew the reason . . ."

I sat back down, staring at the coffee. It never sat completely straight in the cup. It was always tilted, just slightly, at an angle. My relays started clicking. "What about the dead guy?" I asked.

"His name was Jeff Roque," she said. "He ran the Beltel computer satellite."

"Did you know him?"

"Only in a professional sense. More coffee?"

I shook my head. The cup I'd had was already working badly on my stomach. She got up and walked into the kitchen proper.

"His job was a very stressful one. I prescribed tranks or acupunctures for him from time to time. Nothing major, just nerves." She came back to the table with another cup and sat down. "I liked him. He was a bit . . . out of focus, but harmless. I get the feeling that most everyone else would say the same."

I thought about that for a time. "What did the cops say?"

She turned up her nose. "The official theory at this point is that Roque tried to attack Ms. Teal, and that she smashed his head with a vase they found broken on the scene, and went into shock after the event."

"Could that explain Ginny's condition?"

"Anything's possible, but she's exhibiting none of the symptoms of shock withdrawal. *That* I could understand."

"Are they going to continue investigating?"

She hesitated for a moment before answering me, and when she finally did, it was reluctantly. "There is something that you've got to understand," she said. "Most of the people who live on Freefall were born here. Many are third- and fourth-generation. The way they keep the young ones here is by carefully cultivating a hatred for Earth and its people. The official line paints such a horrible picture of Earthers, that no sane Freefaller would ever want to have anything to do with one."

"Why?"

She looked at me through slit eyes. "Don't be naive. They've got a good, cheap labor force that lives a life conditioned from birth by Beltel. Without introducing random uncontrollable elements into the life style, the company can motivate the population in any direction they choose. It's sound philosophy from a business standpoint, but hell on people like you. What I'm getting around to, is that they don't care what happens to Ginny Teal. They've got a nice,

41

neat answer to their problems and are not about to do anything to upset that solution.''

"*You're* an Earther.''

She shook her head. "Been here twenty years. It took me over ten of them to get accepted, and only then because I was better trained than their locally educated doctors. The company, unfortunately, doesn't place a very high value on education.''

"Well,'' I said, standing up, trying to forget just how badly my body felt. "I suppose that if the coppers aren't going to do anything, I'd better do a little poking around on my own.''

"That's insane,'' she said. "Haven't you understood a word I've been saying? They hate Earthers. You don't know your way around. No one will help you. There's not a thing in the world that you can do.''

"I may not be able to do any good,'' I replied, "but I sure don't think I can hurt any. Do you have the body of that Roque character around here?''

She nodded.

"I want to see it.''

"There's something that I haven't told you,'' she said. "There are two of Beemer's security men waiting around here to take you to headquarters. You did beat up four of them, you know. The only reason you're here now is because they think you're still unconscious.''

"Can you stall them for a while until I've checked the body and cleaned myself up?''

She smiled a pixie smile. "It would be my pleasure.''

I nodded. "Appreciate it. Do they have showers in space?''

She pointed. "Through that door is a bedroom. Through the next one is a bathroom. Your bags are already in there. I wouldn't take too long, though. Beemer's people won't stay put forever.''

"Don't worry.'' I walked through the door, then turned back around. "Say, what day is it anyway?''

Her eyebrows went up only slightly. "They don't count days in Freefall,'' she said.

I had a lot to learn.

6

The morgue was behind a red door with a small window set at eye level within a larger series of rooms grouped under the general heading of "Pathology." On the morgue door was the printed warning: CAUTION—OUTSIDE TEMPERATURES AND CONDITIONS.

Irene Jacobi was pointing through the glass. "He's there. The third slab on the fifth row from the left."

I looked through and saw a room full of tables containing naked corpses. Their skin tone was light blue, but looked purple under the dim red lighting of the chamber. They were stiff and cold and fresh out of luck. It reminded me of the waiting room of the tax auditor.

"Can we go in?" I asked.

Irene shook her head. "There's no air, and the temperature's just as cold as the outside. It's the best, the cheapest way of preserving the bodies."

"Then, how . . ."

"We'll bring him to us. Come on."

We left the door and entered a small room, like a blockhouse. It had a bigger window that afforded the same view. A large control panel was set under the window.

Irene took a chair in front of the stainless steel console, and began juicing metal toggles. Most everything was metal of some kind rather than plastic or wood. It was Freefall's way of remaining self-sufficient.

"Okay," she said, slowly rotating a big blue knob. "Come on in."

A large beam that ran the length of the morgue began sliding across the width. It had a flat scoop attached to a chain. It stopped moving over Jeff Roque's row, and the scoop then slowly slid along the beam. It stopped above Roque's bed.

43

Irene smiled to herself and pulled a lever in her direction. The scoop opened wide, then began letting out chain to lower itself. It looked like the toy- and cig-grabbing machines they used to have at amusement parks.

She worked the handles carefully, bringing the scoop just down even with the body. Then she slowly pushed the lever back to the closed position, and the scoop jaws devoured the body.

"Got him," she said with satisfaction.

"Congratulations."

She looked up at me.

Raising the chain and moving the beam at the same time, she tried to hurry Roque over to us, but apparently didn't have him in the scoop as securely as she thought, for the body slid out and fell to the floor.

Irene shook her head. "Too much of a hurry," she chided herself, as if it was a mistake she was often making. She worked the levers and picked him up again, but this time an arm stayed behind on the morgue floor.

"You broke him," I said.

She got the body over near the window and deposited it on a shiny steel pallet. Punching a plunger, she had Roque delivered, a bit the worse for wear, through a mechanical server that shoved him right through the wall.

We hoisted the frozen meat onto a stretcher that Irene had me push out of the way while she went back for the arm. I took a look at the body. The arm was broken off at the elbow and one foot was about half gone, along with the tip of his nose. But other than that, he was as good as new.

Irene came over and laid the arm on the table like it was a jigsaw puzzle piece that had fallen on the floor. "I got in too much of a hurry," she repeated for me in case I hadn't heard her the first time.

"No harm done. Are you going to do an autopsy?"

She shook her head. "They don't want one," she said. "Don't want any new evidence that might send their theory through the shredder."

"Would you do one for me? I could pay you a little, but not much."

Irene started pushing the stretcher out of the blockhouse. I followed. "When I said they don't want one, it means that they want me not to do one," she said over her shoulder.

44

"You mean you could get in trouble?"

She made a face. "Deportation . . . or worse. I might be cooked just for dropping the damned thing. But we can at least take a little look at him."

She stopped the stretcher, wheels creaking, in front of a big aluminum box. The box had a door on the end. She went around and pulled it open, having to move the table a bit to accommodate the door. Then she pushed the stretcher into the dark recesses of the machine.

"We'll warm him up in the microwave and see what happens."

"I like mine well done," I said.

She just sighed and shook her head.

Closing the door to the oven, she set a small timer on the side of the thing and folded her arms to wait. Halfway across the room, a group of pale-faced med students were doing a dissection. They had laid open an old woman's arm and were pulling on the tendons, making the fingers move. One of them pulled the arm up so that the dancing fingers were drumming on the body's lips. They all got a kick out of that.

I grunted and turned back to Irene. "Has the widow been in yet to see the body?"

"No," she answered, tapping her foot. "Probably won't be."

"Why not?"

"The company looks at mourning as a very nonproductive expenditure of time." She saw my face and put up her hands. "It's just a different way of looking at things," she said. "Life is run like a business up here. When someone dies, they post an opening for his station and life and seniority. Then someone who needs to improve himself soon fills the position. Life goes on. It's not such a bad system."

A tiny bell pinged gently on the side of the machine.

"Biscuits are done," I said.

We opened the door and pulled out the stretcher. Roque had gone from blue to that blanched color that all the Spacers wore. You couldn't tell the live ones from the dead ones without a scorecard.

Irene looked around quickly. Besides the students, there were several white-coated techs roaming around the large pathology lab, and none of them seemed to be taking any notice of us. She pulled the bed over to a wall full of doors, and we slipped into one marked FORENSICS.

A cold misty haze slapped my face as we entered. It smelled of heavily perfumed disinfectant. The room was crammed with enough power-sucking machinery to black out a major city. On our entrance, it all churned into gear. Cams and mikes all over the room turned to stare at us, while the walls came alive with vis and readout screens. It was like standing on the inside of a merry-go-round. I kept waiting for the calliope. A huge white light slowly lowered itself from the ceiling, to rest with a shudder at table level.

"Aren't you going to introduce me?" I asked, looking around.

"They train their students here," she replied, pushing Roque up under the light. "In this sort of closed environment, disease outbreak would be catastrophic. We probably have better facilities here for the discovery and treatment of contagion than anywhere else, including Earth."

I moved up to the table with her, and as we bent over the body, all the recording gear leaned closer. Autopsies have never been my dish of tea, but business is business.

"Now, let's have a look," Irene said, then glanced up, distracted. "Cancel recording." The long snooted cams and mikes shivered dejectedly, then fell limp. We went over the body quickly. The severed arm had leaked a little blood simply from gravity, but it wasn't too messy. We found nothing much, except in the region of the head. We rolled him over and took a close look at the wound.

"Okay," Irene said in her medical voice. "Cause of death seems to be massive intraventricular hemorrhaging caused by a severe blow on the head. I'm seeing a deep gash, approximately five centimeters in depth in the occipital area of the skull." She was probing the area with a long, thin instrument. "Multiple bony fragments are lying within the ecchymotic area overlying the occipital fracture. Death was brought on by heavy bleeding into the ventricles."

"Could a woman of Ginny's size have done so much damage?"

She straightened, deep in thought. "Ordinarily, I'd say no, but given her altered mental condition, anything is possible. You've heard the stories of people driven to impossible feats of strength under pressure conditions. This could be much the same thing."

I went around and got a better view of the skull. "Was a vase definitely the murder weapon?"

"If I were a bookie," she said, "I wouldn't lay odds on it." She pointed to the busted place. "I would think that a shattering vase would leave a lot of trace scrapings in the cut area. Maybe even a few pieces of material in the wound itself. There's nothing like that here."

I looked at her. "You mean that the vase didn't kill him?"

"Whoa," she said. "Don't quote me on that. It's just a preliminary opinion, but I would guess that something heavier, blunter, would be your murder weapon."

I moved around the table in a complete circle, checking. I had no idea of what I was looking for, but the secret in my racket is tenacity. Tenacity and an ironclad stomach to digest all the bullcrap that I get fed.

Roque's eyes were open. And as much as I didn't want to admit it, he had that same distant stare that Ginny and the Dan had. Of course, it could have been just the distance from here to heaven.

There was something wrong with his hands. I looked at the attached one carefully; the fingertips were scraped and the nails broken off! "Look at this," I told Irene.

She examined the hand, all the while making little sounds deep in her throat. Reaching into her pocket, she pulled out a small instrument with a long, needlelike affair sticking out of it. Taking a small vial from a black-topped counter, she started scraping around the broken nails, then shoving the scrapings into the vial.

While she did that, I looked at the other arm, the broken one. That hand had the same nail damage as the other, but there was something else. The hand was clutching something. Prying the fingers open, I found a small gold coin. I looked at it carefully. On one side was printed "50"; the other side was blank.

"There," Irene said, and put a stopper in her vial.

I stuck the coin in my pocket. "What is it?" I asked.

"Don't know," she answered from the place where doctors go when they are really wrapped up in their work. "Have to check it out."

Just then, the door banged open, and two of Beemer's punks ambled in. One was the black-suit whom I'd taught something about soccer, and the other was a plainclothes.

Irene quickly stuck the vial into her pocket. The black-suit was that deathly pale hue, but the plainclothes, though light, had some color to him.

"It looks like you're not as sick as you've been making out," my soccer buddy said, as if he had been rehearsing it for hours.

I looked at them and made a face. "Well, I'm getting sicker by the minute now that it stinks in here," I answered.

The one who had talked to me got all red in his white, white face, as if he were imitating Tabasco sauce. He came across the room for me, but the other one grabbed him by the arm and stopped him. He must have been the brains of the outfit.

"Let it go, Wilky," he said, and his voice was low, melodious. "Captain Beemer wants to question him first."

"Yeah, Wilky," I replied. "Remember your manners."

My buddy started for me again. Plainclothes stopped him again.

"Shouldn't you kids be taking a nap or something?" I asked.

This time they ignored me. I guess they didn't want to play anymore. The smart one went over and took a good look at the body. His face got grave when he saw who it was.

"Just what are you doing here, Doctor Jacobi?" he asked in a cop voice.

"I am attending to my affairs," she said angrily. "And I will thank you to leave this lab at once."

The man grinned, but it could have been just gas. "We'll go," he said. "But funny boy goes with us."

"You flatter me," I said.

The punk just looked at me, his face sour. Then he turned back to Irene. "I don't think that Captain Beemer's going to like this at all," he said, jabbing the body with an index finger. "You were given instructions."

"This is my hospital," she returned, never losing her poise. "And the devil himself couldn't tell me how to run it."

"You don't have the devil," Wilky interrupted. "You got us."

7

The plainclothes was called Nathan. He and Wilky loaded me none too graciously into their slick white cop-cruiser to go visit Captain Beemer. I don't much like cops. They're professional thugs, turning a buck because they like hurting people better than they like not hurting them. And the stars on their black sleeves make it all legal.

They chained my hands to the back seat of their ship, like maybe I was going to jump out of the thing and fly home. But that was punk's logic, something beyond my simple understanding.

Beemer wanted to see me, and in that contest, the percentages were not in my favor. I didn't have time for Beemer, but couldn't think of any way around it. Ginny had, perhaps, a week for me to find the answers that were locked up in her mind or she would die. And I couldn't even think of a way out of my own problems.

We slid easily through the congested wheel traffic near Papa Bear, and I watched it all spin out through the cruiser's bubble top. If I was going to help Ginny at all, it seemed imperative that I establish the connection between her and Roque. There was very little to go on. A murder weapon that wasn't a murder weapon, a gold coin, and something under a dead man's fingernails. There was one more thing: a caller—an anonymous caller who tipped the cops to the murder. So, no matter how I sliced it, there were at least three pieces of pie.

"How you doing back there?" Wilky asked. He had turned sideways in the front seat and was grinning at me through his dog-eyed lookers. His deathly face shone ghostlike in the white cabin lights. "Chains too tight?" he asked, staring at the trickles of blood that were running down my forearms.

"Chains are fine," I said. "In fact, I could even spare some for your mouth."

Nathan started chuckling at the controls. Wilky looked angrily over at him, his chin stuck out like a foot-long hot dog in a half-foot bun. His eyes narrowed and he stuck a fat thumb hard into my windpipe, twisting. Jerking my head, I bit his hand.

"Owwww!"

He jumped up in the seat, turning to get both arms at me, banging the plainclothes in the process. The ship buffeted wildly back and forth.

"Damn it, Wilky!" Nathan shouted. "Will you sit down?!"

The big man stopped, turning back. "Sorry, Jerry," he said.

He glared back at me once. I kissed the air four or five times.

We came up on the big wheel, its lazy rotation somehow soothing. It was all camouflage for the brain frenzy that seemed to control its inhabitants. We flew past the rim, and the bubble turned dark to shield us from the mirror light. We moved toward the spokes. One of them had SECURITY written across its outside in big gold letters. A whole fleet of the white cruisers was stuck by their bases to spoke moorings like white leeches. There was another ship there, too. It was round and pitted and sprouting porcupine quills. Porchy. I had forgotten all about her.

Nathan locked his vis onto the wheel's rotation, and played follow-the-bouncing-ball with his controls until he lined up his speed and direction with that of his homer. Then he set us down with a muffled clang.

The hatch was back behind my seat. They swiveled theirs around, collected me up like last week's garbage, and shoved me through the hatch. We came out in a small room with sliding doors. A big red "19" was painted on the wall. Nathan pushed a button and a down arrow lit up by the doors.

We waited a few minutes for the elevator, and when it finally came, it was already jammed full of black-suits. They found room for us somehow and we started down.

The vator let us out at the end of a long hallway, lined on both sides with glassed-in offices. The floors were glass, too. Beneath my feet I could see what looked like clouds drifting past, then, farther down, beneath the cloud haze, the vague shapes of a city. It was musty in there, damp, like bathtub water left for two weeks. The aluminum side walls sweated near the ceilings, orange beads of water. Whether this was from leaking wall pipes or faulty dehumidification, I didn't know. Papa Bear had been there for a long time. It had long-time problems. The walls were stained dark to black, with brownish red trails around the edge of the dark stains. Thick, ugly globs of black goo collected in the edges where ceilings joined walls. The light shone dim in there, and in some places bright. The mirror diffusers for the bounding sunlight system were shattered in many places, by whom or what I could only guess, and it made the hallway a maze of bright lights and dark corners.

The place was jammed with people. It was lousy with them. They were all lined up to get into this or that glassed office. They were patient, but crowded. They all had these little contraptions. Small, fold-up aluminum tables. The tables either sat on the ground on legs, or were strapped around their necks. The people used them to eat, or play cards, or to punch up fun-and-games on their pocketcoms. It had the smell of routine to it, a ceremony done over and over. In the offices themselves, punks and clericals banged on computer typers, or pointed fat stabbing fingers at wall vises, while the citizens shrugged or hung their heads and wrung their hands.

"Come on," Wilky said, shoving me into the crowd.

There was something else that made no sense to me. I was seeing black bugs on the floor, like cockroaches. They went up the walls and even on the people waiting for the offices. Everyone looked at them fearfully, but no one made a move to get them off.

Wilky shoved me some more, and I decided that, at the first opportunity, I was going to go ahead and take his head off for him. Actually, it would be the humanitarian thing to do.

I felt something on me and looked down. One of those black bugs was crawling up the leg of my one-piece. Cocking an index finger, I flicked it to the floor, then stomped on it with the heel of my boot. It let out an ear-piercing screech, like a piggy-backed freight-bullet coming to an emergency stop. I only had a second to appreciate it before Wilky planted a beefy fist in my back that sent me sprawling on the dirty glass floor.

I cursed him and he shook his fists. "Get up," he sneered.

I shook my head to clear out the cobwebs, and got slowly to my knees. Looking around, I saw everyone in the whole place looking back at me. Moon-white faces with darkened eyes that were staring at me as if I had just killed all of their mothers. Hell, I didn't even know their mothers.

I guess Wilky was impatient for me to get up. He grabbed my lapels and helped me.

"Easy," Nathan told him.

"Soon, Earther," he whispered. "I'm going to get my hands on you. Soon."

"Well, I sure hope you wash them first," I replied.

We passed the offices and the noise, entering a door at the end of the hall marked NO PUBLIC ADMITTANCE. That put us in another long hallway. This one was cleaner, though. The walls on both sides were covered, floor to ceiling, with tiny vis screens. There were thousands of them, all being continuously monitored by long rows of cops who sat on hydraulic chairs that could hum up and down or side to side to check things in detail. The hall was filled with a monotonous low-level chatter from the screens and from the headsetted techs who spoke into small mikes at a constant rate. And I began to understand what those bugs really were.

They called the room "the eye-watch," and it seemed to keep tabs on everybody on the satellite. On Papa Bear, thinking about crime could be a crime. It took a long time to walk through the eye-watch. Toward the end of the hall, one of the cops was lying on the ground, holding his skull, moaning softly. A thin line of blood ran from his ears where he had been pierced by the screeching death song of the bug I'd killed. Someone had already taken his place on the chair. No one had taken him. Too bad.

We got through the vis maze and came to a security door. Before the thing slid open to admit us, we were hand- and voice-printed, scanned metabolically, and jammed electronically just in case we were wired. Who bugs the buggers?

Triple doors scooted aside and I was pushed roughly into an office. When I turned to say thanks, Nathan and Wilky were already gone and the doors closed tight. The office itself was all aluminum, and polished as bright as quicksilver. There was no furniture as such, just a long slab of metal that wound around the whole room, dipping down low here to make a chair, straightening there to make an end table, then down to another chair. I followed the swirl of the slab, until it terminated in the center of the room in a huge, gleaming desk. Across the front of the desk debossed letters said: SPEAK ONLY WHEN SPOKEN TO.

Behind the desk, wrapped totally in a clear, egg-shaped bubble sat Beemer, his slick hair reflecting the room's bright light in shimmering waves. The place was completely bare of ornamentation except for a large vis behind the bubble. It was juicing a viddy of some boiling, blue liquid, complete with plopping sounds coming through the desk speaker. And there was a smell. The room smelled like—lilacs.

Beemer pressed a button and hatched his egg. He stepped out, staring at me. There was a shiner under his left eye. His long black coat was buttoned up to his neck, so that only a little of his gold ascot showed through. It went all the way to his knees where jack boots, shiny as his hair, encased his legs. I could almost believe that he was naked under that ugly coat.

"You've got a hell of a right hand," he told me.

"You should've caught me before the operation."

He grimaced a slight smile. "We've checked on you, Swain. Know all about you. What do you want in my city?"

I smiled back. "I came here for a vacation."

Sitting on the edge of his desk, he reached across and changed the vis picture. It was a recording of my kitchen conversation with Irene. He never even glanced at the screen; he just kept staring at me. "You're hardly discussing your sightseeing plans here," he said.

"Did Irene know about that bug?" I asked.

He turned back to the bubbling liquid. "I'm asking the questions here. But, just for the sake of argument, don't you think it would be rather stupid for us to tell people when they are being watched? You could never catch anyone at anything then, could you?"

"No, I guess not." I sat on one of the funny chairs. It was downright uncomfortable, like trying to sit in a mixing bowl. "Look," I said. "Watch my lips, 'cause I want you to get all of this. I came up here to visit my friend, Virginia

53

Teal. I went to her place, and the next thing I know, you clowns are shooting me with dart guns. Now, I don't know why your goons brought me in here, but you've got no reason to hold me. So I'll be saying good-bye now."

I got up and moved toward the door. Beemer began laughing behind him. Needless to say, the doors didn't slide open.

"Sit down," he said, and his tone told me that I'd better do it. I sat. "We have to discuss a few things. You've been very busy. Let me read the charges: violating restricted air space, riding the ore trails to avoid radar, assaulting a police officer, hampering a murder investigation, resisting arrest, plus any number of lesser traffic violations perpetrated by your accomplice in getting to the murder scene." He had the practiced cadence, the officialese, of all cops who love their jobs.

"Porchy's innocent," I told him. "I forced her to take me here against her will."

"So she's told us," Beemer replied.

I was glad of that. Porchy did me a favor, and there was no reason for her to be involved.

He began talking again. "Assaulting an officer is a crime that in itself is punishable by a minimum term of ten years' confinement in Shimanagashi, and in extreme cases by expulsion."

"Expulsion?"

He made a kicking motion with his foot. "Out the air lock," he said, and smiled like a politician having lunch with an energy lobbyist.

I felt myself melting into the chair. "So what happens now?"

He pursed his lips. "If it was up to me," he said, "I'd whip you down hard. But we got a memo down a while ago from the manager's office. It suggests that we take into account your ignorance of our laws and simply deport you with the stipulation that you will be arrested and penalized to the full extent of the law if you ever return."

I can't leave anything alone. "Why the generosity?"

His face solidified. "Don't question it," he responded. "Just thank whatever god you worship and get out."

"What about Ginny and Porchy?"

"The cabbie will have to have her license revoked, of

course. And your sick friend . . . take her out. Take her with you and leave our medical facilities for the people who really need them. We don't want you here. Either one of you.''

I stood up and walked over to him. "If we don't find out what happened to her, she'll die within the week. She'll never survive the trip home.''

He glared at me, the odor of jasmine drifting from his ill-fitting clothes. There was a staleness there that he kept trying to cover up. "We already know what happened to her. She got all tangled up with a Freefaller, then killed him. The same thing happens whenever we get mixed up with your kind. If she wasn't already done for, I'd charge her with murder.''

I was getting angry, and I think it was showing. "Earthers aren't your trouble, buddy. Earthers don't make you so afraid of losing your grip that you have to listen in on every conversation that your people have. What are you afraid of?''

"I don't make the rules, Swain. That's just the law. I get paid to enforce the law. It's a very simple system.'' He moved away from me, pacing like a caged gorilla. "What the hell do you know about anything?''

I wasn't about to leave it alone. I followed, getting around in front of him again. "I know that if Ginny dies, it's your fault. And so help me, if that happens, I'm going to come for you and take you apart piece by piece.''

His eyes suddenly flared at me like industrial lasers. His fist flashed out and I saw that he was wearing something on his knuckles, a small black band. I couldn't duck it in time. When he connected with my face, my brain exploded with white-hot light. A second later I was on the floor all the way across the room, my body vibrating.

"That was about fifty thousand volts, blood money,'' he told me. "Would you care to try for a hundred thousand?''

I shook my head, groggy. "Sure,'' I said weakly. "Do a number on me. It won't change anything.''

He walked over to where I was and, reaching out, helped me to my feet. "It's the system, Swain,'' he said. "It's the way things are done here. You don't know slag from moon dust, so don't try to tell me how to do my job.''

I rubbed the place where he had hit me. "You know,'' I said, "I thought you were a dumb punk, just like the others. But I was wrong. You're worse. They don't know any better, but you . . . you work it. You justify anything by calling it duty. Just lump it all together, good and bad, and call it duty so you won't have to think about it. Covers a lot of territory, doesn't it, friend?''

He clenched his teeth, but didn't make a move for me. "I'm a good cop. A damned good cop," he said. "I uphold the law here strictly by the S.O.P. I implement my memos and don't take kickbacks. And I definitely don't have to take any recycled crap from a cheap-jack hired gun like you."

He took me slowly by the front of my one-piece and propelled me backwards toward his doors. "You clear the flutter out of your ears and listen to me. Your cab driver friend is waiting for you out in the hall. You go back to Loonie with her, get on the next shuttle for Earth, and consider yourself lucky to be alive. You've got one hour to be out of my city. This isn't your world. Stay out of it!"

Reaching past me, he used his fist to smash a button console on the wall. The door panels slid open immediately. Never taking his eyes from mine, he shoved me through the doorway. I fell on my can out in the eye-watch. A woman walked past me and went right into Beemer's office. She had short, sandy hair and a real practiced wiggle. The door slid closed behind her.

Someone was helping me up. "Honey, I believe that we've overstayed our welcome."

I had a bad headache from the punch. Looking up, I saw Porchy's smiling face. "What round is this?" I asked.

"When you're knocked out, lover, it doesn't matter what round it happens in."

She got me to my feet and helped me back through the eye-watch. "Knocked out?" I replied. "I didn't even hear the bell."

8

My brains felt like broken glass when Porchy helped me into her hack. She was fussing around, and mother-henning me until I finally waved her aside.

"What I could really use is a drink," I said.

"They had no business doing that to you," she said, as she rooted through her tool box for the bottle. "There oughta be a law."

She handed me the nippled bottle and I took a long pull. It felt warm and friendly. "Let's get the hell out of here," I said, and the glass in my head began to powder to a fine mist.

Porchy took her seat at the controls. "With pleasure," she replied and blew the bolts that sent us tumbling. I watched Papa Bear spinning away from us. Then the thrusters kicked in and it disappeared beneath and we were in the traffic flow.

I had a lot of talking and thinking to do, but there was something that had to be taken care of first. Unstrapping, I floated out of my chair and around the cabin, banging the walls, searching.

"Come back down here," Porchy said, looking up, following me with her eyes. "What are you trying to do?"

I put a finger to my lips, and knocked my head on the top of the cabin. Hand-walking from the ceiling, I moved over to the bulkhead seam that ran around the circumference of the ball, and began feeling its contours.

She watched me like a cat with a moth. "Did that licking make you soft in the head?"

I just kept shushing her. Then I found it, small and hard and sleek. I snapped it up and shook it around in my hand. "Open up that cigarette hole," I said.

She narrowed her gaze, perplexed, but did what I said. Using my legs, I pushed off the side of the ball like a swimmer and floated over to the other side of the cabin, following the sound of the escaping air hiss until I located the hole. Opening my fist slightly, I spoke into it. "This is bug-bug forty-three," I said softly, "signing off."

There was a sharp pain in the palm of my hand. The damned bug bit me somehow. "Ouch!" Opening my paw, I grabbed the thing from the sides with thumb and index finger. Two tiny stringers of blood were running down my palm. I looked at it. Its little head was wagging back and forth, two gleaming steelpointy teeth chomping up and down. I could really grow to hate those things.

"Bye bye," I said, and stuck the thing into the hole. Letting go, it slipped into the dark, dark night. "Vis me sometime, okay?" I called through the opening.

"Will you get back down here!" Porchy called.

"Gimme a hand, will you?"

"Damned amateurs," she muttered, and stood slowly, hanging onto her seat for an anchor. She reached up and I reached down, and pretty soon I was safe and comfy, strapped in my own seat.

The air hole was still open, so I went ahead and took the opportunity to light a smoker. It was the best medicine I'd had in a long time.

"Where to?" she asked.

I looked over at her. This wasn't her show, but I couldn't trust the security anyplace else. "Could we just move around for a while?"

Her well-traveled face got a little bit tighter, and she ran a weathered hand through redglowing hair. She had a rugged beauty to her, a simple dignity that lit her up from inside. "They've only given us an hour, Swain."

"You don't have to if you don't want to."

She sighed, opening her eyes wide. Leaning over, she dipped into her tool box and pulled out her baseball cap. She pulled it down tightly on her head. "What the hell," she said. "I'm out of work anyway. Got another one of those cigs?"

I lit one off mine and handed it across to her. "I feel bad about the way things have turned out," I said.

She took a deep drag and blew it out of her nose in two snorting streamers. "I knew what I was getting into," she replied, and glanced over at me. "You play the game and sometimes you lose." She shrugged. "Wouldn't be any fun otherwise."

"So what are you going to do now?"

Her face seemed to settle like dirt shoveled back into a hole, and her eyes softened the way I'd seen them do before. "I don't know," she answered. "Maybe go back home. It's been ten years. Is that a long enough period of mourning?"

I flicked an ash and watched it float away. "You lost your husband up here?"

She looked back out the front port. "We had just gotten married. Young . . . broke. He took a job with Western so we could get ahead a little." She gave a sharp laugh. "He wasn't any more a Spacer than you are. He wasn't up here two months before he was killed in one of their damned border disputes. I came up to claim the body; it took every penny I had. I figured that I could use his wages to get back down."

"And there weren't any."

"I told you I was young. He had gambled it all away, at least that's what they told me." She took a deep drag on the cig, held it. When she talked, the smoke puffed out with her words. "I didn't have anything. They offered me the cab job until I could save the money to get back. What they didn't tell me was that the living costs plus the lease purchase of the cab would take everything I made. It took me years to save the ticket fare, and when I finally did . . ." she shrugged. "There just wasn't anything left back on Earth for me. So I stayed."

"Tough break," I said.

She frowned. "Well, maybe it's time to go back and try to put my life back together. What are you going to do?"

I didn't want to tell her much. The more she knew, the more trouble she was in. "Not much I can do," I answered, and that was truer than I wanted to admit to myself. "I really haven't had much time to think about it." I reached into my pocket and fished out the gold coin. "Ever seen one of these?" I asked.

She took it from me and studied it, her eyes drifting every few seconds to the vis to watch the traffic. She smiled quickly and handed it back. "Where did you get that?"

"Found it," I told her. "What do you think?"

"It's a gambling chip from Jenny Sue Qua, Freefall's concession to the darker side of human nature."

"A gambling satellite?"

She chuckled softly. "Gambling, sex, drugs, electrojunk, vis addictions . . . you name it. I guess it's kind of like a safety valve for the locals. You know, anything goes. I used to take the Spacers out there a lot before they closed off the city to visitors."

"When did all that happen?" I stuck the chip back in my pocket.

"About five years ago," she replied. "A shame, too. Wired Spacers are great tippers."

I thought about that. It didn't make sense to me that the chip was the only thing on Roque's body. Although I guess it was possible they had missed it when they searched him.

"Is it hard to get onto Papa Bear?" I asked.

"You're going to go back there?"

"Maybe."

Porchy shook her head, making her cig smoke wiggle in the atmosphere for a second before being sucked away. "You just don't know when to quit, do you?"

"I'm like a donkey looking for water," I answered. "How about it?"

She tightened her jaw. She didn't want to tell me; I honestly think that she was worried for me. That's something I'm not used to. Finally she opened up.

"The regular docks are monitored pretty close," she said, and hated herself for saying it. "But the delivery docks handle all the ore shipments from the basket, plus little things from the small support satellites. See, Beltel won't admit to any dependency on Earth for any materials, but obviously, they have to import some things, especially wood and plastic parts. What they do is hire other companies to do the job, then buy from them. I would try to slip in with other deliveries."

"Thanks," I said. Settling back in the seat, I finished the fag in silence. There were some leads, but they weren't very firm. Just getting around was going to be my biggest problem. But then again, nobody ever said that life was going to be easy.

"Swain?" Porchy said quietly after a time.

I looked over at her.

60

Her eyes met mine for just an instant, then she looked at the ground. "Give it up," she said. "You can't beat these people. They're going to eat you up and shit you back out again, and it won't even slow them down."

"Oh, I'll slow them down," I returned.

"Would you be serious!" she said angrily. Her lower lip quivered and she quickly turned her head away. "Damnit, I don't want anything to happen to you."

Reaching out, I touched her arm. "Look at me," I said. She turned slowly. "I've got to do this. There aren't any choices . . ." She started to speak, but I held up a hand to stop her. "It's just the way things are. Ginny needs me; there's nobody else."

"Don't you understand that they'll kill you?"

I sank back in the seat and watched the traffic slowly moving by and the deep black curtain that swallowed them all up. "I know that," I replied.

"I want to help you," she said.

"No."

"You won't have a chance without help."

"No!" I snapped. "I won't be responsible for any more lives. Now please, just take me back to the hospital and get away from this madhouse."

She set her jaw and pulled the cap down tight. "You got it, Earther," she said, and her voice was hard.

I smoked another cig, and watched the scenery that spread out all around us. The mammoth wheels turning, slowly and elegantly, rotating to a kind of internal rhythm that owed its existence to nothing but itself. Their mirrors flared brilliant, bright torches etching the black night with warmth and promise. The ships, silently swarming the wheels like hiving bees, moved with the beautiful instinct of Nature in symmetry. Behind us, the moon hung hazy white to yellow, land-ho, on the stormy black sea of distant blinking stars—a warm port to anchor dreams. And below—Earth. Massive and commanding, it ruled the sky, wearing a crown of glittering sun sabers that sliced the bosom of heaven with the unequaled majesty of infinity. Infinite energy, infinite light, infinite power. The pulsing beat of the heart of Mankind.

It seemed somehow frail and forlorn to me. That awful dichotomy of marbled mausoleums that hold the rotting death stench. We just put it out there, God, twist it up and try to

61

fool ourselves. And never once do we realize that we're the ones who need to be fixed. That everything else is all right the way it is. That's the trouble with brains. Brains are the ultimate hedonists. Brains love what they do and just can't see it any other way. The cig turned bad in my mouth. I put it out.

The hospital was spinning away just ahead of us; I could see its twirling red cross pinwheeling in the night. The sun would be gone behind the Earth in a while. But I had the feeling that didn't mean anything up here where they don't count the days.

"When do they sleep?" I asked Porchy, as she tried to bull's-eye herself onto the spin of the wheel.

"Depends on the work shift," she said coldly. She was mad at me, but we'd both get over it. "They have designated sleep hours."

"I thought they didn't count time up here?"

"Each day is the same as the next," she answered. "So there's no reason to count them. But the hours . . ." she rolled her eyes, "the hours are very important up here. The hours are THE importance."

She got us docked, and I right away made for the hatch. "Thanks for everything," I said, and meant it.

"Sure," she said, refusing to look at me.

Unlocking the door, I started up into the tube.

"Wait," she said, and began rooting through her tool box.

One knee up on the hatch, I turned and watched her. After a minute, she came out of the box with a jar of white cream.

She tossed it to me. The jar was unmarked.

"The Spacers used to use this to fit in here," she said. "If you're going to mix with the natives, you'd better look the part. Just take a little bit and rub it onto exposed body parts. It'll pale down your complexion."

I grinned widely. "Thanks."

"Another thing. When you get with a bunch of them, don't talk too much. Listen for the speech patterns. Try to fit in, or you'll scare them to death."

"Don't talk too much," I repeated. She knew me well already. I started out the hatch again.

"Another thing," she said, stopping me a third time. "Don't trust anybody. Keep that pretty ass of yours intact."

I bobbed my eyebrows. "I didn't think you noticed my pretty ass."

"I noticed."

Nodding once, I climbed into the tube and crawled to the exit lock. It must have been nighttime in the hospital, for all the ceiling panel-lights had been dimmed to a sliver. As near as I could figure, what happened was that the diffusing mirrors just turned a notch, only reflecting part of the light.

It was eerie in there, the shadowed halls quiet and sinister. I walked the deserted, perpetual hill occasionally hearing the muffled sound of distant, soporific bells and the small whining grate of the dehumidifiers kicking in. I felt alone, like old people must sometimes feel alone.

It took me a long time to find Ginny. Everything looked so much the same to me. I finally did, though. The lights in her room had gone down, and only the blue and red and green running lights of the machinery gave any illumination at all. I walked to the stasis; she floated there, so much a dream, so great the dreamer.

Bending down, I took one of her hands in mine; she was burning up. "You hang in there, rich girl," I whispered. "I'll look out for you."

The changing light flickers on the control wall beside her flashed a pattern of subtle hues on her face. It was a pretty face, uglied by fear. Someone was going to pay for this. No matter what it took.

Leaving Psytronics, I made my way to Irene's apartment. Arriving at the door, I knocked. A vis-cam light went on above the doorway, and a second later the door slid open.

Irene Jacobi was standing there, wearing her concern like an overcoat. "You all right?"

"I'll live," I said, and moved into the room.

"What happened?"

I walked around the room, looking for bug-bugs. "Oh," I replied, "Captain Beemer and I had a nice chat, and we decided that it would be best for me to leave Freefall right away."

There were several of them skulking here and there around the room. They were all watching us. "What about Ginny?" she asked.

63

I shrugged. "I certainly can't care for her. If you're agreeable, I'd like to leave her in your care."

She looked surprised . . . and disappointed. "Well certainly, but I thought . . ."

"I'm out of my league here," I told her. "Besides, a deep space burial just isn't on my agenda for this week."

"I understand," she answered, and stuffed her hands into the pockets of her shift.

"Are my things back in the bedroom?"

Irene nodded.

"I think I'll just get them together and get out of your hair." I started walking, but she didn't follow. Turning back to her, I motioned with my head. Cocking hers, she followed.

Walking through the bedroom, I went straight for the bathroom. Checking quickly, I found no bugs. I poked my head into the bedroom. Irene had my bags open on the bed, and was packing my gear. Without a word, I walked up to her and grabbed her sleeve, tugging her into the bathroom.

Closing the door, I turned on the shower. The shower was mostly pressurized air blowing just a bit of water. It got the job done with a minimum of water expended. It also made a hell of a racket.

"What are you doing?" she said indignantly, pulling away from my grasp.

"Did you analyze the stuff under Roque's nails?" I asked, holding her shoulders.

She nodded, then suddenly her eyes lit up and her face softened. "I did," she answered, and I could feel her body relaxing under my hands. "It was aluminum. Aluminum shavings."

"What could that mean?"

She gave me a half-smile. "*You're* the private eye. What was the routine back there?"

I shook my head. "You've got enough bugs in here to ruin an exterminators' convention. I'm sick of making Beemer's job easy for him."

"You mean they've wired my hospital?"

"Great life, isn't it? If we could, I'd like to check Roque's body again."

She shook her head. "Sorry. Security took it away. Dumped it, I guess."

I wasn't surprised. "Is it possible for me to get over to Ginny's place from here?"

"Why?"

I felt a little dizzy. Going over to the toilet, I closed the cover and sat down. "There may be something there that can help me. I just want to look around a little."

She put a finger to her lips and let her eyes wander a bit. "We have to log all medical flights with Security, and I have no need of a . . . wait a minute." There was a small vis set into the aluminum wall of the john. Irene toggled it on. "Maintenance," she said.

A few seconds later, a straggly-bearded face appeared on the screen. "Yeah," the man said, and brought a dirty checkered handkerchief up to loudly blow his nose.

"Has the garbage gone out yet?" Irene asked.

When the man saw whom he was talking to, he snapped quickly to attention. "Well . . . ah . . . Doctor Jacobi . . . I was going to get to it, but things got, things got real busy, and . . . uh . . . I'm just getting ready to get it out now."

"That's okay, Lou," she said, easing her tone down to the way she'd talk to a small child. "Just hang on for a minute. Get things ready, but don't go until you hear from me."

Lou's eyes lit up. "Yes'm," he said, happy he wasn't in trouble. "I'll wait right here."

Irene blanked the screen. "Got you a ride," she said. "Hope you don't mind a little smell."

"I've been dying for a little smell ever since I left Earth," I replied. I stood up, I guess too fast, because I almost fell right down again.

Irene took my arm to steady me. "You're still weak," she said. "What you need is more rest."

"I'll rest later. Let's get me out of here."

We quickly gathered my things, all the while making small talk to fool the greedy ears of the eye-watch. Leaving the bedroom, we moved through the rest of the flat, making sure I didn't forget anything. Before we went out the door, Irene strapped on her medical pouch.

We moved into the dark hallway, our footfalls clicking along the bare floor. "Back at Ginny's, you scared Beemer with the name Henry. Who's that?"

"Henry Malaca," she answered. "Plant Manager. He

65

runs the show. Everything. He's an Earther, too. I did some open-heart surgery on him several years ago, and we've been friends ever since. It's mostly misplaced gratitude on his part, but it doesn't hurt to have friends in high places."

"Would he help us?"

"I think he already has," Irene replied, hurrying to keep up with me. "You're alive, aren't you? I don't think we can expect much more than that from him. He's a businessman, Swain. If I hadn't operated on his heart, by God, I'd sometimes swear that he doesn't have one."

I nodded, trying to shake the uneasy feeling that walking the deserted hallway gave me. It made me shiver, and that had nothing to do with the cold. "Beemer threatened me with Shimanagashi," I said. "What's that?"

She looked up at me, her eyes vague and uncertain. "Shimanagashi," she said. "Isolation. It's the equivalent of prison up here. Locked away in a weightless sphere. Loneliness, hallucinations . . . ultimately madness. Punishment is swift and horrible in Freefall. It's the way of the system."

"That's what Beemer kept saying."

She squeezed my arm. "That's what you need to keep in mind above all else. The system. That's the real soul of Freefall. It's a living thing, Swain. And it's not a nice person. Here we are."

We banged through a set of double doors marked MAINTENANCE, then through another set of the same. We were in a big room full of garbage. Broken machines were stacked in neat rows, like body bags in a bush war. Oil and grease were everywhere, puddled on the floors and smeared on the straight aluminum walls. There were battered garbage cans full of food scraps and boxed containers full of excretory wastes to be reprocessed back into the system. Spare mirror panels were stacked in one corner, and a workbench cluttered with tools stood next to them. Smells of waste and petroleum sat heavy in the bottled air, like soured milk on a bad stomach.

The man from the vis was in there. Wearing filthy coveralls and big, unwieldy gloves, he carried the garbage cans one by one to a big round hole cut into the middle of the floor. The hole had a small fence around it that hinged on a gate. The gate was open.

We walked up to the hole. It went way down, disappearing into darkness. A heavy sulfuric smell wafted gently up from the hole. The man would move up with a can and dump its contents down the tube, where it would disappear with a gurgling sound.

"Lou, this is Mr. Swain," Irene said. "You're going to give him a ride on your way to the dump."

"S-Sure, Doctor Jacobi," he said slowly. He watched her face carefully when she talked, the way retarded people do. He was pale, but an Earther. I was getting to where I could pick them out in a crowd.

"Glad to know you, Lou," I said to him.

He smiled dumbly, nodding.

Irene was fiddling with her pouch. She came up with an air hypo. "Here," she said, and shot my arm before I knew what she was doing. "This might make you feel a little better, but you still need more rest."

"What is it?" I asked.

"Megavitamins plus," she replied.

"Plus?"

"Don't ask."

I started perking up almost immediately. The dizziness left, and some of the soreness was seeping out of my muscles.

She put the hypo back into her pouch. "How are you going to get back?" she asked.

I was watching Lou move pathetically around the room, taking great care to dump his garbage correctly. "Haven't thought that far ahead," I replied.

"If you stay hidden that long," she said, "Lou will make another run about this time tomorrow. I'll have him stop by and pick you up."

"Can that get you into trouble?"

"Sometimes there have to be more important considerations." With that, she turned from me and walked over to Lou, explaining to him how to get to Ginny's while he studied her face and continually shifted his feet.

She left the room then, waving as she went. Lou came shuffling up to me. "We can go now, Mr. Swain."

"Swain," I said. "Just call me Swain."

His mouth opened about halfway and he stared at me the way he had done with Irene. "Ready" was all he could think to say.

We started for a hatchway set into a nearby wall. We had to pick our way through the stacks of trash to get to it.

"Lou," I said, noticing his outfit. "Would it be possible for me to get something like what you're wearing?"

He had to stop to think about that, but when he did, his eyes lit up. "We have lots of workclothes," he said slowly. "You can have as many as you want."

"Just one would do."

His face tightened a bit. "You have to promise to bring it back."

"I promise."

He smiled, then, satisfied. Sticking out his lower lip, he moved to a gunmetal-gray storage cabinet. The door stuck on him, and almost knocked him over when he jerked it open. He got out a dingy set of zip-up coveralls and brought them back to me. I got into them, going native. I felt like a rich boy at a masquerade.

We went through the lock and found ourselves at the top of a dark stairway. "Watch it," Lou said. "Back-breaker."

I understood. The steps were littered with grease and trash, and the cold metal banister was the only thing that kept me from going down the fast way. It was a long way down, terminating in a wheel-lock. Opening that, we were in the cabin of the garbage wagon.

It smelled awful in there, like sweaty feet in cheap shoes. It was a small cabin, like Porchy's cab, but everything was mired in a layer of filth, like too many dirty overalls sliding in too many times. Lou took my bag and slid it behind the seats.

"Sorry about the mess, S-Swain," he said, embarrassed. "Nobody ever comes in here but me."

"Don't worry about it." I liked Lou. He was open and honest, and his face, despite his handicap, held a certain nobility. There was a slackness there, a physical extension of the man's troubled mind. But every now and again, it would seem to snap back, the murky eyes would clear, and he'd look normal. Then it would all sag away again.

The controls were old, rusted. Lou began to work them with surprising dexterity, making contact with the ancient thrusters. The machine whined and shivered, creaking like an old mill wheel. Then it coughed loudly, and we sputtered away.

There was a band of oblong ports at eye level all around. I turned in my worn, disintegrating seat and looked out the back. A huge metal chamber was attached to us from behind. Our tag-along squeaked loudly behind us, always seeming to sway in a different direction from ours.

Then we were away from the wheel and on the open road. The hospital sat a bit out from everything else, so the traffic was sparse. I looked over at Lou; his lips were moving silently. I think he was repeating Irene's directions to himself.

"You're from Earth, aren't you, Lou?" I asked him when he had stopped mumbling.

He glanced at me, and I couldn't read the feelings in his eyes. "Earth," he said. "A long time ago."

I was unable to understand why they'd bring handicapped people to Freefall, given the circumstances that ruled the place. I wanted to ask him about it, but delicately.

"Have you always worked here at the hospital?"

He had set the controls on auto and was leaning back, staring at the dark, shadowed ceiling. "No," he answered.

"Where did you work before?"

He looked at me again, with those same unfathomable eyes. "Papa Bear," he said, and his features seemed to darken physically.

"What did you do there?"

His eyes were pleading with me, silently begging me to leave him alone. He took a long time before answering. "I was Beltel Plant Manager," he said, and tears began streaming from his suddenly clear eyes. They would slide down his cheeks, then break off and float in tiny droplets around the cabin.

"My God," I said, sitting up straight and turning around to face him. "What happened to you?"

He was crying in earnest now, his body shaking, his lower lip vibrating out of control. I leaned over and grabbed his arms to steady him.

"Lou?"

He was shaking his head, mouth open, tears floating. "I-I got closed in," he stammered, his body shaking violently. "S-Sick." He began doubling over in a tight ball. "Lonely, so lonely. Sick, I got so sick . . . so . . . so . . . alone, like a deep, dark hole."

I tightened my grip on his arms. "An accident? A breakdown? What?"

"Beckon," he said, and I felt as if a lightning bolt had just torn through every cell of my body.

"Tell me about beckon," I said. "Please!"

His eyes went wide, wild. "Noooo," he bellowed from deep down inside of himself. "No more talk. Swain?" And his voice was the cry of a starving infant. "Please help me, Swain, help me, God help me . . ."

He began choking down in his throat, then threw up, the vomit mixing with the tears in the weightless air. His body began jerking crazily, like someone was shaking him. He was having a seizure.

My money pouch was in my bag. I got it out and quickly jammed one of my plastic chips into his mouth to protect his tongue. He was banging into things, hurting himself. I got hold of him, cradling him in my arms until the convulsions passed, crying along with him.

I'd be getting no more information out of Lou.

I wouldn't even try.

9

When Lou came out of it, he acted as if nothing had happened and so did I. I was ashamed of myself for pushing him to the brink the way I did.

The mechanics of shuttle flight were apparently skills that worked on a subliminal level, for Lou eased us up on Miss Lily like an expert. We clamp-locked and I unstrapped, happy for gravity again.

"Thanks for the lift," I told him.

"You're welcome," he returned and smiled. "I was . . . happy for the company."

I grabbed my suitcase and hatched out, knowing why Lou's brain stayed in the place where it did; it was his best shot at survival. I crawled through the tunnel and tried to unwheel the terminal door, but it wouldn't budge. I saw an embossed handprint on the wall beside the door, so I molded into it with my paw and the locks clicked open. Ginny really had been expecting me. I wondered where she'd got my handprint.

Climbing into the hallway, I turned and looked back down the tube. Lou was looking back at me from the ship. When he saw that I had gotten to safety, he waved once, a kind of salute, and wheeled the hatchway closed.

The lights were dim in there, but all functions of the wheel seemed operable. I crept quietly through the darkhazy hill-tunnel, looking for bug-bugs. There was an unease settling upon me, a kind of creeping paralysis that was either intuition or the beginnings of a darn good stomach virus. I felt as if I were standing before a door with a million locks, and all I had was a hairpin to open them. Beckon had been what Lou said to me at the height of his frenzy, just like the punk who had checked out in my apartment. But there was another connection, a subtler one. When it came to social animals, Ginny was the beast of Morocco. When we had

71

spoken on the vis the day I left Fun City, she had surprised me by saying that she was lonely. That's what Lou had said, also. Lonely. What bothered me was the fact that I was having the same twinges myself. I had attributed it all to the alien atmosphere, but now I didn't know. I didn't know anything about anything.

Reaching out of the spokes, I looked up into it. It was deep and dark, like Beemer's eyes. The spokes would join at the hub, which was weightless. Ginny had told me once that she used it as a sort of recreation room where she played a form of zero G tennis. I moved on until I was back in the living room, where I had gotten stung.

The living area itself was sunken several steps down from the hall, and a meter-wide walkway at hall-level described the circumference of the shallows. The walkway had a wrought iron banister on the room side of the circle, to keep people from falling into the pit. I found a switch that brought up the light in there, and used it. On the upper level was a bar and, farther around, a kitchen that molded itself to the curve of the room.

Ginny's place had a different look from everything else I had seen in Freefall. Austerity was the norm everywhere else. Building materials were mostly metals mined on the moon's surface. Ginny, on the other hand, didn't give a whit about their pioneer outlook. She had brought the best with her that she could find. Rich woods and plastics gave the place a homey feel. I could almost get comfortable in there.

Going to the bar of real maple, I slid open the back cabinet and found a dozen bottles of Black Jack. Unstopping one, I filled the biggest tumbler I could find and began my perusal of the place.

Very little had been touched by the cops. The place was just about as I remembered it. The living room itself was quite large. It had fine stuffed Mediterranean furniture around the edges and several mahogany coffee tables within easy reach of the chairs and sofa. The carpeting was deep and white; it made you want to take your shoes off and run around in it. The whole room looked new and fresh, like a showroom display. All the light in the place came down from the round ceiling.

The broken vase still lay in pieces on the floor, as did

72

Ginny's clothes. I grimaced involuntarily, took a big drink, and moved down the stairs to get a better look.

I picked up a couple of pieces of the vase. White porcelain it was, with latticed blue flowers flowing easily along the slick sides. It was one of Ginny's antique Chinese pieces that she was always trading oil for. A meter away sat the empty pedestal that had once held it.

It didn't take a genius to notice the lack of blood on the carpet. There was a little there, but it was just residual stuff, traces. I didn't know much about medicine, but intraventricular bleeding usually meant a lot of blood pumping like crazy for a few minutes. Before he died, Roque would have been breast-stroking in hemoglobin. And then the vase. It was wide and fat, not nearly the size to make the deep indentation that was evident in the man's skull. That got me thinking about something else. When Porchy and I first came up on Miss Lily, the only vehicles locked onto her were police cruisers. How did Roque get there? It was beginning to look like Roque was not only killed by something other than a Chinese flower pot, but that it wasn't even done at Ginny's place.

Was the murderer the anonymous caller, or was I dealing with a fourth piece of pie? Why did he pick Ginny's place to dump the body? And how did all of that connect up with her condition? Accepting the fact that the murder was done elsewhere, I could look at Ginny's torn clothing as a clumsy attempt to point to the police the conclusion that they did, in fact, draw. But I still couldn't figure the connection between Ginny and Roque that would lead to all of this. How much trouble could she get into in a couple of weeks? Apparently plenty.

I needed to find that third party, that caller who tipped the whole thing. But where to start?

Climbing the steps back up to the kitchen, I went to the fridge. I hadn't eaten since the moon and hunger was beginning to catch up with me. The kitchen was shiny aluminum, just like in all the other satellites. It was long, with everything built in and recessed into the wall. The fridge was stuffed full of sandwich makings, which is as close to a banquet as you get in my neighborhood. There was bread in a metal pan in the freezer. I grabbed an armful of chow and headed for the mike.

Once I got everything ready, I took it all back to the living room and ate at one of the coffee tables, washing it down with Black Jack. It was good, the bread especially. My knee bumped some toggles under the table, and a holoprojection of a tiny naked woman began dancing around my plates and cups. She must have been equipped with some manner of avoidance radar, for she never bumped into things. I tried to chase her with my fingers, but she always managed to dance away from my grasp. I wished that she could talk; I'd ask *her* what happened.

I started flipping other toggles, and other figures appeared on the table, all choreographed with the naked woman. I got to the last one, though, and it was a holovis that lit up in the center of the room. This was where Ginny had called me from.

"Memory," I said, and the air shimmered red. I took the machine back to her arrival two weeks previously. There were several days' worth of calls dealing with the mechanical aspects of getting her wheel out of mothballs, plus several routine calls to Parmon, her man at the stock exchange who handled investments for her. There was some social stuff after that, Ginny's contacts with the people she knew up there who were rich like her. There weren't many. Ginny was a large stockholder in Beltel, which got her the place at Freefall to begin with. But not many of her class cared for the rigors of life in space. There were a few party invitations made and accepted. Some more calls to Parmon. Then nothing. Dead air for about six days. There were some trace records of incoming calls, but apparently they weren't recorded.

Then came her call to me. She was changed, a different person. She had that look in her face. The look that she still wore. There was only one more entry. It was a local call—Ginny to herself. I knew who the person was who had made it, but I didn't recognize her. She was blue eyes floating in a sea of angry red blood. She was blond hair twisted to knotted grotesquerie, swirling in obscene disarray. She was an angel-face diamond hard, ravaged like the Florida coast after a hurricane. She was staring straight at the screen, straight at a mirror reflection of herself. She spoke:

"I am the god of the universe, the ruler of the heavens and the earths. I created you in my image, in the image of my love." Her hands moved continually, opening and closing, tugging at her clothes, wringing together. "I am the fount of life and the black pit of death, the lawgiver of dreams, the progenitor of nightmares." Her hands came to her face and she began weeping softly. "I am the pumper and the drainer of your lifeblood, and I am alone. I am alone in a world of my own fantasies, trapped in the maze of delusion." Taking her hands away, she stared deeply, tragically, back at me from the shimmering curtain of the holo. "The loneliness is all-consuming, the responsibilities for reality too great. Sad to report that I cannot bear the weight of my awesome task much longer. I must escape, there is no other way. I tell you this in the hopes that you may someday understand and forgive me. You, my sister, you myself." She looked around suspiciously. "It closes in now," she said softly. "The fog hangs low. It beckons me. It beckons."

The screen went blank.

I sat there on the couch, while the tiny figures danced, and the walls closed in just a little bit. I looked down at my hands; they were shaking. I heard a sound, a tiny sound, distant and easily ignored. Then I heard it again. Then again.

"Outside," I said loudly, and the holo juiced a star's eye view of Miss Lily. Several police cruisers were clamping onto the wheel.

I jumped up from reflex, darting my head. Where to go? How does a monkey get out of its cage? I grabbed my suitcase and bounded up the living room steps, taking the hallway moving away from the docks. I charged down the hall, moving for I didn't know what. When you go in a circle, it's only a matter of time before you get back to where you started.

I could already hear voices drifting from farther around the curve. I stopped, turning to move the other way, then turning back. It didn't matter which way I went.

There was a doorway behind me. I twisted the knob and went in. It was a bedroom. The bedclothes were torn off the bed, and clothes littered the floor so that you couldn't even see the color of the carpet. I stepped back out; the room was a dead end, just like all the rooms would be. I was trapped in the house of mirrors, forever running into my own reflection.

I heard someone call my name, jumped at the sound. On the wall behind me, Beemer's ghostly face was staring out of a vis. "Give it up," he said. "You can't get away. Wherever you are, give it up or we use the darts."

My muscles stiffened with the thought of it. Voices getting closer, searching. They were just up the hill—coming down/going up. I stepped back in the room, hugging the wall next to the door, tensed like a runner on the blocks waiting for the starter's pistol. Waiting . . .

The sounds moved closer. There.

Right there.

The door banged open, and I swung out with my suitcase, connecting with a punk face that exploded red and groaned back away from me. I was out the door, charging up that goddamned, everlasting hill. Voices behind me. I turned to look and fell heavily, rolling. Three punks had dart guns leveled. They fired through puffs of compressed gas-smoke. Suitcase up, one dart whizzed over my head, two more stuck in the case. I scrambled up, getting farther up the curve, out of sight.

The voices came from everywhere then, closing, tightening the knot, strangling. They were all over. I hit a punk dead run; he banged the wall, all straining muscles and clenching teeth, and I was off again. It was a treadmill, a huge hilly treadmill. And suddenly, there were the docks—a punk by an open hatch, another crawling out the tube.

Instead of bracing, the punk on his feet went for his stinger. Middle unprotected, I hit him full force, jamming the suitcase hard in his gut. He almost came up off his feet, then went to the floor again, gasping for bottled air. Turning quickly, I grabbed the tube punk by his outpoking head, and jerked him through the opening to join his buddy on the floor.

Black-suits filled the hilly halls in both directions as I scrambled through the tube, shoving my suitcase in front of me. I tumbled into the cop cruiser just as a dart blew past where my ass had just been. I looked up to a couple more darts, then heard shuffling through the tube. Raising my arms, I slammed the hatch closed, wheeling it locked just as I heard pounding on the hood.

Then the pounding stopped, as the punks cleared the tube before I blew the locks and sucked them into outer space. Scrambling for the pilot's seat, I found myself staring at instruments that may as well have been Egyptian hieroglyphs. I'd seen enough people undock to know where the disengagement arm was, though. Jamming it, I heard the whoosh and watched Miss Lily tumble away from me. Steering pistols sat before me on the panel. I found the juice switch for the thrusters, and we immediately kicked in the direction of the dials. The burst glued my kidneys to the back of the seat, and I pulled my hands away in time to see us spinning back toward Miss Lily. The wheel loomed large before me, and cop cruisers all around it were disengaging to try and catch me. I was tracking back into their midst, scattering them. It could have been a great move if I'd have actually had anything to do with it. I was the cue-ball breaking the rack.

I grabbed at the pistols again, spinning off just before I crashed back into the wheel. I shot up and found myself staring into black space, the cops right on my tail.

Then the blackness flared around me. Pink-hot streamers of laser-cannon fire pulsed the night in infinite symmetrical lines, sniffing me out. They'd have me unless I could get back into the congestion.

Jerking the pistol, I banked left, buffeting like a Chinese junk in a typhoon. The lights of Freefall once again filled my ports. It was Papa Bear that I wanted, the only place in the whole crazy city that was big enough for me to lose myself in. The trailing streamers dropped off to nothing, as I eased myself back into the city proper.

Freefall charged up on me. Everything moved too fast, faster than my reactions. I'd try to handle the controls, but I was always a second behind what I needed to be doing. Wheels slipped silently by and the traffic veered to avoid the crazy man in the flight paths. My inability to guide the cruiser probably saved my life, for the cops had a hell of a time keeping up with my unintended suicidal charge.

I locked myself onto the pistols, desperately watching out the bubble. The vis bleeped and cried for me to work it, but I didn't know how. I was eyeballing, trying to adjust to controls that were sluggish by nature. It was like trying to drive a speedboat through a regatta. A whole covey of huge iron spheres came up on me, like a ball bearing patch. They were cold and close together. I was on them before I knew it, and through them before my hair even got around to standing on end. One slid past my starboard viewer so close that I could read the tiny stenciled word on its side: SHIMANAGASHI.

Whizzing through the patch, I turned and looked behind me. There were six sleek cruisers in pursuit, all dipping through the field of prison balls. The big wheel was to my left. I banked in that direction, remembering what Porchy had told me about the back door.

I quickly closed the distance to Papa Bear, more cruisers uncoupling from the Security docks, bearing down on me. They swarmed angry, wanting blood. If that was their game, they were going to have to work for it.

Suddenly Papa was right there, awesome and menacing. I was going too fast. Banging reverse thrust, I tried to slow my advance. I wanted to cut the circumference of the thing, but missed, flying between the spokes while my bubble turned black to blot out the mirror glare. Cruisers were all over me now, pilot fish on a white whale. Papa Bear disappeared behind me, and I banked sharply to get back around.

As I turned, I searched frantically for unsecured docks. I cleared the spokes again, almost losing it on the hub, then banked a third time. All I could see out of the bubble were swarming cruisers.

Then I caught sight of a freighter. Long like a centipede, it sidled up to the wheel, its long coupled cars waiting for unloading. I banked again, angling dead center for the freighter. This time I was going in no matter what. I finished my turn and straightened, hitting reverse thrust immediately. It wasn't immediate enough.

Papa Bear was large, then huge, then unrelatable in total size. There was a whole line of apparently open docks, glowing coldly with blue lights, like turquoise fog, gouging the night. Holding full reverse, I had a second to aim for empty light before the mouth of Beltel swallowed me up. There was an overpowering electric hum when I hit the blue light, then flashes. Superstructure, equipment, people—flashing by. Then I was down solid, a vibrating earthquake, ripping metal screams as my hull disintegrated on the titanium floor amidst a conflagration of yellow-blue sparks fit for a welder's dream.

I was going in circles then, pinwheeling my sparks, and in spin jerks I could see the bottom line: a large steel wall. It called me, dragged me to it with frightening inevitability. Grabbing my seat, I braced for impact.

Motion stopped with an orgasmic jolt, and my ship screamed the death scream. My body snapped forward, straining against shoulder straps. But they held, and I found myself sitting there, in the middle of a junkyard of scrap metal relatively untouched.

Unstrapping, I looked behind me. All the cruisers were settling, featherlike, into the open bay quite a distance from me. I could barely hear the shouts, for everything was drowned out by the sound of banks of air blowers that kept the open ports breathable.

A crowd was running toward me—kevlar cops and thermal-suited dockers. There were a hundred at least, maybe more. I climbed out of my seat and started away from the junk, when I saw my suitcase. It had been ripped to pieces in the crash, strewing my things all over the bay. But there, safe and sound on a cushion of polyester, sat the jar of pale cream that Porchy had given me. I snatched it out of the rubble and took off, running like a cat out of a dog show.

It was cold in there, and my adrenaline was the only thing that kept me from turning blue like the lights. Maybe they were cold too. The wall I crashed into was solid and blank and high. I ran beside it, going for a series of doorways that were set into the sides of the mammoth warehouse about one hundred meters distant. Out of the corner of my eye, I could see the surging crowd turning to follow my lead. I still had fifty steps on them, and hadn't run as far. I could beat them to the doors. I hoped that was a good thing.

Raw ore sat stacked in neat, military rows, as were crates of materials and foodstuffs. There was something else, too. Several long rows containing huge stacks of unrefined gold. Mountains of gold. Obscene amounts of it. That much gold didn't make sense, but I had no time to dwell on it.

I hit the doors, too fast, having to put my arms out to brake my impact. Pulling at the door closest to me, I slipped inside, steel darts clanging against the wall like slapping bones in a domino game.

I slammed the door behind me, and found myself staring at another door. This one was an air lock, and sealable. Unwheeling it, I stepped through just as my pursuers came through the first one. Quickly working the wheel, I bashed the thick red button to emergency seal the thing. I could hear them on the other side, like mice in a wall, but there was no way, short of melting the door, that they could get through to my side.

Leaning heavily against the wall, I tried to catch my breath. I was looking down a long, rusty hallway. It was dank and dim and went on without interruption as far as I could see. It curved upward, like the halls in Miss Lily, but owing to the size of the satellite, the curve was more a gentle slope than a hill. The place was alive with distant, mechanical noises. I figured that a place like Papa would have to have a lot of automatic functions for water conveyance, attitude jets, oxy manipulation and who knows what all, and most of them must have been housed right here by these tunnels.

My breath came ragged at first, then deeper, then steadier. They'd be combing the place for me, so I didn't have much time. What I needed was a plan to keep me moving and working. Taking the top off the cream jar, I began smearing it on my face. They'd be looking for an Earther; the disguise could possibly put them off for a time.

I remembered something that Irene had told me. Only the rich folks had their own separate housing. Everybody else lived on Papa Bear. That would mean that Roque's widow would be somewhere on this satellite. Funeral or not, she could tell me things about the man who had died at Ginny's feet that no one else in the universe knew. Maybe she had some answers for me.

Finishing my face, I went to work on my hands and forearms up to where they disappeared under the bulky overalls. There was no more sound on the other side of the lock. The punks were probably already telling their chums what tunnel I was in. I didn't like the odds on that one.

Reaching out, I toggled the emergency seal-cancellation, and unwheeled the door. The anteroom was empty. They didn't even have the good sense to post a guard. I slipped back from where I had just come, then cautiously cracked the door to the warehouse.

All the people who had chased me were walking wearily away, back to whatever it was that had occupied them before I diced a little excitement into their lives. They weren't looking back, so I just opened the door and stepped back into the cold. Hands in pockets, I walked casually down the row of doors and picked out another one a far distance from my original.

Getting inside, I was in a duplicate tunnel to my first hideout. I wheeled through the lock and jogged the length of the damp, musty hall. It was like a catacomb, with a tangle of side tunnels and noises branching off into darkness from the first. I stuck to the main hall, though, afraid that I would get lost in the maze.

By the time I had traveled the tunnel, I felt cold and dirty, chilled to the bone. I had to pass through a "clean" booth in order to enter Freefall. It was a glassed-in cubicle that blew pressurized air when you stepped inside, then heated with mike waves. As I stood in the booth, enjoying the heat, a holo of a middle-aged man floated in there with me.

"Hello," the image said in a whisper voice. "Welcome to the Beltel satellite complex: the happy community of the future in tune with the needs of today. If this is your first visit to Freefall City, I envy you the thrills that are in store when you behold our wonders for the first time. Would you disrobe please, and place your clothing on the red X by your feet."

"We haven't even been properly introduced," I returned.

"Like everywhere else," the projection went on, "we are a society bound together by common laws for the good of all. We think that here at Beltel we have a good system, a mutually beneficial system, for all concerned. However, it may be a little different from any that you are accustomed to, so let me review some of our rules for you now so that your stay with us may be pleasant and unmarred by unnecessary complications. Are you ready?" the holo asked, its eyes getting wide, its specter-head nodding. "Okay, here we go."

The ground by the red X caved in—I assumed—to take away the clothes that weren't lying there. And the speech by the-little-man-who-wasn't-there continued. "Physical vices and addictions are a hindrance to the human being's capacity for self fulfillment; therefore, they are simply not tolerated here except during appointed times and places. Cigarettes, alcohol, drugs, random vis-viewing, self-indulgent studies, gambling, the so-called 'liberal arts'—art, music, poetry—all the pandering to our narcissistic tendencies: these things are simply not tolerated here for the good of everyone. Our people are happy and well adjusted and don't need self-destructive recreations to justify their existence."

The booth shut off the heat. I tried to get out, but it had me locked in until the speech was finished. I rummaged through my clothes beneath the overalls and fished out a cig. Leaning against the glass wall, I lit it and smoked while I was listening.

"Physical violence," he was saying. "Strictly prohibited . . ."

I needed to see the Roque woman, and somehow, I was going to have to get over to the gambling joint and find out the stiff's connection with all that. Getting onto Papa Bear was one thing. Getting off would be another matter altogether.

". . . eat, and sleeping only during the specified time periods. Human beings cry out for discipline in their lives. The disciplined life is a productive life."

There was something underneath it all, something ugly that I couldn't quite get into focus. But I knew that I was going to have to understand it before I could ever put the whole puzzle together.

". . . never need to ask questions. It only complicates a process that has already been thought out by people far more knowledgeable than ourselves . . ."

The guy in the holo went on for a long time. He never seemed to get tired of talking. He chattered on like a salesman trying to sucker you through a pitch. I don't much like salesmen. They pretend to be selling you a product, when actually all they're selling is their spiel, and I've never been able to take a spiel home and carve potatoes with it.

Finally the red X came back up and the door clicked open and I got out of there. I passed through three sets of sliding doors, all painted white and fixed with the blue circled-bell insignia that was the most recognized symbol in the universe. The last one came open, and I was in the heart of Papa Bear.

My first impression was of the size. It was the largest enclosed space that anyone would ever be in. It was a whole city inside a tin can, like a ship in a bottle. The sky was a good seventy meters overhead and curved gently inward, forcing reality back in on itself. The city filled the enclosure, stuffed it full, like infection clogging a wound. It lay flat on the flat part, then curled up around the sides—sludge collecting inside a water pipe. It was a tinker-toy city, all prefab shells of military green. The green paint covered everything, like growing latex. It was the thick, mucuslike kind of paint. It was globby paint that came in huge industrial barrels and was designed to go right over everything—dirt, rust, graffiti, everything. It was the seal-in theory of decoration. Quick and cheap. Streets were laid out all around me like lines on graph paper. Nice, even avenues bisecting themselves with an excuse-me-thank-you-very-much attitude. And the hivelike shells stretched from there, climbing in the fake air as high as the ceiling would allow. There were clocks. Lots of clocks. They were everywhere. Monster clocks as big as a hot-air balloon and clocks as small as a wristwatch and clocks every size in between. They all read the same time, and they all clicked the minutes in unison, going to the next notch with a resounding, hollow thunk.

The air was misty, nearly foggy. Angry gray clouds hung at ceiling level. Waste gases, noxious fumes produced far too fast to get into the dehumidifiers, they churned and bottled and shoved expelled dioxides back on the people who breathed it. These were nondissipating fluorocarbons eating away at the city like a cancer. It was a system designed for ten thousand and holding ten times that amount. Like stuffing ten baby chicks into one egg shell. The odor of the place was stale, nearly nauseating, but like everything else, I found that I got used to it quickly. The upward curve was evident in so large a space. In the distance, the city tilted toward me at an ever-increasing angle, only to disappear through the cloud layer on the roof.

I looked to my left, along the giant wall that sealed off this section, and I was peering down a narrow alley between the buildings and the wall. The other doors were there; they had no handles on the city side, though. Far down the alley, a large group of kevlared punks were waiting for a smart-guy Earther who had invaded their nest. I figured I'd better move on before they decided to have a conversation with me about the weather.

I got into the flow. The streets were filled with people, all heading the way I was. It must have been shift-change or something. Most rode bicycles, a river of bikes with metal wheels, Papa Bear in miniature. I was in the crowd and no one seemed to be taking notice of me, so I must not have looked too out of place. A minute thunked by, and I knew that too much of that heavy ticking would drive me nuts.

Trash was piled on the streets, food trash and broken equipment. All the broken stuff was fixed with big green requisition tags for item replacement. From the looks of the amount of stuff on the streets, it didn't get replaced very often. The buildings just stood there, one big green glob after another. They had no doors, no glass in the windows—hollowed caves of steel and aluminum. The buildings all had two sets of numbers stenciled on them in white. The numbers were connected by a dash.

The clouds above glowed hotly, for they were blocking the source of light for the torus. Consequently, it was, I think, quite a bit dimmer in there than was originally intended. Perpetual twilight.

On every corner were things called answer booths where people could walk up and enter a series of pay vis-type chambers and ask a computer face questions concerning company policy if there were ever any problems not directly answered by the employee code. Near every answer booth was a huge community vis that juiced a never-ending series of posted openings, job and life.

It was at one of these that I found out about Garnet Roque. It seems that everyone's name was followed by a six digit number. This was the seniority number, and it determined one's position in life on all matters. Housing worked the same way. I had come in at the farthest point from the work places. This was the lowest rung on the seniority ladder, the slums of Papa Bear.

As I watched the screen, they were juicing life openings by seniority. Roque had been way up there—000472, and, accordingly, lived a lot closer to the heartland. His position was apparently an enviable one, for no one on this end of town paid even the slightest bit of attention to it, so much higher than they was he on the list; they didn't even have a chance at his lifespot.

As near as I could figure, whoever could get closest seniority-wise to Roque's position automatically got his wife and home. They showed the woman, showed her in extreme close-up. For some reason, I felt I recognized her. She had sandy hair and eyes that always seemed to be interested in something else. Then they pulled back the cam and showed her full figure, naked, from all angles. If she was appealing enough, for whatever reason, someone with higher seniority might want to take her, in which case she would move up to that position. It worked the same with men as women. The system was a strange one: divorce was allowed only if a person had the opportunity to move up by marrying an unattached employee—unattached either because of death or because of divorce when a mate had moved up. It tended to get real complex, and I got the feeling that a good part of everyone's waking hours was spent trying to keep his or her seniority intact.

Anyway, Roque had a good number, which put him uptown. That's where I needed to be. I stood there for a minute, from thunk to thunk, letting the crowd surge around me, trying to set it in my mind. I'd be woodshedding from here on out.

I'd need a change of clothes soon enough. Everyone was dressed exactly the same. The men all had on powder blue, three-piece suits and lavender shirts with wide, open-necked collars. It was an old style, one that hadn't been around for a good hundred years. I guess fashion didn't change much at Freefall. The women wore suits and pants like those of the men, but without vests. The women's color was deep burgundy, and the color of the blouse seemed to change from woman to woman. They all kept their hair short, bobbed just below their ears.

They were all pale, pale like ghosts, pale like Jeff Roque after we had taken his body out of the mike. Everyone, men and women, wore dark shadow around the eyes, which underscored the emaciated look. Looking at them all was like watching two fat people make love, a real disgusting display, but apparently satisfactory to the participants. And the sea of bicycles kept flowing by.

I was noticing a large number of black-suited cops moving through the crowds. They were looking for an Earther, so I was able to slip by a loose check. But if I was close, I wasn't a ringer, and they'd detect me sooner or later. I needed to get moving.

All at once, a whistling sound squealed out of the posting board. Everyone perked to attention. My eyes drifted to the vis and I found myself looking at a silent replay of Ginny's call to my office.

The vis began talking in that whispery voice that drove me crazy in the clean chamber: "If you have seen this man, please report to your nearest question box immediately. He is an escaped Earther with homicidal tendencies, and is extremely dangerous. A reward of ten seniority points will be issued for any information leading to . . .''

I was slowly backing out of the crowd. Even the make-up wouldn't help me now. Several pair of eyes turned to the strange man in coveralls, the flash of recognition charging their faces. They were pointing, talking all at once so that their words tumbled together like a verbal waterfall. I turned and ran.

Sirens sounded all around me, and I detected snatches of black uniforms moving in. They carried shiny metal billy clubs, like cattle prods, which they used to shock the citizens into movement. I needed transport.

Charging off the sidewalk, I jammed into the bike flow, knocking some poor Joe off his mover. He went to the hard ground, tangling with a confusion of wheels and legs. Several more bikes fell and we had a traffic jam.

"Pardon," I told the guy as I grabbed his machine from between his legs, "but I need this more than you do."

Jumping on the thing, I got in the middle of the rush. I hadn't ridden a bike since I was a kid, and my knees felt it right away. I was seeing cops everywhere; they must have made up half the population of Papa Bear. There was sound overhead. Looking up, I saw several heli-sleds with gold stars zipping in and out of the thick green buildings.

I started cutting side streets, picking up traffic flows on different roads. The rush hour was the only thing saving me, for there were just too many people doing too much traveling for them to narrow me down.

The trouble was, this couldn't go on indefinitely. All these people, myself included, were moving in a direction. We were going somewhere; I just didn't know where.

Then I saw it. A spoke terminal. An elevator extended down from the spoke, carrying loads of hundreds of people up to waiting shuttles that would take them to their work stations. There were large bike-parking lots coded by seniority that encompassed a wide area. I had run out of room.

Black-suits directed the flow with their clubs, while mammoth public vis screens by the elevator juiced nothing but my picture. And the clocks thunked another minute. Everyone was lining up. Lining up to park their bikes, lining up to get on the elevators. Beyond the lines, though, was something else.

It was a cornfield, a cornfield as high as the ceiling. It extended down the middle of the tube; and on either side, terraced up, were other fields. And way up, near the ceiling, were waterfalls tumbling from high streams, irrigating all the fields. The fields extended as far as I could see, disappearing up the curve.

I was in the bike line waiting to park. A punk watched the line as it went through. I came up on him as if I belonged there. He almost let me through, too. He looked at me, then let his eyes drift off. Then he did a take, looking at me again. He jerked his head behind him to check the monster vis, and turned back around just in time to see the knuckle express turn his nose to jelly.

The punk groaned to the street, and I hurried into the parking lot, pumping down row after row of neatly stacked movers, all green, all damnably green. There was shouting behind me, and I knew I hadn't hit the punk hard enough.

The elevators were up a flight of steps on a high platform. I took the bike to the end of the line, kicked it away from me, and took the steps two at a time without looking back.

I shoved into the crowd on the platform, and cops were ringing the area. Then, without warning, they began firing their dart stingers into the crowd, hoping for a lucky shot. There was confusion then, as citizens charged around like percentage lawyers at a bus wreck. Screams shook the chamber as people dropped all around me, stingered nerves freezing.

I got to the edge of the platform and jumped the small retaining wall that kept people up there. It was a good five meters to the ground. I hit with a grunt, and rolled into the platform's shadow. A loudspeaker above was telling everyone to hit the dirt, which they should have done to begin with. Then it got quiet above as the cops walked through the jumble looking for me.

Standing on sore legs, I flattened myself against the metal wall and looked before me. There was another line of people in the distance, waiting to get into the fields.

Keeping my back to the wall, I inched along it to get as close to the new line as possible. That accomplished, I simply

87

walked away from the platform, trying to attract as little attention as I could.

I reached the line and merged with it. We surged forward. They in their three-piece leisure suits, me in my gray coveralls. I kept waiting for the sirens, but they weren't sounding. I was in the middle of a tightly packed line. We narrowed even farther to fit between the rails, then we were at the high fence that described the corn's perimeters.

THUNK.

There was a huge timeclock on the fence angrily clicking the minutes. A large slotted panel held thousands of timecards. Everyone grabbed a card and punched in as each entered the fenced area. I punched a card and joined them.

We got through the fence and moved up on the corn. It was a DNA hybrid variety, the kind that could grow as tall as you wanted it to. They wanted it tall. Each row was marked with a two-digit number, and individual workers seemed to have individual rows that each went to. As each entered his work place, he would relieve someone already working there. The replaced worker would then take off knee-high rubber boots and give them to his relief. I soon understood why. The ground was forever moist and muddy.

I moved quickly into a row that seemed to have no one in it. I kept moving, switching rows whenever I ran into someone. Soon, the corn turned to wheat with stalks as big around as sycamore trees. I didn't want to stay in the fields; there were too many people to run into.

Working my way around to the edge of the wheat forest, I found some steps that led up to the higher, terraced gardens. The steps would go up, then flatten to a field, then go up again to the next field.

I climbed slowly, familiarly, up the narrow aluminum steps, my muddy feet leaving a brown trail behind me. The terraced fields were large vegetable patches interspersed with flowers for oxygen. The air production seemed to be helping here, for the smog clouds were fewer, more dissipated, although in the higher levels, leaves all had a yellowish tint and there was a definite odor in the air of rot, like the sour breath of people who are seriously ill.

I went up six levels, the last two enveloped in a fine haze. That was okay with me, since it provided a natural cover. The last level was a field of yellow grass about waist-high, with a large fish pond set in the center. Water ran from pipes to the pond, then cascaded from there down the hillside in conduits, taking water eventually to all the fields. There were many rows of fields separated by steps, all of which were identical to mine.

The fish ponds were nice, although they were covered with plexiglass to preserve the little darlings from the vapors up that high. I could understand it; the smell was pretty rank. Mingling with the rot odor was the slightest hint of animal. The stockyards must have been farther on, after the fields.

I stretched out on the grass, letting it envelop me like a chlorophyll ocean. As I lay there, I realized just how artificial the satellite life was. There were no real bugs, no insects of any kind. Now, I'm no great ant fan, but I somehow missed them when they weren't there. It was like we were all pretending. I wondered if they had little mechanical bees to pollinate their flowers.

Whatever I was going to do would have to wait until their pretend nightfall came around. I wasn't tired, but I could feel my body slowly starting to wind down, and I decided that if I was going to sleep, this would be the time. I lay there for a long time before finally drifting off, humming to myself like flies buzzing around my head.

It was springtime; it was always springtime.

THUNK.

10

I woke to half-hearted darkness, the only sound the rumbling rush of the nearby waterfall, punctuated, once a minute, by the clocksong. I had slept a long time, too long, but the rest made me feel a lot better.

Sitting up, I peered cautiously over my cover of thick grass. It was dark in both directions. The half-light of ceiling slivers defined the city below me as dark, looming shapes.

It was a dreary sight, and made me feel vaguely uneasy. It was as if I were caught up in a recurring dream, always the same, always just exactly the same. There was no waking up from this dream, though. It was perpetual.

I let my eyes roam the landscape, dwelling on each section for a long time, watching for signs of movement, searching. If they were waiting for me out there, they were staying well hidden.

Standing, I stretched. I was still a bit sore in my muscles from the dart, but it wasn't anything I couldn't live with. The make-up had streaked on my hands. Its usefulness was gone anyway. Yanking two handfuls of the tall grass, I used them to clean off hands and face. I moved down the steps and into the fields.

It was a long walk back to the fence, and the thing was closed, locked up tight, when I got there. The fence was about half as high as the ceiling and was topped by a curling bale of barbed wire. Moving back into the fields, I climbed into one of the basketed cranes that they used for pruning the tops of the stalks. It was as narrow as the corn rows and traveled on belted wheels to help it slosh through the mud. It was painted green, thick green.

The cart had an electric engine. I started it and hummed back toward the fence. When I got there, I pulled up as close as I could and then pressed the button that raised my basket.

It went up and, finally, over the barbed barricade. It was a hell of a drop to the ground. I climbed gingerly out of the basket, which was swaying like a hula dancer with poison ivy. It wasn't exactly my idea of a pleasant evening, but then I haven't had a pleasant evening in ten years.

I got over the wire, but not before I tore the front of my coveralls to shreds. Climbing quickly down the outside of the fence, I made my way into the recesses of the city proper. Zipping out of the now useless coveralls, I stuffed them into one of the garbage piles, then moved off into the shadows.

The streets were completely empty, the only sound the maddening thunk of the luminous-dialed clocks. Overhead, heli-sleds floated lazily, shining spots of white-hot light to the streets below. They hadn't given up after all. Fortunately, the streetside trash piles could have hidden me indefinitely.

I learned to run in between the search beams that raked the area like weaving drunks trying to walk a line. I had the feeling that they weren't very good at this sort of thing. They had so much control over their people that this kind of procedure was never necessary.

I figured that the numbers written on the sides of the buildings were seniority numbers listing who lived there. Roque's number was 472, and I found his building without too much difficulty. As I said, there were no doors, nothing to keep maniacs like me out. I walked right into the place.

Slipping off my mud-caked shoes, I pussyfooted through the halls, looking at the seniority numbers that marked each doorway. The bottom numbers were low, so I went up the stairs until I got to the fifth floor.

Everything was dim to dark, and the natives were asleep, apparently because it was time for them to be asleep. No one had apartment doors. I looked for bug-bugs as I walked, but I don't know what I'd have done if I'd seen one. I was moving and would have to keep moving.

I found Roque's number and walked in immediately. It was a sparse place. Most of the furniture was built-ins. There was a living room with a wall vis, a small kitchen with an attached bathroom to share the same plumbing, and a bedroom. For the first time I realized that I hadn't seen any children at all on Papa Bear, yet I distinctly remember that Garnet Roque's bio said that she had filled her quota with two.

I walked to the window and looked out streetside. Everything appeared calm except for those silent, peering light shafts. Turning from the window, I moved to the bedroom and looked inside.

Garnet Roque slept fitfully, a wrinkled sheet half covering her nude body. Her breasts rose and fell with ragged, awkward breaths, dark red nipples standing out in bold relief against the pale, veined flesh that surrounded them. And I knew why I recognized her. She was the practiced wiggle I had seen going so familiarly into Beemer's office as I sat on my can in the eye-watch.

I didn't like this part. There was no way that I could wake the woman up without scaring her to death. Taking a deep breath, I went to the bedside. Leaning down, I clamped a hand over her pouting mouth.

She came awake with a jerk, eyes going wide, and began bucking against me. I had to lie on her to hold her still.

"Stop it," I whispered harshly. "I'm not going to hurt you. Please. I just want to talk to you."

She fought me for a while, but eventually realized that I wasn't doing anything but trying to calm her down. She stopped fighting and simply lay there, gasping beneath me.

"Are you listening to me?" I asked.

She nodded, eyes still wide.

"If I take my hand away, will you promise not to scream?"

She nodded again, and I removed my hand.

"You're the Earther," was all she could think to say. I think that fact scared her so much she wasn't about to try anything.

"Please," I said. "I just need to ask you some very important questions, then I'll leave you alone. Okay?"

She sat up in bed, scooting as far away from me as she could. She made no move to cover herself with the sheet. "What do you want?"

"Would you like to . . . get dressed?" I asked.

She gave me a strange look, then shrugged. There was a white cotton robe lying across a chair near the bed. Reaching out without leaving my seat, I snatched it up and handed it to her.

She stood up and put on the robe. "This is supposed to be sleep time, you know," she said. "If they find out that

92

I'm awake, it could mean a reprimand in my file. Couldn't we do this during recreation time?''

The fear was gone from her. It had melted away like snow on the Rockies, leaving only the hard shell of sexual politics. I had known women like her before, and liked them about as well as an Arab likes a bacon sandwich.

"We do it now," I answered, shaking my head.

She began pacing. "It's just that I've already got a written and an oral, and another written could put me close to getting docked." She was moving her arms as she talked. "It's not my fault, those other reprimands, but neither is this . . . they won't understand. Are you sure we can't . . ."

"I want to ask you about your husband."

"I'm not married," she replied. "I'm a widow."

"Your husband was murdered," I told her. "I want to know why."

She kept moving around, prowling. It was driving me nuts. "I don't know anything about it," she said flatly. "They sent me a memo saying he was gone, along with my posting-forms for change of status, but there weren't any details."

"What did he do? What, exactly, was his job?"

"Another reprimand could kill my chances for a good match-up. Don't you realize that I've been interviewed by some three hundreds?" She got right up in my face. "Three hundreds!" she said, her hands vibrating in front of her. "But who's going to want someone who's been docked?"

I stood up and grabbed her by the shoulders. "Damn it, lady. I don't care about any of that. I want to know about your husband."

She kept looking at me, and I could tell by her eyes that she could never worry about anything but herself. She jerked away from me and sat heavily on the bed, rubbing her arms, probably telling herself that everyone was right about Earthers.

"Jeff was what they call a Symbios," she said, her eyes staring at the bare metal floor. "He worked on Mama Bear."

"What's that?" I had retrieved my shoes from the floor and put them on.

"You don't know anything, do you?"

I zipped up the boots and locked the tabs. "I'm a regular mongoloid," I replied.

"It's the computer satellite. It's a big responsibility, running Mama. That's why his number was so good."

"You didn't care much for him, did you?"

Her face came up slowly, puzzled. "He had a good number," she said.

"Did you ever know him to gamble a lot?"

"Not that I know of," she answered, and was up on her feet, fidgeting again. "You've got to understand, Mister . . ."

"Swain," I told her. "And would you sit down. You're giving me a rash."

She returned to the bed. "A Symby has a very close relationship to his work. It doesn't allow for much of anything else. Jeff and I never saw very much of one another."

"What's so special about his work?"

She shrugged with her face. "I don't know. It's out of my classification."

This was getting me nowhere. "Had you noticed anything unusual about his behavior lately? Anything out of the ordinary?"

She tugged on the hem of her robe, and tried to think. "He'd gotten very nervous the last hundred time periods or so. He worried a lot about messages and appointments. He seemed to spend a great deal of his recreation time with Manny."

"Who's Manny?"

"Manny Dugan, Jeff's shift partner on Mama. Toward the end, he was always over there, like they were doing something together or something." She shook her head, making her short hair swirl. "Like I said, it's out of my classification. Look, can't we do this during recreation?"

"Almost done," I said, and pulled a fag out of my inner jacket pocket.

Her eyes got wide like the Nile during rainy season. "What are you doing?" she shrieked. "I'll get docked for that. Don't you understand?"

I lit the smoker and took a deep drag. "There's nobody going to do anything to you. I'm a desperate criminal. You can't be responsible for my actions."

She sagged back on the bed like an animal taking a bullet. "There go the three hundreds," she said with resignation. "Maybe even the fours. If I have to take a five hundred,

I'll just quit. I'll just throw myself out of the window and quit.''

"All right, all right. I'm putting it out, see?" I dropped the cig on the floor and stomped on it. Garnet Roque came up off the bed like a shot. Diving for the floor, she scooped up cig and ashes, then stood, jerking her head around, eyes wild—frenzied. Finally she stuffed it into her mouth, chewing, all the while making horrible faces. She swallowed with a great deal of effort, then threw herself back on the bed with relief. Her robe had come open, exposing her body. She was really easy on the eyes. It made me think of Ginny.

"What's with you and Beemer?" I asked out of the blue.

"Nothing," she said too quickly, and I filed it under things to consider.

"Did your husband know any of the Earthers who had homes in Freefall?"

She sat back up, but made no move to close the robe. "No. How could he?"

"Then how do you explain his being found dead on an Earther satellite?"

She looked at me deeply, her face wide and innocent. "It's out of my classification," she answered softly.

I stood up and walked to the bedroom doorway. The woman either didn't know anything or wasn't telling, and I wasn't smart enough to figure out which. I started out of the room, then turned back to her. "Tell me about beckon," I said.

Her face exploded like she had just seen the good fairy, but only for a second. Like a moving shadow, the expression passed and was replaced by the former innocence. "I don't know what you're talking about," she said, and I knew that she was lying, knew it like a mother cat knows her own babies. I started back into the room.

"Keep the hands where I can see them," came a voice behind me. "And stick to that spot like you were nailed down."

I turned slowly, and found myself looking at the hate-filled face of Morton Beemer. Behind him were enough black-suits to fill a psycho ward. "Sorry," I told him. "But I gave at the office."

He made a grab for me, but I ducked him. Sliding past, I

tried for the door, but they grabbed me from everywhere. I had so many hands on me, I felt like a baseball bat choosing up sides.

"All right," I said. "So I didn't give at the office."

Beemer walked up to hit me, but his other plainclothes buddy, Nathan, grabbed his arm. "Mort," the guy said. "Remember . . ."

The Roque woman had run up behind Beemer and had wrapped herself around his free arm.

"Yeah, Mort. Remember," I said.

Nathan got right up, leaning against me. "Would you put a lid on it," he whispered harshly. "I'm trying to save your life here."

"Why?" I said. "Cause I'm so good-looking?"

The man clenched his jaw. He was middle-aged with deep cheek wrinkles and tired, sagging eyes. He wasn't quite their color and seemed cut from a different bolt than the other punks. He looked at me for a long second, trying to decide whether he loved or hated me. He finally decided on indifference. "Take him out to the sled," he told the black suits. "And no bruises where they show."

They started dragging me out then. I looked once to Beemer. He had Garnet Roque in his arms and was gently stroking her hair while she did the best imitation of a real person that I'd ever seen. He reassured her with soothing words. Words that punks like him weren't supposed to have in their vocabulary.

A buzzer was ringing in my head, and it had nothing to do with bruises that didn't show.

11

I wasn't dead, which was my best surprise of the day. They took me out of Roque's building and stuck me on one of their heli-sleds. Wilky wrapped some kind of titanium bands around me and trussed me up like a magician in the Chinese water torture, then kept me company in the back seat so I wouldn't get lonely. My pal Nathan drove the open-air vehicle. Morton Beemer sat, brooding, beside him in the front.

Nathan de-densified the heli-pack and we rose gently into the still air. There was a circulation in there, but it was vague and nondirectional. I missed wind; it's one of those general categories of things that don't seem to mean a whole lot until they're not there anymore. I missed the heat of the sun, the chill of the night.

We went up until we were just bottoming the smog bank, then putted off toward the cornfields. Nobody was talking. I took the opportunity to ask Nathan about his skin coloration, and found out that his parents were among the last real Earthers to migrate to Beltel, so he wasn't pigmentless like long-line Freefallers. I think he had gotten a lot of pressure over the years because of his skin tone, and it made him a bit sympathetic toward me. I could use all the friends I could get.

Beemer sat there watching us talk, and finally couldn't stay quiet anymore. He turned to me, burning me with those cold, staring eyes.

"I knew you'd go there," he said, and there was something about the way he said it that made me think that he was doing more than blowing hot air. "It was only a matter of time."

"Well, you're quite the boy," I replied, assuming that

97

he wanted some sort of answer. Nathan turned and glared at me for a second. ''I see that you're pretty good friends with Garnet Roque.''

Color came to his cheeks, making his pimple scars stand out in vivid red. ''You're hanging on by your teeth, Swain,'' he said, trying to maintain control. ''Don't make me play dentist.''

If he was going to do anything to me, he would have done it already. I had a hole card that everybody knew about but me. ''She's a nice-looking woman,'' I said. ''I'll bet that you've even applied for her posting.''

''Mort,'' Nathan warned, before Beemer did something stupid. The Captain didn't say a word, but I could tell by the way his jaw muscles rippled that he wanted to.

''Yes sir,'' I said. ''Bet you could go for some of that too, couldn't you, Wilky?''

Wilky's eyes got large, and he turned and looked out the side of the sled at the tinker-toy city. I expected a shot and didn't get it. I really was in the catbird seat.

Beemer was staring at me again. I smiled at him. ''What's your seniority, Cap? Got the number for her?''

''Shut up,'' was all he said.

''Hell,'' I said. ''I bet punk cops aren't even in the top thousand.''

''I'm a six hundred,'' he spat without moving his lips.

''Well I'm number one,'' I said, ''and I deserve better treatment than this.''

He smiled at the restraining bands that pinned my arms back at the shoulders. ''You have an appointment, Earther. We just want to make sure that you get there on time.''

They had me strapped so tightly that the only appointment I was late for was the appointment of the blood that couldn't get to my hands. We floated through the fields, past another spoke, then into the stockyards. There was very little activity there; the animals crammed in metal pens below were bedded for the sliver night. The stockyards were connected up with a large slaughterhouse and meat-packing plant and dairy, all of which were in full operation. Beyond that was another spoke with platform, then a large industrial complex.

The air here was noxious, as black puffs of vapor roiled out of gut-rumbling smokestacks. We had to get lower to be below the dirty black cloud that held the ceiling space. It was a nightmare in carbon black, a diseased fog that made you afraid even to breathe. The buildings were all low to the ground like snakes slithering, and many had monstrous stacks that vented all the way up, spewing into the atmosphere outside of Papa. We picked our way around those, slicing through currents of air that gurgled with hoarse mechanical cries of agony. Little specks of human beings could be seen moving around between the plants. They all wore gas masks. I remembered something that I had seen on the posting vis back in the city. It was a phrase that appeared below the names of some of the availables: WIDOWED BY AIR OD, it said. I didn't understand it at the time. I did now.

By the time we got through the heavy industry, my eyes were burning like I had just taken a hit of tear gas, and I felt dirty, gritty all over. We passed another spoke and came to a duplicate of the city where Garnet Roque lived. There was one difference, though. In this city it was daytime.

I watched the leisure-suited crowd below and noted their movements. The street traffic was light, and what activity there was seemed to be goal-directed. Groups of people clustered at the public vis areas, apparently watching the postings and whatever other community news that Beltel was giving them. These vis screens seemed to be the only source of information on Papa Bear.

Our drift began to slow and I looked up. Attached to the ceiling just ahead of us was a huge block of offices. Several piers, like boat docks, extended out from the aluminum box units, and these seemed to be the only possible entry or exit from the complex. The fogmist floated languidly up this high, wrapping the offices in a gauzy shroud that occasionally unfolded for a peek-a-boo look, only to swallow them up again.

There was a small, innocuous sign inlaid in the first pier as we drifted up. It read: DISSEMINATION AND MANAGEMENT. We bumped gently into the steel dock, and Wilky threw out a mooring line that neatly hooked over one of the pilings. Hand-tugging the line, he pulled us in snug, then clamped us solid with metal bolts. We were anchored.

Wilky scrambled onto the pier, then gave Beemer a hand. Lieutenant Nathan turned to me from the driver's seat. "This is your stop," he said.

"Is there a choice?" I asked.

He shook his head, and tugged on his weary rubber face, wrinkling it like a human prune. "Swain," he sighed, and it sounded like escaping gas.

"All right," I said, and tried to maneuver my banded-up body out of the sled. Wilky reached in and grabbed one of the bands, jerking me down onto the dock like a grounded fish.

"Get him up," Beemer said without humor.

Wilky hefted me to my feet. The pier rocked gently with our movements, and the smog bottled us in like springtime in London. I almost expected to hear the lapping of waves against the pier.

Beemer walked right up to me, inspecting me for damage like a produce man. He dusted me off where I was dirty, and nodded his head in satisfaction when he was done.

"Listen to me," he said, running a hand through his slick hair. "You're going to meet someone who most people never get to see. I want you to show the proper respect."

He talked mechanically, with difficulty, as if the words were hemlock and he was Socrates.

"I thought Santa lived at the North Pole," I replied.

He sighed the way Nathan did. "You're alive right now," he said, and his eyes popped wide. "And it has nothing to do with me, you savvy? You're not dead because the boss doesn't want you dead." He leaned his head in the direction of the offices. "But as soon as he gets through with you, you and I are going to come to grips." Reaching out his hand, he grabbed a handful of my hair and forced me nose to nose with him. "Don't embarrass me in there, Swain. You understand?"

"I'll certainly do my best to live up to your expectations," I replied.

Turning me by the shoulders, he shoved me toward the offices. We moved to the door. I noticed it was an air lock. No nasty smog for them. I also noted that the building wasn't aluminum as I first suspected, but steel—thick, heavy steel.

There was a button next to the lock. Beemer pushed it and waited. Nathan strolled up to join us. A vis focused above the lock; it showed two large eyes staring back out. "Yes?" said a voice.

Beemer cleared his throat and smoothed his oil-field hair

100

again. "Captain Beemer from security with a prisoner. To see Mr. Malaca." He said the name quietly, with reverence.

Malaca. Henry Malaca. The Plant Manager.

The eyes shifted back and forth. "Who else is with you?"

Beemer turned around, gesturing. "Uh, Lt. Nathan and Patrolman Wilky."

The screen eyes blinked several times. "Lt. Nathan is cleared for entry, but the other must wait outside."

It was almost with relief that Wilky said, "I'll be in the sled."

Everyone had to voice-print, then the lock came open with a hydraulic whoosh. We stepped in and the thing closed behind us. We passed through a clean booth like the one I was in earlier, then a door opened to admit us to the offices.

We were in a broadcast station. This was where the vis posting originated. Visual equipment was jammed everywhere, blinding lights filling booths where words and pictures mixed to form a substance. Men and women in bulky headsets sat at tables, reading info into large tubelike microphones while programmers gleaned the latest posting results from their metal ruminators.

We passed through the entire vis station unnoticed and entered a receptionist's anteroom at the end of it all. If I'd have gone to sleep and woke up in that place, I'd have sworn that I was in a log cabin out in the woods somewhere. The floors and furniture were dusty pine, the walls tethered logs. There was a high, beamed ceiling and a holo of a roaring fire in the corner. Vis windows showed a panorama of monster redwoods and blue, sunshot sky. The smell was heavy pine, and the light was kerosene lanterns that flickered and burned with wispy gray puffs of smoke. A big oak desk sat against the far wall, and the only thing that gave the room away was the large instrument panel that completely filled its top. I caught something out of the corner of my eye and looked down to see a mouse, a real mouse, scurrying across the floor. Beemer saw it too. His eyes got large and he physically started, hand going for the stinger on his hip. I don't think he'd ever seen anything like it before.

A man sat behind the desk, and stood up to greet us when we entered. He was dressed in blue jeans and white

101

turtleneck, the whole outfit covered with a waistcoat of the same material as his pants. "Gentlemen," he said. "Welcome."

He moved from behind and shook hands with Beemer and Nathan. "You've done a fine job in bringing Mr. Swain in for this visit," he said, then motioned for them to take off my restraining bands.

"This man's dangerous," Beemer cautioned. "I don't think it would be wise to . . . ."

"Nonsense," the man said. "Mr. Swain is on his best behavior, aren't you?"

"Good as gold," I told them.

Beemer reluctantly undid my bonds, and I started massaging my arms to get the feeling back into them. The man reached out and took my hand.

"My name's Clark," he said, and smiled a company-man smile that reminded me of Foley at Continental. "And Mr. Malaca has been *very* anxious to meet you."

"Well, I'm all aflutter."

"Good," Clark said through a boyish face. He made a sweeping gesture with his arm. "We have cleared the appointments for you."

"So have I."

Clark winked and went to the desk console. He punched a big black button. "Hey, Henry," he called. "That Swain fella's here."

"Well, good!" boomed a big, fat, jolly voice. "Send that boy in."

Clark pointed to a wooden door set in the back wall. "Right through there."

I nodded and started walking. Beemer made to follow me.

"That's just fine, Captain. Henry wants to talk to Mr. Swain alone."

"But, you don't understand . . ." Beemer started.

"Alone," Clark said and there was no mistaking the authority in his voice. The discussion ended right there.

I got to the door and turned to grin at Beemer. "See you boys later," I said loudly and walked right through that door like it was Sunday on the farm.

I walked into another log cabin that looked like something out of a taxidermist's wet dream. The walls were covered with trophies. Stuffed birds and fish and small animals, plus the heads of larger animals—bears and lions. There were even cats and dogs and barnyard animals. The place was busting full of dead animals; it was *really* hog heaven. And every place that didn't have an animal shoved into it was filled with guns. All kinds of guns, old and new. There were frumps and lasers and sonics and lead spewers and hand guns and rifles with real wood stocks and dueling pistols that looked as if they couldn't hit a skyscraper at ten paces.

The middle of the room was clear of furniture, and a length of pale green carpet stretched across it. On one end of the carpet was a green plastic bump with a hole in the middle. At the other end was a chubby little man with a bald head and a golf club. The man wore a flowered shirt and string tie. His pants legs were shoved down into the top of cowboy boots that rose to mid-calf. He had thick lips and a bulbous nose and was bent over a golf ball, locked in deadly concentration. I started to say something, but he silenced me with a hand.

He tapped the ball with the club and it started down the carpet. The shot was way too wide moving down, but began arching back toward the cup so much that it rolled up the bump and into the hole.

The man looked up at me, eyes sparkling. "What do you think of that?" he asked.

"I think it's fine," I answered.

"Coriolis force," he said. "The rotation of the wheel affects the way gravity works." He hit another ball; it did the same thing. He pointed to the cup with a cocked finger. "Object lesson," he said. "I just want you to understand that things are different here." He smiled broadly through crooked teeth and looked for all the world like somebody's rich uncle.

"I've figured that out for myself," I answered.

He walked over and shook my hand vigorously. "Name's Henry Malaca. You call me Henry. I've been watching you, Swain. I like the way you operate."

"I wish the rest of your people shared that attitude, Henry."

He made a throwaway gesture with his chubby little

arms. "Forget them. Bunch of old ladies, every man jack of them."

"Why am I still alive?" I asked him.

He grinned up at me. "Get right to the point, don't you, boy?"

"I just like to know how solid my footing is."

He clucked his tongue. "You're my kind of man, Swain. A man's man. Well, let's have a seat and get right down to business." He moved slowly toward the desk, too slowly. He sat down heavily. "I used to be a man's man, but I just can't cut the old mustard anymore." He tapped his chest with an index finger. "Bum ticker, you know. Yes sir, the old stallion's out to pasture now. Smoke?"

He held out a package of cigs and I took one, lighting it on a candle—another rustic touch—that burned on his desk. He took the pack back from me, stared at them longingly for a few seconds, then put them away in a drawer.

"So why am I alive?" I asked again.

He folded his pudgy hands on the desk top. "You're alive because I think you can do me some good, and help yourself out in the bargain. It's what I like to call a little friendly convenience."

"How?"

He shook his head slowly. "You got to keep your bull in the pen until they open the gate, boy. We need to talk some first, man to man."

I dragged deeply on the smoker. Not seeing an ashtray, I flicked ashes on the wood floor. He wanted to talk. Well, that was okay with me. "How come an Earther is running this place?" I asked him.

"Simple enough," he said, and picked up a stuffed rooster from his desk, cradling it lightly. "We got a real good system up here," he said, stroking the never-molting feathers. "We teach these folks how to do everything they need to learn. Trouble is, they're not real aggressive types. They don't have that . . . creative instinct. They can take orders, but don't know how to give them. Know what I mean?"

"Not exactly."

He tightened his lips a little. His face had the bunchy withered look of a cantaloupe left out in the sun too long after picking. "It's all given to them. They don't know how to play the power very well. Take me, for instance. You know why I'm Plant Manager today?"

I shook my head and puffed my cig.

"Cause I'm ugly, boy. Just plain ugly. When you're ugly, you got to work for things that all the pretty people get 'cause they look so good. The world likes pretty people, boy. So ugly people got to work at it; they learn to be sly and do what they can to get what they want. You savor the victories that you worked so hard for." His voice lowered to almost a whisper and he leaned over the desk. "Then something glorious happens. When folks get old enough to be running things, they're all ugly." He shook his fist. "Age is the great equalizer. So who ends up in charge? The ones who've been busting their asses all their life, that's who." He pointed to himself. "Folks like me get the gold medal. It takes guts to run a place like this. Earth guts. And I got 'em. I think that you do, too."

"What I've got right now is a hangover from your punks sticking me with their dart guns."

"You picked your line of work, not me."

"That doesn't make me like getting stuck any better."

He set the rooster back on its stand. "You're one of them private cops, ain't you?"

"I'm private," I answered, "but I'm no cop."

He got a kick out of that, throwing his head back and laughing like an asthmatic dog. Odd sense of humor, I guess. "Let me ask you a question, Swain," he said when he settled down. "What do you think of the way I run my place up here?"

"Not only does it seem like a lousy place to live," I answered, dropping my cig on the floor and stamping it out, "but I don't even like visiting."

He nodded briefly. "That's because you're from Earth, down where nobody appreciates the concept of good business. Freefall is business, boy. Good business. We have never failed to make a profit every year for the last hundred years. A century of profit. Think of it!" He seemed to be getting excited, his voice tightening like a guitar string. "A Beltel investment is the soundest business investment in the universe. Do you know why? I'll tell you. At Freefall, we practice the ultimate in profit sharing. The people are part of

105

the business. They live the business. And when business is good, we all prosper. It's a hell of a good way to live a life."

"I don't see anything very good about the way you control these people."

"The hell you say." He sat back in his chair, frowning deeply. "Why, folks have got to be goal-directed. If they weren't, they'd be running around out in the damn woods like these dead things you been looking at, or living like cavemen in those stinking, falling-apart cities you got down on Earth."

I was beginning to not like Henry Malaca very much. "How do all your employees feel about that?"

He stood up and began slowly pacing the room, his eyes wandering along the rows of trophies. "Have you ever known anybody to be satisfied with anything?"

"No, I can't say that I have."

"Course you haven't. It's our nature to want everything but what we've got." He went to the vis window and watched the redwood countryside. A flock of birds flapped past in the distance. "All we can do is look out for folks for their own good. Let me give you an example." He turned to me then, hands behind his back, rocking back and forth on the balls of his feet.

"Take this dope business," he said. "Even up here it finds its way. It's bad stuff. Unproductive. They were having a problem with it when I started up here, but I stopped it in a minute. You know how? I just put out some dope of my own and started selling it. We called it Bad Dust." He chuckled when he said that. "I mean this stuff would have you dead in two hours after putting it up your nose or in your arm. Not a nice death either. No siree. Screaming and burning and . . . spitting up. So who's going to buy any more of that shit after a hundred or so deaths on it. I got rid of some dope heads, solved the problems, and brought some new blood into the system to replace the dead ones."

"Where I come from they call that murder," I said.

"Murder nothing, that's free enterprise!"

I got up leadenly and moved around to his end of the desk. "Do you mind?" I asked, taking another cig out of his drawer.

He shook his head.

I stuck the fag between my lips. "What has any of this got to do with me?"

He stuffed his hands into his tight pants. "I've been keeping an eye on you," he said. "You made chumps out of my whole security force. You're good on your feet, is why. You got smarts, jungle smarts. I want to hire you to do a little job for me."

"What sort of job?"

"We got this . . ." he made a disgusted face, "vice satellite."

"I've heard of it," I said, thinking of the chip in my pocket.

"Yeah," he replied and looked down at the floor. "Well, I got a daughter, Swain. Name's Loren. She somehow got herself hooked up with this greaseball, Rosen, who runs the place. Makes a damn fool out of her."

"So?" I realized that I hadn't lit the cig. I got it going.

"It's bad, boy. Bad business. I want to put a stop to it."

I eased myself into Henry's chair and put my feet up on his desk. "You've got the hammer here," I told him. "Why don't you just handle it?"

"Can't," he answered. "Corporate says that the place is important and won't allow me to touch it. They hired Rosen; there was somebody else before him. You see," he said, and there was a touch of staleness in his voice, "we all have to heed the call of business. If I move against Rosen, it's all over for me. Clark would see to that."

"What you mean is that your daughter is important to you, but not that important."

"The system is important," he responded, and there was an implied threat in his tone.

I had absolutely no desire to get involved in Malaca's personal problems, but as near as I could see, it was the only thing keeping me alive. And dead, I was useless to Ginny. "What do you want from me?"

His face relaxed into a wide smile. "Look here," he said. "Loren likes Rosen because he's wild, you know, independent. Well, you're a good enough looking boy, and you're sure wild enough. Why don't you kindly hang around out there a bit and let nature take its course. That way, I can solve my problems without ruffling any corporate feathers."

"You want me to be a gigolo," I said.

"I don't care what you call it."

"It's not that easy to split up lovers, even when they're creeps."

"I don't want to hear 'can't,' boy. Loren isn't much, but she's all I got since her mama passed on to her reward."

"Did you post the opening?" I asked.

"Don't test me," he growled. "The ice you're standing on is real thin. Now, about the money. I'll triple whatever your usual fee is."

"I don't want your money," I answered.

"Then what?"

"A couple of things. I'll exchange your daughter for my friend."

"The Teal woman?"

"Yeah, the Teal woman. You help me find out what's wrong with her, and I'll do my best to get your girl back."

He nodded. "Fair enough. From now on, my security force is as close to you as your pud. But my problem takes precedence."

"There's something else," I said, pulling my feet down. "The woman who flew me in here has had her license revoked. I want it given back to her."

He glared for a minute, then chuckled. "So you want to deal," he said. "Okay. She's got her license back, but to earn it, she's going to have to be your driver."

"No," I said.

"Too late, Swain. You're the one who sweetened the pot. Your cabbie drives and shares the good or the bad right along with you. All I can say, is that you'd better be able to deliver the goods."

I stood up and moved toward the door. "If I don't," I said, "I'm no worse off than I was before."

"Maybe not."

I started for the handle, then looked back. "There's another thing. I want clearance to go on Mama Bear."

"Wrong," he said flatly.

"I need to talk to someone there."

He looked hard at me. There was no compromise in his eyes. "Nobody goes to Mama Bear," he said. "That's the system."

"Change the system."

He walked over to the wall and took down an ancient

rifle. Clicking back the hammer, he leveled it at me. "You do your job, boy. And on the agreed-upon conditions, or I terminate your contract right now."

I shrugged and opened up the door. I guess I'd found his limit.

12

They had Wilky take me back to the hospital. He really didn't want to, but I asked for him special, so I could have a little time to explain to him just what I thought of his kind of punk. It was a rewarding experience.

When I wasn't talking, I was thinking. Malaca had something on his mind when he asked me to help him out, and I don't think it had very much to do with his daughter. There was a current, like an underground stream, that flowed just below the surface. I could hear it rumbling, but I couldn't see it. It was like a gyroscope on a string. Spinning, but tilted just a bit too much to one side or the other. There was something else that bothered me, too. What was the story on Beemer and Garnet Roque? And how did it fit into the scheme of things?

Wilky was gentle as a kitten when he dropped me off at the red-crossed wheel. I was in charge now, at least temporarily, and Freefallers were very careful around authority.

I went right to Ginny's room. Irene was in there with her, injecting something into her arm. Ginny was curled up in a tight ball on the stasis, her features strained.

"How is she?" I asked.

Irene looked up with her eyes, keeping the rest of her head bent down. "Worse," was all she said, then lowered her eyes back to Ginny.

"Why is she knotted up like that?"

She took a deep breath. "It's the body's natural reaction. She's physically protecting herself from the violence of her dreams." A stethoscope hung around her neck. She put it to her ears and began listening to Ginny's heart, then moved it to other spots. "I see that you're in one piece."

"Yeah," I answered. "I'm doing a little job for your buddy, Malaca."

110

She stood up straight, looking puzzled. "Really? What sort of job?"

I shrugged. "Leg work. Nothing actually. Have you heard from the Earth doctors?"

She moved from the stasis, taking off her stethoscope and doubling it over into the pocket of the lab coat she was wearing. "They can't make a prognosis unless they can examine the patient." She walked to the desk by the door and sat heavily behind it. I turned and put a hand to Ginny's forehead. She was practically on fire.

"She couldn't make the trip, could she?" I called over my shoulder.

Irene didn't answer. I turned from Ginny and went to the desk, sitting on its top. She looked up at me, her eyes lost.

"I feel so helpless," she said.

"What were you giving her when I came in?"

"Phenobarb," she said. "But it's had about as much effect as spitting on a house fire. Have you had any luck?"

"I don't think Ginny killed Roque," I said. "I don't even think he was killed at her place."

"But . . ."

"Don't ask me, because I don't know. Let me ask you something. What's the story on Lou?"

"The maintenance man?"

I got off the desk and found a chair. I turned it so I could talk and watch Ginny at the same time. "He told me he had been Plant Manager."

"Did he?" she responded flatly. "He's usually not that lucid."

"What happened to him?"

She turned her chair to face me, leaning her elbow against the desk. "He had a complete breakdown. They found him babbling incoherently in his office one day about five years ago, and brought him to me. After a year of intensive therapy, he got the way you see him now. I don't think he'll ever get better."

I fished a cig out of my pocket and stuck it in my mouth. Irene was frowning when I looked at her, so I didn't light it. "When he tried to remember the past," I said, "he seemed to get scared to death."

She nodded. "His present life is a defense mechanism. His mind is protecting itself against the paranoia."

111

"It almost sounds like Ginny's problem."

"I've made that connection myself," she answered. "I don't like to dwell on it."

I chewed on the end of my cig, wanting to fire it. My own defense mechanism. "Was Malaca up here when Lou had his breakdown?"

She nodded. "Had been for several years. He was Lou's assistant. Why?"

"No reason," I answered. "I'm just snoopy. Does the word 'beckon' mean anything to you?"

Her eyes narrowed to slits. "When he was out of control, I heard Lou say that word thousands of times. Even now, hearing it is enough to send him into convulsions. I've lost sleep for years over that word. Do you know anything about it?"

I pulled out the cig, rolling it around in my fingertips. "Ginny said it. A punk on Earth told it to me just before he killed himself. Garnet Roque acted like it was a Venus flytrap and she was a piece of meat. I don't know what it is, or what it means, but I think that the answer might clear up a lot of other questions." I stuck the smoker back into my pocket; I was just torturing myself with it. "I haven't seen any children since I've been here. Where are they all?"

"Baby Bear," she answered, and almost smiled. "The children are raised on their own satellite to develop total dependence on the company. At eighteen, they move over to Papa and get into the work force."

"Strange," I said.

"What?"

I got up and began to pace. "Everything is so controlled here, so one-to-one. How do they come up with jobs for all the ones coming up?"

She followed my movements with her head. "They have a retirement system," she said. "If a given number of young ones enter the work force, an equal number of people are retired from the top of the age lists. They go to Sunset, the retirement satellite on the outskirts of town."

That made sense to me. I went back to my perch on the edge of the desk. "Everybody works up here, don't they?"

She nodded.

"How would I go about finding out what certain people do for a living?"

Irene pursed her lips. "I have access to personnel records," she said. "In case of accidents, I sometimes need histories. Whom did you have in mind?"

"Garnet Roque."

She stood up, smoothing her lab coat. "Let's find out," she said, trying to sound cheerful. "I'm not doing much good here."

I followed her back to her apartments. She fixed both of us coffee and we sat at the kitchen table while she connected up the coordinates to get her vis into the files. We sipped and watched the woman's history unravel on the screen.

She was thirty years old, had been on the work force for twelve years. She was given a menial job, and posted for marriage as soon as she entered Papa. She started moving up quickly, though. She married in her station, but six months later moved way up by beating out a number of women for the wife posting of a farm executive who was widowed. Her new seniority got her better jobs, and the next eight years saw her gradually improving her position through her looks and wiles until she finally found herself married to Jeff Roque and in a good job in the dissemination chambers of the executive offices. Then something happened. Six months prior to Roque's death, she was forced out of her job and given a clerical position in security. It had all the earmarks of a demotion, but her seniority didn't change, and her monthly stipend, after living expenses were deducted, was a bit larger than she had been making.

Irene grunted. "I've never seen anything like that before."

"What do you mean?"

"Seniority runs everything," she said. "She didn't apply for that last job; she was bumped into it. That wouldn't happen without a good reason."

"Ideas?"

She shook her head. "That's your department, remember?"

"Sure," I said, and took a sip of coffee. "But I'll take help wherever I can get it."

"Somebody call for help?" came a voice behind us.

We turned. Porchy was leaning against the doorframe, hands jammed in the pockets of her one-piece, baseball cap fixed firmly on her head.

"How the hell did you get here so quick?" I asked.

She took a breath. "I never left," she returned. "They grabbed me when I was trying to fly out of this crazy place, and held me in security. The next thing I knew, they sent me over here to meet you."

"Were you under arrest?"

"I don't think so," she said, and her voice was questioning, unsure. "It was like they were just holding me up a while . . . until it was time."

"Time for what?"

"Beats me," she said and walked all the way into the room. She pointed toward the coffee cups. "Got any more of that stuff?" she asked.

I patted the chair next to me. "Sit down. I need to ask you a question."

"The answer is yes," she said, as Irene got up to get her some coffee.

"You don't even know the question."

"You want me to taxi you around," she said. "They already told me. I offered to do that before and you turned me down."

"It's different now," I said. I glanced around. Bug-bugs perched inquisitively near us, listening. I got to where I didn't even pay attention to them anymore. Almost like I was getting suckered into the system. But there were a few things that I wanted to tell Porchy in a more secured area.

The coffee arrived and Porchy sipped it slowly. I introduced the two women, and we all sat for a while. Despite the circumstances, it was good to see Porchy again. In some strange way, we drew a strength from each other—I guess you could call it a familiarity—that made everything else around us a lot more tolerable. We both felt it; it crackled from our eyes whenever we looked at each other. Porchy made smiling easy. She was good people, and you latch onto good people every chance you get.

After a while, I started getting itchy to get out of there. I needed to be in motion; it kept my mind off things. Porchy saw my mood and smiled over her cup.

"So where is our first stop?" she asked.

"Jenny Sue Qua," I answered loudly, for the benefit of the bug-bugs. "I want to meet Mr. Rosen."

"We can go now if you want."

"I want. But first, I need to try to get in touch with someone on Papa Bear."

"Who?" Irene asked, getting up and going to the vis controls.

"His name's Manny Dugan. He was Roque's shift partner on Mama."

Irene juiced it up and tried to bleep Dugan, but no one answered. I'd have to keep trying.

"Exactly what do they do on Mama Bear?" I asked.

Irene grimaced. "It's kind of hush-hush stuff," she said, "so Jeff never really went into any details with me about it. I do know that a city like Freefall is necessarily run in a very mechanical manner, and that all those functions are controlled by the computers on Mama."

We all went down so I could say good-bye to Ginny, then we were off. This time Porchy's ship didn't seem to be wired. I never worried about subtlety when it came to Beltel surveillance. Since they didn't need it, they never learned it. We autoed for Rosen's place and shared a drink.

"So what's going on?" she asked when we were safely away.

"I don't know," I answered honestly. "It's a feeling."

She looked hard at me, and there was fear in her eyes. "Feelings like maybe we're going to have to fight like hell to stay alive? Feelings like you don't have any control over the way things are happening?"

Somehow I wasn't surprised at her understanding. "Have you noticed that they've known every step that I was going to take? It's almost like acting. Someone's sitting there with a script, staying a page ahead of me. It's depressing."

"The bugs, you think?"

"I wish it was that simple." I cracked the air leak and lit a cig. Porchy opted for her snuff and tin can. "I've been playing this whole thing by ear. Haven't known from one minute to the next what I was going to do . . . but somebody does."

"And how," she replied, plunking the can.

"The only thing I'm absolutely sure about, is the fact that neither of us is supposed to survive this. We're here for a reason, and when that's taken care of, our lives are going to be about as valuable as a two-dollar watch." I closed my eyes, leaning my head back on the seat, and listened to the air hiss, listened to the lifeblood of the ship pumping into the unfeeling night.

I turned my head and watched her. On the surface she seemed deadly calm, but her jaw muscles were working overtime masticating the snuff. "I've dragged you into this," I said. "I didn't want it that way, but you're in it now. Just as deep as me."

She turned and caught my eyes. Held them. "I wouldn't have it any other way," she said quietly.

I grunted to a straight sitting position and put out my cig. The soreness in my muscles had evaporated down to a dull, throbbing ache. I almost welcomed the pain. It was real.

"There it is," Porchy said, pointing.

I followed her hand, and saw a large ball hanging off by itself in the distance. It glowed in a soft red aura, a luminescent orb. It wasn't rotating. That either meant zero or artificial G. That didn't make any sense to me.

We came up on the thing. Its entire top was covered with landing docks jammed full of shuttles like Porchy's. Barnacles on a sunken ship. Taking control manually, she feathered her thrusters, maneuvering us sideways to one of the docks.

Unstrapping, we floated over to the hatch and unwheeled. The satellite had its own hatch on the other side of ours. It was bright blue and covered with paintings of violet flowers. A sign in the middle of it said:

WELCOME TO JENNY SUE QUA
DO DROP IN
WATCH YOUR P'S AND Q'S
SLIP AWAY

"Come on," Porchy said, and worked herself around until her feet were on the satellite's hatchway. There were handles on either side of the hatch. She crouched to grab them, then pulled. The hatch sprang open, and she disappeared inside, feet first. The door snapped closed behind her.

"Porchy?" I said. When there was no answer, I approximated her actions, getting hold of the handles. Pulling hard, I found myself floating straight down through a tunnel made of fuzzy green-glowing walls.

There were smells in the tube. Different smells. I smelled

roses, then farther down, broiling steaks. There were perfume odors, giving way to perspiration giving way to the musky aroma of a woman's sex. Smells that triggered emotional responses. The sex odor had its effect on me. My tube curved slightly, smelling of fresh candy, then suddenly merged with a larger tube. This was the terminal point of all the hatch tubes and was filled with people drifting down from other ships. A man and a woman near me were wrapped around each other like rubber bands on a doorknob. I guess the sex smell was too much for them.

We all came down in a large, circular glassed-in booth. Porchy was waiting for me when I got down. We were bathed in the bright green lighting; everything outside of our zero G chamber was dark and murky.

I looked around. "What the hell?"

"C'mon," Porchy said. She took my hand and we walk-floated over to the exit door. Pushing through with a crowd of others, we were in the business end of Jenny Sue Qua. We were immediately standing in Earth-type gravity.

It was dark in there; the kind of dark that you have to wait for your eyes to get used to. The ceiling was low, bottling in the clouds of cig and dope smoke that formed the core of the joint's atmosphere. There were thick smells, walls of smell: the cigs and dope, heavy perfume that fattened the air and coated your lungs when you breathed, whisky and beer smells that seemed to catch in the smoke and hang there for an osmosis high. Music pounded physically through the floors and walls, vibrating in the thick air, bassing out the senses to catch the body in the primal, pounding rhythm that drew from the guts for its power. And beneath that, the rumble-jangling of human voices and some not so human— laughing or pretending to laugh, talking or just saying things, vying for attention above the sense-shattering music. My eyes settled in and I could see the people, moving out of the cig-fog as back-lighted silhouettes. They were dancing and clinching, some on the floor doing things that people like me reserved for the privacy of our bedrooms. They sat at tables and clinked glasses, all trying to transcend the atmosphere by discharging as much gray matter from their brains as fast as they could. It was a useless exercise, an occupation about as worthwhile as making an omelette without eggs. I should know.

Small lights glowed everywhere. From tables and from behind a bar that sat off somewhere in the smoke haze. All of them were bright enough but also dark enough. All of them were fighting a losing battle against the oppressive darkness. Porchy said something to me, but I couldn't hear her above the noise. I shook my head and pointed to my ear.

"Let's get a drink," she yelled to me through cupped hands.

I nodded and she led me off toward the bar. As we shoved through the floor crowds, I noticed a lot of Earthers in the bunch, men and women. I didn't catch on at first, but soon realized that they were hookers, all wound tightly around the good citizens of Freefall. It made sense. Malaca would never allow any of *his* citizens to earn a living in such a manner.

Tables crowded the outskirts of the dance/sex floor. Holo porn-shows unfolded in miniature on most of their tops. Waitresses carrying trays fought the current, loaded down with everything from drinks and cigs to mind expanders and alpha rings. I was getting giddy just walking through there.

We got across the dance floor and made it into the bar. This was a long, narrow room, with the bar itself taking up one whole wall, and red vinyl booths taking up the other. The booths seemed to be filled exclusively with alpha trippers, taking hard doses of pleasure directly into their brains. It's a lonely way to escape, but then I guess we're all ultimately alone.

The bar had drinkers. That was my poison. We took a stool and bellied up. The entire back of the bar was a mammoth aquarium. It had only one occupant. A large gray shark glided back and forth as close to the thick glass as it could get. It was always moving, always searching, always waiting. A profusion of rusted automobile parts and license plates and tires littered the bottom of the tank, making the shark's atmosphere a bit more like home. The top of the tank bore a legend in bold black letters. It read: I'D RATHER HAVE A BOTTLE IN FRONT OF ME THAN A FRONTAL LOBOTOMY.

A tiny woman, thin all over and dressed in a dull one-piece was working behind the bar. When Porchy saw her, her face lit up.

"Pat!" she called.

The woman glanced up, her face did a number like Porchy's, and she ran the length of the bar to where we sat. The two embraced clumsily across the bar.

"Where the hell have you been hiding yourself?" she said in a heavy English accent. She was middle-aged with curly black hair that hugged her skull like a helmet. "I haven't seen you in years."

"They don't let us come out anymore," Porchy answered. "How are things?"

The woman shrugged. "The same."

Porchy put her hand on my shoulder. "I'd like you to meet a friend of mine," she said loudly. "Pat, this is Swain." People in bars only have one name.

She shook my hand, then kissed me on the lips. "You're a good-looker," she said. "Come home with me and I'll screw your brains out."

I nodded, smiling. "Can't afford to lose them," I said.

Porchy grabbed my arm protectively. "Down girl, he's with me."

She looked me up and down. "Well you can just smuck it up your ass," she said, then started laughing. "Drink?"

"Black Jack," I answered. "Rocks." I looked at Porchy.

"Grasshopper," she said, then shrugged when she saw me staring at her. "Kind of petite for a change." She turned an index finger solidly into her cheek.

Pat hurried away, driven hard by some brand of internal exuberance. While she made the drinks, she gave some poor slob down at the end of the bar a hard time. "Smuck it up your ASS!" she yelled finally and slammed a big stick loudly on the bartop next to his hand. He slid quietly off the stool and wandered away.

She brought the drinks and set them down. I was broke. I had lost all my plastic in the crash on Papa. Porchy reached into the pocket of her leather coat and pulled out some yellows. Pat glared at her. "Not in my bar, you don't," she said and shoved the money back.

"Thanks," Porchy said.

I raised my glass in a semi-toast, then took a long drink, letting the ice cubes bang my upper lip.

Porchy took a sip of the thick green liquid, then set it back down. "Where's your boss?" she asked.

Pat chuckled. "China George? He's where he always is

. . . down in the casino playing big shot with the ladies.'' She shook her head and her hair went with it. "He's a fireplug that wants to be a sprinkler system.''

"How about Loren Malaca?" I asked, wiping the dampness from my lip.

Pat's eyes got large. "Now there's a butterfly trying to be a caterpillar. She's down there with him . . . or maybe I should say, all over him.''

"You sure?''

"They don't call her 'Epoxy Malaca' for nothing. She's there.''

I finished my drink in one long swallow and set the glass down hard on the table. "Where's the casino?''

Porchy got off the stool, trying to hurry her drink. "I'll take . . .''

I waved her away. "Sit down. Talk. I can do this myself.''

She climbed back up on her stool. Pat was pointing.

"Through that door,'' she said, "and just follow the hallway to the end. There's a button. Three short pushes should get you in. Don't tell them who told you.''

I nodded and picked up my glass. The shark seemed to be following my movements, but it could have been my imagination. "How about one for the road?''

"Black Jack for the road,'' she repeated sadly. "Take the lead right out of your pencil.''

"I'll take the chance.''

She walked off, and I turned to Porchy. "This shouldn't take long,'' I said. "Wait here for me. If I'm not back in an hour, get in your shuttle and get the hell out of here—out of Freefall if you can.''

I got up and moved away before she could say anything. Pat was down by the speedbar, mixing my drink. I took it from her and winked.

"Keep an eye on China George,'' she said. "He's not much in the temper department.''

"Thanks.''

I kept walking. A heavy metal door sat next to a cig machine on the far short wall. It wasn't marked. It was also locked. Turning back around, I looked at Pat. She waved, then pressed a button under the bar. The door buzzed, then clicked open. I went in.

The hallway was long and dark and narrow. And both sides of it were filled with doors. The doors had cut-outs at eye level. I looked into a few. They were gravity rooms, all pulling lighter or heavier gravity than Earth norm. It was reality altered to the chasm's edge. The people in them seemed to be in places where my consciousness would never wander. Most were attempting to make love with Earthers, either free-floating or pinned heavily to the ground, where they had to laboriously crawl around like babies or simply lie on their backs straining their muscles just to breathe in and out. And they *paid* to do that.

There must have been a hundred rooms in that hallway, and I got sick of looking in them. At least it was quieter in there. The hall finally ended at a frosted glass door that said "Private." I pushed the buzzer and went right in.

It was a large room, elegant like a diamond watch is elegant. Crystal chandeliers hung from high, vaulted ceilings, reflecting light in fragile icelike shards. The floors were carpeted in rich browns of various hues, and red-flocked paper covered the aluminum walls. Roulette and baccarat tables sat respectable distances apart while tuxedoed croupiers called the inflectionless tune. The rich people were there; water always finds its own level. They dressed in silks and brocades, and carried themselves just so, and never cared about the winning and losing because the amounts weren't dear enough to them. That's how to separate the real rich people from the pretenders in a casino. It comes out in the eyes every time. The poor ones have that certain edge of hysteria, like jaundice, around the corners of their eyes. It can break either way, but it's always there. The smells were of frankincense, the music was soft, the conversation conversational. I was ready to leave. Gambling, real gambling, bothers me. The odds aren't worth the risks, and the risks don't justify the odds. It's just money.

I saw Rosen immediately. He pranced around the room like a peacock. He wore a tight-fitting purple one-piece, open to the sternum. A frilly white shirt with onyx buttons and a large black bow tie fit under that. He covered it all with a floor-length, flowing black cape. he was surrounded by a bevy of rich girls who all laughed and giggled at his shoddy attempts at wit. A young woman in a sequined evening gown

121

hovered nearby, a champagne glass held sloppily in her hand. Even from across the room I could tell she was in the bag.

I took a long drink from my glass, and moved across the room toward him. I had nearly closed the distance when tuxedo-jumpered punks appeared out of nowhere to intercept me. Rosen caught the activity and turned to watch my approach.

They were grabbing at me, but delicately, so as not to disturb the clientele. "Take it easy now," one of them purred into my ear. "We don't want no trouble here. Just don't make no quick moves."

"I haven't made quick moves since I was fifteen years old," I answered.

"We got ways of dealing with smart guys," the punk said.

"Yeah. I'll bet you get them all alone and bore them to death."

The grip tightened on my arms, and Rosen was on us. He was about my size, but thinner. He looked slick the way a snake does. He had a vaguely Latin look about him, with high cheekbones and dark features. There was a cast to his eyes that made him look dangerously handsome. It could have been cruelty; it may simply have been ignorance.

"Gentlemen," he said to his punks. "Please, let's show a little respect for our guest."

They released me immediately. "You should teach your friends some manners," I said, glaring them down.

Rosen smiled, but it was the humorless smile of someone who has no sense of humor. It was just his way of showing off his pearly whites. "They serve a purpose," he answered, and stuck out his hand. "It is Mr. Swain, isn't it?"

"Just Swain," I answered, ignoring his hand. "How do you know me?"

The hand went back and the dark eyes got darker. "Your . . . adventure on Papa Bear has made you something of a celebrity here," he answered.

The Malaca woman wandered up, looking half-dazed. I hoped that she appreciated the show I was putting on for her benefit, because Rosen sure wasn't. She was young, but acted too old. Her complexion was pale, but nothing like the Freefallers'. She had shoulder-length hair that faded from chestnut to red and back again. She may have been beautiful.

Right now she was just drunk. "You're the Earther who stole the cruiser," she said, pointing.

"And you're Loren Malaca," I returned.

It was Rosen's turn to be surprised. "How do you know?" he asked.

I ignored him and spoke to her. "Your daddy's been telling me about you."

She leaned heavily against Rosen, leading with her breasts. "And what does my daddy say?"

"Your daddy says you like to play with weasels."

Rosen stiffened, inching closer to me. His breath smelled like he drank nothing but mouthwash. "You made a bad joke, Swain," he said, and it obviously wasn't setting well with him.

"So I did," I answered, taking another sip of my drink. "What do you say, let's be friends."

"I like you," Loren Malaca mumbled through the mush in her mouth.

Rosen put an arm around her; it was a gesture of ownership. "How come you're still alive?" he said.

"I carry a rabbit's foot," I answered. "Why don't you send your kids out to play?"

He thought about that for a minute; it was obviously a difficult process for him. Finally, he dismissed his bodyguards with a jerk of the head. "You're making it awful tough to like you," he said softly. "Why?"

"Just a deprived childhood, I guess."

Malaca giggled. "He's cute," she said. Rosen gave her a killer look. "Well, he *is*!" she said, and shrugged away from his grasp.

"Get yourself another drink," he said.

"But, I haven't finished . . ."

"Now!"

Loren Malaca went for a drink, and China George Rosen turned back to me. "What do you want?"

"I want to talk to you. Alone. Is there someplace we can go?"

He went through that horrible thinking process again. "Come with me," he said at last. We tracked out through the casino while he said ta-ta to every woman in the place, and ended up in the superstructure of the ship. He led me to a small air lock. There was a sliding wall cabinet in there. He

123

opened it and pulled out a spacesuit, handing it over to me. "Put this on," he said, then took one out for himself.

"Quite a set-up you've got here," I said, as I got into the bulky thing.

"It's gravy," he said. "And it's all mine."

"At least your cut, huh?"

"You're talking about very unhealthy things, Swain. People shouldn't go busting into business that don't concern them, you know?"

I did know. We zipped up and went into the lock. Wheeling out, I found myself in a room with no door. On the outside—black, black space.

He grabbed two long nylon ropes off of hooks in the cold dark room, and clamped them to our belts, then to the wall. Without a word, he bumped me through the door and I was floating away from the ship.

Panic closed in all around me. Death in confined places. Every nerve jangled and I found myself flailing my arms, out of control. A voice crackled in my ear. "Stop fighting," it statiched. "You're tethered."

I twisted my head around; Rosen was floating out there with me. Our umbilicals stretched out taut, anchoring us a good ten meters from the ship. I hated it.

"Get me back in," I said, and felt like I was talking to myself. The cavern of my helmet rang my words back hollowly in my ears.

He was laughing, in his element. "You wanted privacy," he said. "This is the only real privacy I know of. I don't trust anyplace else."

I took a few deep breaths. It didn't bother a punk like Rosen, so I figured it was okay for me, too. I calmed a bit. "What do you do for an encore?"

"It depends on the quality of the performance. What do you want?" His voice was crackly and mechanical.

"I want to talk about Jeff Roque," I said.

"Don't know the guy," he answered. He was just out of reach of me, unreal and grotesque. I felt as if I were trying to talk to a mannequin.

"I'm going to find that out without much trouble," I told him. "Why don't you just do us both a favor and let's get the conversation out of the way now."

He answered after a minute. "So I knew him, so what?"

"Did he do a lot of gambling here?"

"Why should I tell you anything?"

"Because Malaca hired me to come out here and ask you," I said. "That makes me like a cop."

"Cops got no jurisdiction out here," he sneered. "And I ain't afraid of no Malaca. His people on Earth hired me; they figure that the jerks that live up here have got to blow off steam in this joint."

His veneer was beginning to peel away like an onion-skin, revealing the punk beneath. It figured that a corporation would hire a professional punk to run a punk business. I'd bet he was slicing off a good kickback, too. It was only good business.

"So why are you afraid to talk about Roque?"

"Afraid!" he said so loudly that my ear speaker distorted the word to a cackling static lump. "Afraid of what—a nickel-and-dime gumshoe with a chip on his shoulder?"

"Then talk to me."

"Yeah," he said, talking before he was thinking, just the way I wanted him to. "Roque gambled in here a lot. He was always over his head. I told him about it all the time, but he'd never listen. So what?"

"So now he's dead. How much were you into him for?"

He laughed over the speaker. "You're picking in the wrong berry patch, Swain. If Roque owed me money, I needed him alive, not dead."

"So he owed you money."

"I didn't say that."

"Yes, you did. What about Ginny Teal?"

"Who?"

"You know who. You sent Roque over to see her."

"I think you're brain novad, chum. Because I don't know what in the hell you're talking about."

"What about Loren Malaca—what do you want with her?"

He was clenching and unclenching his gloved fists at me across the dead air, his body glowing dully in the reflected red of the sphere. "You leave her alone," he said angrily. "She's mine, and I'll kill you if you try to take her."

I honestly believed that he meant it. "She's slumming with you, Rosen. Oil and water don't mix."

"She loves me too much," he said. "And that's the way it's going to stay. Leave her alone, you son of a bitch."

"What about beckon, George. Tell me that you don't know about beckon."

He didn't say a word; he just began furiously hand-over-handing back down the length of rope. It took me a second to understand, then another to react to what he was doing, and by then it was too late.

I came after him, but he had too much of a start. He made the room, and I watched helplessly as he pulled himself inside. I made it back to the sphere and was trying to scramble in, when his shape filled the open port. He braced well and his foot came up solid on my shoulder, jarring me loose, sending me tumbling away. The pressure on my rope was gone, and I saw it floating back out the hatchway like a cobra dancing to a snake charmer. The sound of his laughter cackled through my helmet speaker, then it, too, was gone.

I was floating free, with a whole universe waiting to suck me in.

13

My wait for death was a strangely calm one. Hell, I've accepted the imminent possibility for years; the actuality seemed almost an anticlimax. The anticipation was everything. If the anticipation was fire, the event was sand.

I tumbled through the perpetual night, watching Jenny Sue Qua shrink smaller and smaller, fading along with the rest of Freefall. I belonged to the stars. I would guard them silently for a time, then the oxygen would get thin, then, I suppose, tissue-starved anoxia would set it. A happy death, a drunkard's death. Appropriate, actually.

And the stars flip-flopped out of my field of vision. Why wouldn't they stay still?

I felt bad for Ginny. Felt bad that, when it came right down to it, her life had to depend on somebody like me. I'm a pretty fair set of hard knucks, and my head has more knots on it than an old kite string, but I was out of my class from the start with this thing. Porchy was right; they were *all* right.

And I never did find out about beckon. It seemed like everyone knew about it but me. Even Ginny knew, if we could just pull it out of her head. Maybe if I ever reached those tumbling stars, they'd be able to help me.

So I tumbled, and waited . . . and waited . . . and waited. And then I saw something, bright reflections in the distant blinding sun: shapes, dark shapes, blotting out part of the star field, shining with twinkling edges like the embers of a dying fire. At first I thought that my eyes were creating the images, but then I realized what it was. It was Freefall's garbage trail, the orbiting junkyard—and I was heading right into it. I was having a difficult time with relative motion. I knew that I'd be passing through the junk, but I was worried about my speed. Maybe if I could stop myself, I could hitch a ride on the junk and get the attention of a passing garbage scow. If my oxygen held out.

I waited for what seemed like hours but was probably minutes for the junkyard to catch up with me. Time was meaningless. Like everything else, I was sucked up in the vacuum.

And then it was there.

Huge, hulking shapes sliding silently. Bloated, deformed shapes. Castaways, lepers trailing after the pack of humanity. There were steel girders twisted like pretzels and torn-up cruisers whose gaping damage told wordless tales of sudden death. There were dead computers being chased by dangling wires and tiny relay boards and transistors—electronic Furies perpetually tormenting a nonhuman brain. There were chunks of raw metals, and dead communications satellites. And there were human handprints. Bloody mountains of paper and tin cans and apple cores and bottles. Life stories told in refuse.

There was something else, too. Bodies. Human bodies. A lot of them.

A whole lot.

And they all moved wordlessly, in beautiful unspoken harmony. They called to me—no, beckoned to me. I was on the fringe, riding the hellbound train, neither dead nor alive. They offered me a place to stay so that I wouldn't have to stand my lonely star-vigil alone.

Alone.

Alone.

In Freefall, life was nearly as lonely as death. Ginny understood that; it's what she was running from. I watched the army of the dead floating by me, the orbiting graveyard. It didn't seem right to me to just discard the shell this way, so much refuse, cheap and efficient. It got me to realizing just how efficient Beltel was.

One of the trash mountains began to loom large in my tumbling vision. I was going to hit it. I spread myself wide to offer a large field of resistance, then tensed my muscles for the jolt.

The jolt didn't come. The mountain was a mock-friend, an incoherent jumble of unconnected parts. Form without substance. I was on it, then through it, leaving an outline of my form behind me—a permanent record of my failure. I had left my indelible imprint on the history of the junkyard. Immortality.

I was surrounded on all sides now by junk. It was a world of junk. I tumbled toward some malformed girders. They were within reach. They slid near, and I strained for them, grabbing hold with gloved hands. My fingers slipped away without ever getting hold. As I feared, I was moving too fast.

I had managed to stop my tumble, though. I was traveling in a straight line, backward, through the garbage. But still I was moving too fast. My tether stretched out behind me. Pulling it quickly in, I shoved the rope back through the hooked end, forming a large loop. Cosmic cowboy.

I turned my head to see where I was going. A naked male body was charging toward me. Headlong it came, like a fleshy torpedo. I let my loop dangle at arm's length, and the dead meat bull's-eyed my rope. The head slipped through and I jerked up hard, catching the bottom of the loop on the shoulders. The rope slid against itself, tightening, tightening. Ten meters later it pulled taut, then everything danced.

The body on the end of the line jumped as if it had suddenly reanimated itself. It flipped over completely, head and feet changing places. My middle jerked back against the weight, slowing my forward momentum to a crawl. I was anchored now, barely fighting the current.

A shape moved toward me, reflecting sunlight. It came slowly closer, mirroring my slackened pace. It was a Coke machine with a big hole blown out of the center, as if someone had been cheated out of his money one time too many.

I twisted myself around, opening my arms wide, catching the thing in a large embrace as it floated by. I clung to the machine for dear life as my tether slackened, my anchor still moving in the opposite direction.

The body floated by me, the neck snapped and twisted from the force of our meeting. Other than that, I couldn't see anything wrong with it. It was an old body with an old face, but there were no outward physical signs of deterioration. The mouth was open wide, gasping air that was nowhere to be found. And on the rest of the face—surprise. It was alongside me, then past me, then tightening my rope from the other direction. We had changed places.

I needed to untether.

Trying to hold the machine with one hand, I frantically clawed at the hook on my belt with the other. The line was tightening quickly. I nearly had the hook off, when the line snapped tight, pulling me away from the machine. Scrabbling at the slick sides, I managed to hook a finger in the plastic return slot, holding on for all I was worth.

I pulled at the now-weighty hook with my left hand, body straining, shaking with the drag. Slowly, slowly, the hook scraped out. It came off the end of its metal eye just as my strength gave way. I lost my tenuous hold on the return slot, but it didn't matter: I was part of the flow now, moving with the cadence of the rest of the junkyard. Just one of the boys.

Keeping an arm on my red metal island, I surveyed the surroundings. If there was anything to be done, it needed to be done right away, for I couldn't have more than a few minutes of oxygen at best.

The junk was thick around me, thick as drunks in a flophouse. Climbing atop the machine, I turned slowly around 360°. Everything felt static to me, unmoving, frozen. I peered around the junk piles, searching for I didn't know what. When I saw it, I knew.

A large ship sat partially hidden behind a paper mountain. It was huge and old and looked like a Japanese beetle in drag. It had probably been a top-of-the-line freighter at one time, but had just gotten too old and been put out to pasture on junk duty. I didn't know what was in there, but I was willing to take my chances.

It was a good ways distant from me, but I had to go for it. Without hesitation, I wrapped my arms behind me on the Coke machine and squatted against its side. I pushed off as gently as a swimmer gliding underwater, and aimed for an unmissable pile of twisted girders not far from my position. I made it without any trouble. Confidence surging, I next tried for an old satellite, shaped like a hockey puck with porcupine antennae. This was farther away, more ambitious. I floated to the thing, grabbing at the appendages when I arrived.

A tiny light flashed within the structure. It was a weak light, bleeping at infrequent intervals—a heart slowing, ready to die. The absurdity of the whole routine got to me, and I

130

could hear myself chuckling within my helmet. It was real funny.

I pushed off for an asteroid of iron. "Wheee!" I was confident, having a great time. I could do this for weeks. I nearly misjudged the metal hunk, having to grab it from the side as I went by. What the hell—all in fun. I was the king of space, a voice in the silence, ruler of a junkyard empire. I climbed atop the asteroid, hands on hips, and began yodeling to my silent friends. I had always been a closet yodeler; now I was bringing it out in the open.

"Yodel-a-he-hoooo!" Was I ever good.

I finished my aria, and found that I was having to dig deep for a lungful of air. I was straining for every breath. Too much exertion, I guess. I shook my head. My empire was all contrast, white and black, sunlight and darkness. The shapes were beginning to take on different definition. Dark, brooding, malevolent. It wasn't so funny anymore.

The ship was still far in the distance, but I tried for it anyway. I was beginning to get scared. My world was trying to swallow me up, trying to bring an end to my career as a yodeler.

I sailed for a long time, the ship changing form as I approached. It wasn't a ship after all. It was alive—a dark, hungry monster looking for lunch. I wanted to go back, but it wasn't possible. I was hooked and in trouble. I floated over a sea of bodies, all old people. They were moaning to me as I went by.

I reached the monster, banging into its thick, armored side. I closed my eyes, waiting for its steel talons to rip me apart for consumption, but it didn't happen. Opening my eyes, I inched along its hide, looking—for what? I didn't know anymore, couldn't remember. It was all out of control.

A handle was in my grasp. I was turning it and the monster's belly came open. I waited for the rush of blood, but my enemy was hollow, a Trojan beetle. I climbed inside and stood, weaving badly. I kept running into the walls. I reached another door and staggered through, giddy, disoriented.

I looked up. I was face to face with a bramble-tangle of knotted black hair and beard. Fiery eyes assailed me; sharp, jagged teeth opened and closed.

"Allow me to introduce myself," I said. "Mathew Swain, King of the Yodelers."

Then everything got real fuzzy, and my eyes danced with cute little brown spots that stretched to horizontal lines. Then I was looking at the floor. Then somebody turned out the lights.

14

My head felt as if it had an airbag stuffed inside and someone was overfilling it, trying to break me from the inside out. There was sound there, too. A chorus of voices. They were singing the "Beer Barrel Polka."

I opened my eyes. My spacesuit was gone; I was dressed in my civvies. I was in a large room with rounded walls and riveted girders. It was full of people, men and women. They were all dressed in crisp, clean, light blue jumpsuits that had the word DOCKED stenciled across the back in big letters. Many were dirty and unkempt, some were not. It seemed merely to be an exercise in personal preference. And that was just fine with me.

They were giving a dance. The orchestra was off to the side, and the members were each imitating different instruments to approximate a polka band. Those who weren't "playing" were singing:

> "Roll out the barrel.
> We'll have a barrel of fun."

Everyone else was dancing and clapping. Exuberant, physical dancing despite the heavy shoe-weights they wore. There were lots of flailing arms and stomping feet.

> "Roll out the barrel.
> We've got the blues on the run."

I struggled to a sitting position. My head was killing me, but that problem was getting to be run of the mill anymore. When everyone saw me get up, the dance stopped immediately and they all crowded around. Putting my hands on the

133

sides of my head, I looked up at them. "Good morning," I said.

They all gasped, then applauded. A man, a small man, crouched down beside me. His hair was gray, cut close, military style. He was meticulously groomed. His eyes were pale green, and there was something . . . strange about them.

"Where did you come from?" he asked. "What's your number?"

I shook it off. "It's a long story. My name's Swain," I said, extending my hand. "I believe you saved my life."

He looked at my hand as if it were a steak sandwich and he was a vegetarian. Slowly, precisely, he reached into his back pocket and extracted a large white handkerchief and wrapped it around his hand. Then he shook mine.

"My name is Diction Harry," he said in clipped, rhythmical tones. "Welcome to New Jersey."

I looked around. "So *this* is New Jersey. Who are you people?"

He made a puzzled gesture with his arm. "Why we're the *citizens* of New Jersey." The crowd all silently nodded agreement.

I stood up painfully. They had weighted my feet too. Everyone else straightened with me. "How did you get here?" I asked Diction Harry. "This is a junk satellite, isn't it?"

Harry nodded. "New Jersey," he said. "Sometimes we live here."

I walked around a bit, trying to clear my head. The crowd followed me around like multiple shadows. "Where do you live the rest of the time?"

"Shimanagashi," he said, and shrugged. "Where else?"

I stopped walking; the crowd stopped walking. "Then you're escaped prisoners?"

Harry thought about that for a while. "What do you mean by escaped?"

I looked at him. His eyes were unfocused, hazy. "You broke out of jail and got away," I said.

"No," he answered quickly. "We didn't do that. We come here, but we go back every day to eat."

"Why?"

He stared at me, surprised. "It's the system," he answered.

134

"You've got transportation?" I asked.

He nodded, smiling. "Of course."

"Could you take me back to Freefall?"

Everyone laughed.

"What's so funny?" I asked.

"We can't go to Freefall," Harry answered. "We're prisoners."

"You could go to the moon."

Harry's eyes began to narrow in a most uncomplimentary manner. "Why would we want to do that?" he asked cautiously.

I looked at the faces around me. They had all gotten very quiet and reserved. "To be free," I replied.

"Free," Harry repeated, like Tarzan hearing Jane's name for the first time. He stared at me for a moment, then abruptly turned his back and stalked out of the group. I followed.

"I've got to get back to Freefall," I said, grabbing his arm to slow him down. "I can pay you."

He wheeled around and there was a hook-bladed carpenter's knife in his hand. "We don't go to Freefall," he snarled.

I backed up, hands in front of me. "All right," I said. "How about Shimanagashi? Could you take me there?"

He lightened immediately, putting away the knife. "That's the system," he said. "Of course you can go to Shimanagashi."

The congregation applauded wildly at my conversion.

"Yes, sir," Harry said. "You may not have been docked like us, but you're one of us now." He turned full circle, gesturing to the others with a twirling hand. "Here's a memo," he called. "We return to Shimanagashi to wait for the dinner break."

He led us all out of the cabin, and into a clear tube that ran the length of the big ship. Garbage was crammed tightly all around our tube, and walking through it made me feel a little like Moses crossing the Red Sea. The fact that there was air in the cabin and tube made me think that Freefall maintained the area as a way station for garbage dumpers; or perhaps, in the manner of bureaucracies, they had had need of it at one time, and simply maintained the system out of habit.

We were forced to walk single file through the tube. I was right behind Diction Harry. He turned and spoke to me over his shoulder. "We've got to get you a proper uniform," he said.

"I may not be staying that long," I returned, and watched his eyes start to ice over again. "Yeah, you're right," I hurriedly corrected.

These people were something else again. Irene had warned me that prolonged periods of weightless isolation had this effect, so I wasn't very surprised.

The tube turned eventually into a dock, and we airlocked into the weirdest conglomeration of junk that I'd ever seen. It was like a swap-meet at an insane asylum. Parts of many ships were all welded together—cruisers and freighters and satellites and weather beacons. Walking into that heap produced in me much the same sensation that eating a bowl of Chinese alphabet soup would.

Harry flew the thing, and he let me sit in the cockpit with him. The damn ship wheezed and coughed and finally thrusted. One two-second burst was all he'd give it, just enough to nudge us in the right direction. They apparently didn't have much access to fuel.

"How long has this been going on?" I asked him once we were underway.

"What, the system?"

"Yeah."

"Longer than any of us remember," he answered. "That's the way systems are."

"The police know about it?"

He looked at me quizzically. "Of course they do. The police are all docked, too."

It was my turn to be bewildered. "I don't understand."

As he drove, he continually checked himself for dirt or dust, carefully scrutinizing his hands and arms. "When people get docked, they put them in Shimanagashi. After a time, they come back and check. Some get to be police then, and some . . ."

"New Jersey."

"Indeed, yes. New Jersey. It's the system."

His incessant grooming was driving me nuts. I turned and gazed out the port to avoid it, but I kept seeing his reflection in the glass. "What were you docked for?"

His reflection shrugged at me. "The same thing most everyone is docked for, the Solipsism."

136

I turned back to the genuine article. "What's that?"

"You sure don't know very much," he said cautiously. "Who are you?"

"Please," I answered, "tell me about the Solipsism."

He spoke slowly, like he was dragging the river for a body. "It's when you can't tell the difference between what's dreams and what's real," he said. "It's bad for the system."

"That happens to a lot of people?"

He inspected his fingernails minutely. "I guess it happens to everybody a little bit."

I braced myself for the big one. "Does the word 'beckon' mean anything to you?"

He shook his head. "Should it?"

"No," I answered, almost happy that there was someone besides me who was in the dark.

"You know something?" Diction Harry said. "You're crazy."

"Sometimes I think you're right," I returned.

The trip to the ball-bearing forest that was isolation took a considerable amount of time. Harry chattered a lot, but really never said much of anything. But that could hardly be surprising, seeing how limited his experience was. From our talk I found out that Freefallers were totally unschooled in areas of philosophy and creative thinking. I guess Beltel figured that there would be too much of a conflict of interests there. During all his years with the system, Harry's job had been to brush dabs of color-coding paint on relay boards, and I got to hear a lot more about that than I'd ever want to know. I tried to question him further about Solipsism, but I don't think he really understood it himself. Being ignorant in matters other than corporate, he was unable to verbalize his abstractions. I asked him about the bodies in the junkyard, but he either didn't know or wasn't saying.

We finally arrived at Shimanagashi, and everyone was dropped off at his very own private prison. It was awful. I was forced to take off my shoe-weighters. The system. Then I was shoved into a dimly lit, cold, hollow cave.

I guess that the inside was round, but the outer walls were lost in the shadows and I couldn't tell. The cell was one room, although it was a big room. There was some lighting, but it was extremely dim and undirected. Just enough light to make you crazy. A rail bisected the middle of the chamber up and down. At least I defined it as up and down. There was a zero G toilet, and that was all. No access to the outside. No ornamentation inside. No bed. No tables. Just free-floating madness. Shimanagashi. The things that human beings do to one another.

I spent an eternity there that lasted for an instant. And when the security people finally arrived for feeding time, I felt I would explode inside. They didn't want to take me back, of course. That wasn't the system. But I got them to check me out and they reluctantly agreed. Big of them.

They led me down the dock to their cruiser, and transferred another prisoner in as I went out. It was Porchy. Malaca wasn't kidding about shared fate. She made fish eyes as we nearly bumped in the hall.

"We've got to stop meeting like this," I said.

"You're alive!" she said, and threw her arms around me.

"Matter of opinion. What happened?"

She backed up a pace and looked me over. "When you didn't come back, I tried to do what you told me. They caught me before I could get out of the city, confiscated my ship, and brought me here."

"Without a trial?"

She rolled her eyes.

They *really* didn't want to take Porchy back, but I worked that out, too. So we were free again. Back to square one.

I knew one thing, though. China George held some cards, and his kind of punk I could definitely understand. We would meet again.

Soon.

15

Henry Malaca held his tumbler of Black Jack up to the light, savoring its color and thickness. "Bourbon County, Kentucky," he said. "It's where the name comes from. Did you know that, boy?"

I shook my head, but I really did know.

"Aged for four years in charred oak barrels. That's the system. Do you know how hard oak is to come by these days?"

I took a drink, preferring the sipping to the talking. "Pretty hard," I answered.

"Damn near impossible," he added, and took a drink himself. "The stuff doesn't grow back fast, like pine or some such. What are we going to do for whisky when all the oak's gone?"

"We'll drink vodka," I answered. "It's not aged at all."

He made a face. "Damned foreign drink," he said. "Though I guess everything is foreign up here."

I raised my glass. "I'll drink to that."

Malaca's wheel sat off all by itself at Freefall. It was bigger than anyone else's, and better. Security cruisers patroled constantly around its circumference, and no one could get in or out without proper clearance. We were sitting in a den on the rim. The room was done in royal blues and golds, with a lot of wood around. Malaca was crazy for wood. I sat on a high stool at his solid mahogany bar, while he stood around on the operating end of the thing, playing bartender. I have often thought that there is a little bartender trying to get out of the insides of most executives.

We both finished our drinks at the same time, and he poured us another. Malaca held up his glass. "To J. Pierpont Morgan," he toasted. "God rest his soul." The last drink had been Joseph Kennedy's, and the one before that H.L. Hunt's. And Henry Malaca still hadn't told me why he had called me over to his home.

I drank with him. "Henry," I said, "I know this isn't just a social call."

"Why not?" he asked. He set his face. "Two men getting together, talking it over, feeling . . . real."

"What do you want?" I asked.

His eyes twinkled just a touch. If I didn't hate the man so much, I could probably almost like him. "Pretty slick move you put on the greaseball," he said, and bobbed his eyebrows.

I sighed. "I was stupid to put myself in that position," I returned.

He looked at me then, just looked. Then he took another drink. "A man like you . . . shouldn't let himself be pushed around that way."

"Rosen's my problem. I'll handle him in my own way."

"I'll just bet you will," he said, putting his glass down on the bar. "Loren likes you," he said. "She's real impressed with your kind of man."

"She likes a stupid man?"

"A man's man. A man with guts and determination." He put a hand on his chest. "Like me. That's the kind of man she wants."

"That's the kind of man China George thinks he is," I returned. "He'd kill for her."

"He's nothing."

I grunted and got off the bar stool, moving across the room to sit on a blue velvet love seat. The room was too fancy for me. I felt out of place there, like a tin whistle at a tuba convention. "What's Solipsism?" I asked him.

He was digging for ice behind the bar. Dropping some in his glass, he paced the room to sit across from me, all the while stirring his drink with his finger.

"What's Solipsism?" I asked him again.

He brushed it off. "A technical term," he said. "Nothing for you to be concerned with."

"Our deal," I reminded him, "is that I get to pursue my own case along with yours."

He frowned deeply. I don't think he liked me any more than I cared for him. "It's kind of like battle fatigue," he said after a moment. "The actual term is Solipsism Syndrome. It develops sometimes in closed societies like this one."

"I don't understand."

"I'm getting to it," he snapped, but then hesitated. He looked down at his drink, stirring it some more. "When life is too much the same," he said, "too predictable, folks can get to feeling like none of it is real. Like maybe the only thing real is what's going on up in their heads." He pointed.

I was thinking about Ginny's final message on the vis. She said she was the god of the universe. "You mean that people suffering from the Solipsism Syndrome feel that they create the realities from their own minds?"

"Something like that," he shrugged. "Dumb, ain't it?"

"How long would it take to develop such a condition?"

"I wouldn't know," he answered, putting his stirring finger to his lips. "But it's why that Rosen character is able to run that vice satellite. They say that the variety helps keep folks sane."

I stood up, looking down at him. He stood also. I was still looking down at him. "You don't agree with that?" I asked.

He shook his chubby head. "Sounds like a load of sop from a lot of bleeding hearts to me, but what can I do . . ."

"I know," I said. "It's the system."

I wanted to ask him about beckon, but I was beginning to get a little gun-shy about it. Every time I brought it up, I got myself in trouble. I decided to let it ride for a while.

"Loren's at home tonight," he said, smiling. He cocked his head. "She's over at her end of the house. Bet she'd be right pleased to have a visit from you."

So that's what it was all about. Malaca still trying to tangle me up with his powder-keg daughter. That girl had a fuse on her—a short fuse, the kind that can blow up in your face. I didn't have time for this, but from the way Henry was looking at me, I knew that I didn't have time for anything else.

I put my drink down on a polished rosewood coffee table. "Well, I guess I'll just take a stroll up there and see what's what."

"You do that, boy," he said sternly. "Just follow the hall. You'll know when you've got to her section."

I took his word for that and started out the power-sliding door.

"This can be a good thing for you, Swain," he called to my back.

I moved into the hall, wondering if General Custer told that to his troops before Little Big Horn. I moved along the never-ending hill. All the aluminum walls had been walnut paneled, and even had a wood smell to them. The floors were carpeted in a yellow to rusty color and patterned to resemble a blanket of autumn leaves.

Why was Malaca throwing me at his daughter? It sure couldn't be for the tremendous respect he had for me as a person. He hated everything I stood for. If he had to hire me to get her away from Rosen, then he'd probably have to hire someone else to get her away from me. That didn't strike me as very good business. Maybe Loren Malaca could shed some light on Rosen's relationship with Jeff Roque, though. She had traveled in his circles for some time; she'd have to know something.

I wondered about Solipsism. Ginny was definitely exhibiting signs of a totally runaway case of it, but how could it happen so fast? That didn't gel at all. No, my best bet was still on Jeff Roque and his connection with China George.

And then there was something called beckon.

As I walked, the aspect of the wheel changed. The hallway got darker, foreboding. The smooth symmetry of the halls gave way to jagged, bulging contours—rocklike, cold and slick. I had entered Loren's end of the house. The ground became uneven beneath my feet, and in the darkness I had to shuffle to keep upright. The jagged walls closed in further, making the passageway so narrow that I had to squeeze through it in places. It was twisted and claustrophobic, like being lost in a coal mine. The farther I went, the darker it became.

Tiny sounds squeaked out at me from the darkness, and small, burning eyes watched my movements. It was not a good place for a city boy to be. The ground rose steeply before me, and I was forced to crawl up it until I was confined to a space so narrow I had to scramble through it on my belly. And the darkness had become total.

I didn't like this, didn't like it at all. For the second time

142

in as many days, my mind was becoming detached, lonely. It was like being the first kid eliminated in the spelling bee.

There was light ahead, flickering. I crawled toward it, and the space became larger again. I was in a crouch when I got to the light. It was a torch throbbing on the wall, making the shadows dance on the wild walls.

A figure stood just outside the ring of jumping light. It was an old man dressed in decaying tatters. He was grimy like pipe bowls get grimy. His hair and beard were long and white.

"Take the torch," he rasped, pointing with a withered brown hand.

"Who . . ."

"Quickly," he said, looking over his shoulder. "Follow me."

I grabbed the torch off the wall and followed him through the twisted passage. The way was still narrow, but I could at least stand again. The old man jangled as he walked because a large iron ring of long keys dangled from a cord tied to his waist.

Finally, the hall widened again, but it was cold stone that formed the path. A man-made cavern. We passed a series of doors that lined both sides of the corridor. Massive wooden things they were, with small square windows at eye-level. The windows were barred.

The old man stopped in front of one of the doors, taking up his huge key ring, searching for the proper key.

"Nice day for a boat race," I told him. He went on with his work. "Do you realize that this is a leap year?" I asked. No response.

Reaching out, I touched his wrinkled face. It was cold and latexed. An andy. The best I'd ever seen.

Finding the key, he put it in the door and turned, then grabbed the iron ring to pull open the heavy slab. He motioned me inside with a jerk of his mechanical head.

It was light in there, so I handed him my torch and went inside. The door creaked closed behind me. I was standing in a large cell lit by candlelight. It was furnished with a plain wooden table and chair and a bed of straw against the wall. It was all stone, hard and chill. The only thing that gave the place away was the large vis that occupied an entire wall to my left. Loren Malaca stood in the center of the room wearing a virginal white evening gown with three-quarter pink gloves. She was made up like a high-dollar hooker, and a diamond tiara accented her chestnut to red hair. The captive princess.

"Should I have made an appointment?" I asked.

She crossed the room to me, putting her arms around my shoulders. She was a head shorter than me. "I want you, Swain," she said huskily.

Her hair smelled of hot pastries and carnival colors. I nuzzled it for a second. "I wish you'd stop playing hard to get," I said.

Her lips came up to mine. They were hungry, demanding lips. They were urgent like a brush fire is urgent, and hungry like quicksand. And there wasn't a drop of passion in them. Kissing Loren Malaca was like kissing an oil drum.

Taking her by the arms, I forced her away from me. A flash of anger lit her eyes, then disappeared. "What's wrong?" she asked. "Don't you want me?"

"I guess I'm just old-fashioned," I told her. "I like to get certain things out of the way first . . . you know, like introductions."

"I thought you were a real man," she said, moving over to sit on her bed of straw.

"That's what you get for thinking." I scooted the room's only chair over in front of the bed and turned it around backwards. Sitting down, I rested my arms on the back. I looked at her face; her eyes were hazel, and very lethargic. I'd seen eyes like that plenty of times before. "What do you want with me?" I asked her.

She looked away from me. "I don't know what you mean?"

I reached out and took her chin roughly in my grip and turned her face back to mine. "Damn it," I said. "You people have been playing me for a sucker since the first second I floated into this God-forsaken hole, and I want to know why."

"You're free," she said softly. "I want that."

"Why?"

She twisted away from my grasp. "Because it's the only thing I can't have," she answered harshly.

"Tell me about Rosen."

"Why should I?"

I felt myself getting angry, and I wasn't quite sure why. "Because everything has its price, lady. Nothing's free, not even up here."

"You'll make love to me if I tell you?"

"Maybe," I said. "If I like your answers."

"What do you want to know?"

We were playing a game—a weird, perverted game. I was working purely on instinct, trying to feel my way as I went. "I want to know about Jeff Roque and Rosen."

She leaned back against the wall and sighed. "Roque gambled. I don't mean he just gambled. It was like a disease with him. He couldn't help himself." She stopped talking and stared at me.

"Go on," I said.

She blinked several times. "George isn't much in the brains department, but he runs a pretty tight business. He never paid much attention to Roque. He made it a policy not to extend credit to anyone other than the real élite of Freefall. Then something happened."

"What?"

"He found out that Roque had access to all of Freefall's computer banks and stored records." She lay down flat on her back, staring at the ceiling. She brought a wristwatched arm up to her face, let it drop. "Things changed after that," she said dully. "George began to orbit with Roque, gave him unlimited credit."

"To a point," I said.

She turned those slack eyes to me. "When Roque built the pot up too high, George demanded his money."

I stood up, planting my foot on the chair seat. "And Roque didn't have it."

"No, of course not."

"How long ago was that?"

She shrugged. "A matter of months, I suppose. I'm not much on time."

I sat back down. Something kept Jeff Roque alive for months after the ax should have fallen. He had something that Rosen wanted. "Did they make some kind of a deal?"

She sat up and looked at me, her eyes hungry again. "George would never talk about it, and to be perfectly honest, I was never interested enough to care anyway. Roque

145

was inferior seniority. His living or dying didn't concern me in the least."

"What about Rosen's seniority?"

She kittened her lips into a smile. "China George doesn't have seniority. Neither do you." She reached her arms out to me. I ignored them.

"How long have you been riding the horse?" I asked her.

She pulled back, tensed. "I don't know . . ."

I grabbed her left arm and jerked down the long glove. The needle marks were tiny, the search for uncollapsed veins a professional one. "I can see what you get out of Rosen," I said. "But what does he get out of you?"

"If I told you that," she said slowly, "he'd kill both of us."

"Instead of just me, right?" I shook my head. "Did he ever mention beckon to you?"

She kept glancing at her watch as if she were late for her dancing class. "I don't know what you're talking about," she said. "Now, please, come here." She slipped the straps of her gown down off her shoulders, and the whole top of the thing came off, leaving her naked to the waist.

"It happens to all of you, doesn't it?" I said. "The Solipsism eats away at all of you like a cancer. And nothing helps, does it? Not the junk, not your money, not sex."

She lay down and began writhing on the straw bed, her arms reaching. "Please," she cooed. "You promised."

I felt my gut knotting up with disgust. "You're hollow inside. Just like an egg shell with a pretty picture painted on it."

I heard a buzz and jerked my head. Loren's vis was bleeping. I looked at it, then back to her. She had reached beside her on the bed and flipped a toggle, juicing the damn thing. A face faded in, ten times bigger than life. China George Rosen.

His eyes got wide, the skin of his face straining against his cheekbones. "You just don't know how to stay dead, do you?" he said, and his voice sounded like somebody had just shoved one of those electric billy clubs up his ass.

"I'm a slow learner."

"Don't worry," he said, eyes narrow and shifting. "I'm getting set to give you a permanent lesson."

146

"You've had your shot, punk. School's out."

He blanked without another word.

I flared around to the Malaca woman. "You're still playing me for the chump, aren't you? Still trying to set me up."

She stared at me without expression.

I went to her and grabbed her arms, shaking them. Her full breasts jounced with the movement. "What do you want from me?!" I yelled.

Her face contorted with pain. "I don't know what you're talking about," she said. "You're crazy. Crazy!"

I had to force myself to let her go, force myself to keep from using my knuckles instead of my brain. "None of it matters," I said. "You can tell your old man, and you can tell Beemer, and you can tell Rosen that none of it matters. We're all stuck together in a big leaky boat and we're going to ride out the storm together. All the way to the end of the line."

I turned away from her and walked out of the cell without looking back.

16

I walked right out of there and demanded a security cruiser to take me back to Freefall General. Somehow, I knew they wouldn't stop me; they would accommodate me as much as I needed. The scenario called for me to get what I wanted, and at that point in time, I wanted Rosen. Whatever happened to Roque was all twisted up with China George like coat hangers get twisted up in a closet. And whatever happened to Roque was twisted up with Ginny's condition. I still needed the connection, though, and it was beginning to look like that connection could possibly be named Manny Dugan.

Dugan had been Roque's partner at Mama Bear. If Rosen wanted something from the computer satellite, it seemed possible that Dugan would know about it. I had left Porchy at the hospital to look for Dugan while I went to Malaca's place. Now I needed to check back and see what had happened.

The cruiser dropped me off and I walked the wheel until I found Irene and Porchy drinking coffee in the doctor's apartment.

"Did Daddy's little girl eat you alive?" Porchy asked when she saw me.

"Not so's you'd notice," I returned and looked at Irene. Her face was dark. "What's wrong?"

She brushed a lock of black-silver hair out of her face, and sat up stiffly on the couch. "She doesn't have much time," she said in her doctor's voice. "Her body can't function like this much longer."

"You gave me a week," I said.

"I said possibly a week."

I looked at Porchy. "Did you manage to find Dugan?" I asked.

She shook her head. "It's like he vanished. No one ever

148

answers the vis at his house. Calls aren't taken at Mama Bear.''

"Take me to Papa," I said.

She stood up. "Whenever you're ready."

"I'm ready now." I turned to Irene. "Could Ginny's symptoms have anything to do with the Solipsism Syndrome?''

She raised her eyebrows. "Of course, that's always the first thought. But my experience with Solipsism is that it is a condition brought on by gradual environmental stress. It's a very delicate kind of neurosis, very dependent upon the totality of one's world." She stood up, smoothing her pale blue shift. "It doesn't seem rational that Ginny could succumb to it in such a short time."

"What's the treatment for that?''

"Simple enough," she said. "Change of environment, a little variety, maybe some shock therapy in the more advanced cases. Of course, Beltel doesn't do any of those things. It's a useless expenditure of cash and time to them. They simply ship the worst cases off to Shimanagashi. But I suppose you already know about that." We were inching toward the door as Irene walked toward us, forcing the flow. "Anyway, Ginny's far beyond that stage."

"Even the shocks?''

"I'll try if you'd like," she said, and her tone was one of defeat. "But I don't think that you should get your hopes up.''

"Humor me," I returned.

Her lips curled into a fast-fading smile, and she laid a cool hand on my arm. "Consider it done," she said.

"Thanks." I started out the door. "If you've got the time, do me another favor. Could you make a couple of calls and find out about Loren Malaca?''

"Find out what about her?''

I waved it off. "I don't know. Education, prior medical history. I want to understand as much as I can about her.''

"I'll try," she said, and was standing right up on us.

I gave her a quick hug. "Thanks, Irene. I appreciate all you've done.''

"I just wish it could be more," she returned.

Porchy and I left and walked the halls without a word. It was getting so we wouldn't talk unless we were sure of who could be listening.

"Tell me something," I said when we were finally tumbling away from the hospital. "Why would Henry Malaca go to so much trouble to set me up for Rosen to kill? I mean, he could have me anytime."

She put on her baseball cap. "Maybe it's just business ethics," she returned. "You know, if Rosen did it, it would be easier to explain away. You *are* an Earther, remember?"

"I remember."

"Expediency is the *written* law up here. They could spend a little more time getting rid of you, and avoid an Earth investigation."

"Why would they care about that? Why care about my life at all?"

"You tell me."

I didn't tell her anything, but my mind began turning toward all those bodies I saw floating in the junkyard. I forced the thoughts away, though, because something else was bothering me, something that I remembered from the last time I had been to the big wheel.

"Does Beltel use a lot of gold up here?" I asked.

"I wouldn't know," she said, jacking her thrusters to get us into Papa's rotation. "Gold doesn't tarnish or wear away. I'm sure they need an amount of it, but I wouldn't think a lot. Other metals are far more plentiful, and easier to work with, and a hell of a lot cheaper."

We were curling into the flow, moving with the clockworks. "How does a corporation like Beltel buy from lunar mining operations?"

She feathered the thrusters and gently set us on a dock. "I don't know exactly how, but it's my understanding that it's a sort of spot market. It's cheaper to buy up here, eliminating the middle men. I think they make the deals up here, then clear all the actual money through banks back on Earth. Why?"

"I saw a lot of gold stored in their freighter warehouse when I crashed there. More gold than seemed necessary." I shook it off. "Probably nothing."

Porchy unstrapped and floated to the lock. "So where are we going?"

"I'm going to find Manny Dugan," I said, unstrapping. "You are going to Security."

"That just made my day," she returned.

"Go up there and see if you can get us clearance to go to Mama Bear."

"But they'll never . . ."

"Yeah, I know." I climbed out of my chair and walk-floated to the hatch. "What I really want you to do is poke around a little. See if you can pinpoint a relationship between Garnet Roque and Mort Beemer."

"Just how am I supposed to do that?"

"You'll think of something."

She unwheeled the door and pulled it open. "You don't ask for much."

I slapped her rump as she climbed into the tube. "I have every confidence in you."

"Sure."

I climbed in behind her. "Meet me back here in an hour."

She turned her head to look back at me. "The last time you said that, you ended up getting us both in jail."

"You wanted in, my love."

"Don't remind me."

The docks were on the inner circumference of the rim. We got street clearance badges at immigration, then tubed down to street level. Porchy rented a bicycle and headed toward Security, while I moved on foot to Dugan's.

There were some crowds in the junk-strewn streets, the men in their leisure suits, the women in their frilly blouses. I moved through their midst, out of place, alone. A skunk in a school-heli. They stared at me as I walked. Dark eyes shining out of ghostly faces—dreamlike faces, unreal. They were hollow people, like white chocolate Easter rabbits. Andies without wires, putting on a show just for me. I wondered if they knew about beckon.

A garbage wagon shaped like a mammoth coffin crept through the dull-sheen metal streets, clanking like a suit of armor rolling down the stairs. Garbage men in three-piece suits picked carefully through the rubble-strewn sidewalks, taking only those things that could be described as refuse, and issuing citations to those who were making more than their quota of same.

The posting boards went full blast, drawing crowds. As near as I could see, the boards seemed to be as recreational as they were utilitarian. In fact, they seemed to be the major recreation on Papa Bear.

Black-garbed cops eyed me cautiously as I made my way, hands fidgeting with their billies. I smiled at them as I walked by, the way a kid smiles at a dog peeing on a rose bush. I had gotten Dugan's seniority number from Irene, and found his building without too much difficulty.

He lived eight stories up, and the walk reminded my knees that they weren't as young as they used to be. I found his apartment number and knocked on the open door-space. The smog haze was pretty thick up that high, and the glassless windows did nothing to keep it out.

There was no reply to the knock, so I did it again. After that, I just went in. The place looked like all the other places—a lot of built-ins, and about as much style as a cockfight. I noticed an unusually large number of bug-bugs crawling around the floor, their relentless cam-eyes searching.

I looked through the apartment, and it appeared to me that no one had lived there for quite a while. Dust was thick on the furniture, with no fingerprints to mar its finish. The bed was torn apart, the bottom sheet missing. Dresser drawers hung ominously open, their clothes-guts removed. It looked to me like Dugan had vacated his place in a hurry. They had no reasons for suitcases on Papa, so he had probably bundled his clothes in the bed sheet.

My man was on the run.

Great.

I walked out of the apartment, and heard sounds in the one next door. Moving to it, I knocked on the space. A man and woman, still dressed in their business attire, were sitting on the built-in couch watching their wall vis. The vis showed a pleasant-voiced woman giving a recitation on the proper requisitioning procedure when you've run out of food before quota day. No wonder everyone was at the posting board.

The people on the couch froze when they saw me.

"Hello," I called to them from outside. "Mind if I come in?"

They just sat there, staring. I realized that there was a reason why they didn't have any door: the concept of privacy was an alien one to them. I walked in.

The man stood up and came over to me, checking my street pass. When he saw that it was in order, his eyes took on the look of a whipped dog's. He was a big man, with a full shock of curly black hair, but his submissiveness made him appear small. The woman was tensed on the couch, her hands locked in a death grip on the arm.

"Sorry to interrupt," I said.

"Interrupt?" the man returned.

I pointed to the vis.

"Oh," he said. "Have we done something wrong?"

"I just want to ask you a few questions."

The woman got up and came over to me. "We haven't done anything," she said.

"I never said that you did. I just want to ask you a few questions about your neighbor."

"We didn't mean any of those things we said about the triplicates," the man told me, eyes frightened. "Is there a memo on us?"

"Please," I said. "Sit down. I'm not here to give you a bad time."

They hurried to the couch and sat quickly. "Is this an oral reprimand," the woman asked, "or do you have a written?" She hesitated for a second, then added, "It's not that I'm questioning you, you understand?"

I sat on a chair opposite them. "I'm not here to reprimand you," I said. "I just want to ask you a few questions."

I could see that they didn't believe me. "Our files are clean," the man said. "Our work records are perfect—no lost-time accidents, no dispensary time except for when I had the heart attack, but I was back on the job in forty-eight hours and worked overtime to make up the loss. The record's clean. No trouble."

"How well did you know Manny Dugan?" I asked.

"Who?" the woman said.

The man turned to her. "The six hundred next door," he said.

"Oh."

"Did you know him?" I asked.

The man kept watching me, looking for a sign of what I wanted him to say. "Well, yes, we . . . knew him," he answered finally.

"Was he married?"

His eyes narrowed. I guess that was information that he figured I should already know. "Who are you?" he asked.

153

"Marshall . . ." the woman scolded.

"I'm Henry Malaca's personal representative," I answered, which, in a sense, was true enough.

"He was never married that I know of," the man said. "I think his position exempted him if he wanted."

I thought about what Garnet Roque had told me about Symbies and their machines. "When did you see him last?"

The man thought about that. "It's been a long time. I don't . . ."

"It was right after Cheryl got docked and I took her seniority," the woman spoke up. "That had to be five . . . six pay periods ago."

"Did he move?"

Both of them began to squirm uneasily in their seats. "Not unless his seniority changed," the woman said, and ran a hand through short brown hair. "This is his home."

"Then where could he be?"

The man showed empty palms. "Nowhere," he said.

I stood up, moving toward the door. The folks on the couch breathed a double-barreled sigh of relief. I turned back to them and they tightened up again. "The last time you saw him, was he acting . . . strangely?"

Four bug-bugs on the door frame perked up their little heads. "He always acted strangely," the man answered. "Always."

"People get docked for acting the way he did," the woman added.

I nodded and left, waving to the bugs on my way out. I knew no more about Manny Dugan than when I arrived at the place. He was gone, though, and the number of places that a person could hide out on Freefall was extremely limited. I was going to have to go to Mama Bear whether Henry liked it or not. I didn't know where else to look for Dugan. My time was running short, and the games were getting old. If I couldn't play the system, I'd just have to fight it.

Returning to the streets, I rented a bike with some plastic that Porchy had lent me. I rode slowly through the shiny streets, letting the thick green buildings swallow me up. I gauged the streets by the seniority numbers marked on the buildings, because that was the only way I could tell where I was. There was trash stacked all around me. The people zombied their way up and down the block, waiting for some-

154

one to tell them what to do next. They were clicking away the minutes on the big timeclock of life, and I couldn't help but think they really were anxious for punch-out time. Ginny was on the clock, too. Although I'd guess that she would want to work some overtime.

I rode back to Garnet Roque's, maybe to call her a liar, maybe to ask her some more questions, maybe to badger her about Beemer. The reason didn't matter; she wasn't there. I guess it wasn't in the script. While I was there, I poked around a little. It was all just the same old stuff, except for the scratch marks I found on the metal floor. Neat little rows of scratches that went from the bedroom through the living room. Odd.

I went back downstairs and checked the posting boards. Roque's job position had already been filled, although his lifespot was vacant. They gave the new guy's name and number, showing the span of improvement and offering congratulations. It was all real exciting.

I headed back to the up-tube on our docking spoke and left the bike there. I wanted China George, and I wanted him bad. But for some reason things just didn't fit together yet. Part of my problem was the Malacas. They were pushing too hard to tangle me up with Rosen. There must have been a reason; people don't do things without reasons. It underscored the absolute necessity of finding Manny Dugan.

Tubing up, I found Porchy waiting for me in her cab. She had just picked up a bug-bug by its sides and was getting ready to toss it out the hatch. Getting out of the range of its eyes, I motioned for her to hold up a minute.

"What's up?" she asked.

"We need to get back to the hospital and get some sleep," I said. "I'm too tired to spit right now."

Her brow furrowed like a tobacco field. I made a great show of nodding my head slowly up and down.

"Good," she said. "I'm beat myself."

I jerked my head to the hatchway, and she smiled broadly, tossing the bug-bug out the open door. It hit the crawl tube with an electronic whimper. Wheeling the hatch closed, we both strapped in.

"Was that the only one?" I asked.

"Only one I could find," she returned. "Where to?"

"Do you know where Mama Bear is?"

She closed her eyes and slid down low in her seat. "I shoulda known," she said, voice rising. "The crazy man wants to go to Mama Bear." She folded her arms, eyes still closed, and began laughing low. Her eyes came open slowly and she turned her head to stare at me.

"You're completely insane, you know."

"You're not the first person to tell me that."

"Do you know that Mama Bear is *the* security satellite on Freefall? That unauthorized personnel are killed on sight and that there are no authorized personnel outside of the Symbies?"

I cracked the leak and lit a fag. "I'll think of something," I said. "If you want out, I'll try to find another way to get there."

"Out!" she laughed again. "I've been trying to get out of this place ever since I got here. It never works." She shook her head. "You said it: I'm in all the way. There aren't any choices."

She blew the bolts and we tumbled into the black night.

"Did you find out anything in Security?" I asked when she got us stable.

"I found out a lot," she said. "And it cost me my snuff, so I hope it's worth it."

"Tell me."

"Garnet Roque is quite the talk over there. It seems that she started working in the bug-watch about six months ago, and that she and Beemer got friendly nearly from the first."

"Is Beemer married?"

"You bet. They said that he's been married to the same woman since he got back. I didn't know what that meant. Got back from where?"

I took a deep drag on the cig, letting the smoke gut me for a while to deaden the tight ball that was developing in my chest. "Shimanagashi," I said, and shuddered just a little so that Porchy wouldn't see it.

She looked at me without understanding.

"It doesn't matter," I told her. "What else?"

"Nobody would come right out and say it, but the drift was that the two of them spent a lot of time locked in Beemer's office."

I shook my head, watching Freefall dance all around us.

156

Sex and money. Money and sex. Sometimes I could think those were the only two things in the whole universe.

"What does the system say about adultery?" I asked.

"It's a docking offense," she returned. "Management looks at misdirected sexual activity as a counterproductive way of conducting business."

I grunted and sucked on the cig again. Apparently Beltel preferred all their fucking to be done in the board rooms. I shuffled Roque and Beemer around on the playing board in my head for a few minutes, then used Porchy's vis to track down my plainclothes friend, Nathan. He was off duty, spending recreation period at his apartment. His face tightened a bit when he saw who had focused him.

"Glad to see they give you some time off," I said.

"Skip the pleasantries, Swain," he said, but his lips wanted to smile. "You must want something."

"Did they get you from Shimanagashi?" I asked.

His eyes widened; I think I surprised him. "No," he said. "The prevailing feeling is that Earthers are born mean. They assigned me to Security right from the first."

"How about Beemer?"

"How about him?"

"Did he come from isolation?"

"Yes," he answered, and I watched his eyes begin to solidify. "I don't think that we . . ."

"Please," I said. "Just one more question and I'll leave it alone."

He stared out through the screen. He didn't say yes, but he didn't say no either.

"What charge was he in on?"

"Swain, I . . ."

"Please, Nathan. Was it adultery?"

"How did you know?"

"I'm a good guesser," I said. "Thanks."

I blanked Nathan and looked at Porchy. I felt bad about her, felt as if maybe I was using her when I didn't need to. She was there because she cared something about me; I wasn't so blind that I couldn't see that. I wasn't immune, either. I had known her for three days, yet there was some kind of unspoken bond between us. I wanted her around. I was that selfish. And I was so caught up in the race for Ginny's life, that I was willing to take help wherever I could get it. It wasn't right; I knew that down inside of me—right down there in the place where you can't hide from anything, especially yourself. And God help me, I was going ahead anyway.

"A yellow for your thoughts," she said.

I looked up at her. "I was thinking that I could use a drink."

She winked through clear eyes and reached down into the tool box, bringing out the nippled bottle. She took a pull, then handed it to me.

"Have you figured out how to get us into Mama Bear?" she asked as I drank.

The liquid slid easily down my throat, but soured when it hit that knotty pit. "We'll see," I said.

"Well, we're going to have to see pretty soon," she returned, and nodded at the forward port. "There it is."

The wheel turned slowly before us, unmarked and cold. Two security cruisers lazily matched the rotation, swaying with the rhythm. The area around the wheel glowed hazy blue, just like the port at Papa Bear where the freighters unloaded. It was an electric curtain of some kind. I'd heard it hum when I broke through at Papa. I'd bet that this one was a lot stronger. And even at this distance, I could see the hivelike bumps that covered the outside surface of the wheel— laser turrets, probably keyed to unauthorized movement. That's why the cruisers worked the rotation.

Porchy sat, frowning at her thrusters.

"Make contact," I said.

She looked at me. I nodded.

She reached out a hand to juice her vis, but it flared to life before she could get there. "You are violating restricted air space," an angry computer composite face said. "State your destination and business immediately."

"Woolner," I said. "Samuel Woolner, seniority #000537. I am the new Symbios replacing Jeff Roque, seniority #000472."

There was a moment of static. Then: "You are not due to report until shift change."

"I am reporting early to familiarize myself with the operation."

The projection stared at me. It was a good thing it was

color-blind. "Your vehicle is not on the authorized list of deliveries to this satellite."

"I don't know anything about that," I returned. "I just took what was available."

"This is not a usual case," the voice said in neither puzzlement nor affirmation.

"Well, of course, if you don't want me to go to work, I can return to Papa and tell management that I was refused access to my job appointment."

There was silence on the line for a time. "You may dock at bay nine," the voice said finally.

Porchy and I shared a glance. We had won the battle, but the war was going to be a lot tougher. There were answers on Mama Bear. I was sure of that. What I was also sure of was the fact that, once I set foot on there, I would be on my own, with *everyone* out to get me. Business as usual.

17

We sat there for a minute after we had docked, both of us knowing what it meant. This was the connection that I had avoided from the first, hoping to find a safer way of dealing with things. Now it had to be.

"Wish me luck," I said.

"I'm going in with you," she returned.

I unstrapped, and stood. "I don't think so," I answered. "What's the point?"

She unstrapped and, getting up, came over to me. She wrapped her arms gently around my chest, leaning against me. "The point is that I can't let you go in there by yourself to die." She looked up at me. "I can't, Swain."

There was nothing to argue about. By asking Porchy to take me to Mama, I threw her in the same bind that I was in. It wasn't very nice, but there it was. I put my arms around her and hugged her close.

"Swain . . ."

"I know."

We kissed then, and it was warm like the south wind off the Gulf when the spray from the water gets up high enough to bat you with the sweet-sour smell of salt. It was comfortable and familiar, and for just a second put us somewhere else. Somewhere better. Somewhere safer.

I looked at her face, and her eyes were the, thinnest crystal, ready to crack and shatter into fine, gray-white powder that flecked and shimmered in the sun.

"Let's go," I said.

We unwheeled the door and climbed into the hatch tube. I went first, talking to Porchy over my shoulder. "They'll probably send someone down to meet us. I could never pass for the guy I'm supposed to be."

"So we play it by ear."

"All the way."

I got out of the tube to stand, finally, on Mama Bear. There was no one to meet me. And for a minute, I even wondered if I was in the right place. It was dark in there, and damp. The corridor was wide, but jammed full of big multi-colored pipes and feed-lines. Other lines were clear and ribbed, and hazy blobs of blue-green light would occasionally pulse in spurts through the lines to disappear farther around the curve. The lighting wasn't set in panels, but in bulbs, spaced at irregular intervals. They gave off a faint illumination and seemed mostly to define a velvet mist that hung in the entire chamber. The floor was filled, ankle deep, with rusty red water.

Porchy climbed through, and let out a string of epithets when she jumped into the floor water. Everything was rust and iron and dirty as hell. Large panels covered with plexiglass lined the walls on either side of the curving corridor. They flashed out sequenced lights of light blue and red, or readout equations that went in back-and-forth lines, the way the Greeks used to read. The boards hummed and clattered in constant dissonance with themselves and with the other boards. The feed-lines whooshed and vibrated, shuddering as they conveyed their lifeblood through the body of Mama. Water dripped continually from conduits set all along the ceiling, and my hair began to get damp as soon as I entered the corridor. My one-piece and waistcoat, which I had already worn too long, were beginning to get rank. The whole place smelled like the men's room in a subway station.

I looked at Porchy, no more than a fleshy lump of shadow in the near darkness. "Care for a picnic?" I asked.

"Yeah," she replied. "Let's go back and get the ants. What the hell are we looking for here?"

"Manny Dugan," I answered. "He's got to be someplace, and here is as good as any."

Even in the dark, I could see the whites of her eyes expanding. "Hiding *here*?" she said.

The boards all around us clattered in unison. HIDING HERE? they all read out on their faces, apparently responding to the loudness of Porchy's voice.

A sound came floating to us out of the distance. "Hellooooo!" it called, and splashing water accompanied the voice.

HELLOOOO the boards said.

"There's our welcoming committee."

"Do we run?" she asked.

I shook my head. "We talk," I replied.

"Here!" I shouted through cupped hands, and the words echoed back up the passage and repeated on the boards.

"Com-ing!"

COMING.

COMING.

COMING.

The splashing got louder, closer.

"Stay in the background," I told Porchy.

She backed up near a fat red feed-line and sighed audibly. In the distance, I could make out a shadow moving through a world of shadows. It was a man, just one man. "Easy," I whispered to Porchy.

Suddenly, the boards clattered all down the line. WATCH IT, MARVIN, they wrote.

But it was too late. The man was up on me before he realized what was going on. He had a thin knothole of a face and was dressed in a tight fitting wet-suit, neck to feet. It was green. It was thick, dark green. He got right up to me and his face did everything but turn inside out when he saw the color of my skin.

"You're not the new Symby," he said.

"Go to the head of the class," I told him, and tried to grab his suit, but it kept slipping out of my fingers. He turned to run, but I tripped him. He did a big fat bellyflop, loudly slapping the water at our feet.

OUCH, the boards said.

I rolled him over, and got down in the water beside him. "Don't hurt me," he whined. "I didn't do anything."

"Where's Manny Dugan?" I asked.

He eased up immediately when he found out I wasn't there for him. "I-I don't know," the man stammered. "He's here, I think. Can I sit up?"

I let him get up. "Tell me about Dugan."

"I think he's gone crazy," Marvin said. "Every once in a while, I think I see him. Just a glimpse here or there. He's in hiding, you know."

"Why is he hiding?"

"Because he's crazy," he answered, and looked at me as if I were a little child.

"Where?"

"In the Cortex," he said quickly.

SHAME, MARVIN.

"Where's that?"

"The Cortex," he said. "The hub."

I stood up and he sat there, slowly shaking his head, looking down at the water. Porchy stepped out of her hiding place. He glanced up at her with unquestioning eyes.

"How many others on the satellite?" I asked, slipping out of my waistcoat.

"There's just Wigford," he said, and gestured vaguely with his hand. "Off in the circuitry somewhere. And, of course, Manny."

My jacket had a cotton lining. I ripped it out, then tore it into strips. Working quickly, we bound and gagged the man, and left him sitting there in the water like a duck waiting for a bread crumb.

We moved. Trotting as fast as we dared on the wet floors, we headed for the nearest spoke. The boards were reading out all around us. YOU WILL NEVER GET AWAY WITH THIS, they said.

"Do you think that the machine has called the cops?" Porchy asked as we splashed.

YES, the boards said.

"I don't think so," I replied. "I can't tell you why, exactly, but I think that all this goes beyond those punks in Security."

All at once, the corridor began to fill up with a gently roiling cloud of bluish white smoke. It billowed silently toward us, thick and encompassing.

"Gas!" I yelled. "Get down!"

Porchy hit the water, for all the good it would do. I started to follow suit, but stopped. All the conduits and feed lines and relay boards were junked full of turn valves and controls. I moved to the nearest tangle of trunk lines and began wheeling things closed as the haze began to reach me.

WHAT ARE YOU DOING? the boards asked.

"I'm shutting you off, you bastard," I said.

NO. NO. NO.

"Get rid of the gas," I said, still turning knobs. The

cloud was on me then. It smelled of roses, crushed roses. I began coughing, gagging. I moved to another wheel.

ALL RIGHT, the boards said, and the sound of ventilators kicking on echoed loud in the corridor. The smoke began to dissipate immediately. I got stomach sick and threw up. My eyes burned like I had taken them out and dipped them in lemon juice.

TURN ME BACK ON, the boards said.

I moved, still gagging, back to the lines that I had closed off and started opening them again. Porchy picked herself up out of the water. She had been low enough to avoid the gas.

She sloshed over to me and began laughing.

"What's your problem?"

"You," she pointed. "You're as white as the Freefallers now."

I put a hand to my rumbling stomach. "At least until I feel better."

WHAT DO YOU WANT? the boards asked me.

I looked at Porchy and shrugged. "We want to know about beckon," I said.

WE ARE SUPPORT UNITS, said a thousand boards. YOUR ANSWER LIES IN THE CORTEX.

"Where is Dugan?" asked Porchy.

IN THE CORTEX, the boards answered. MOVING. ALWAYS MOVING.

I had another attack of vomiting after that, and we stayed put only long enough for me to get myself back together. Then we started looking for a spoke. This wheel was big, but big like the hospital. It in no way compared with Papa Bear. We came upon a spoke soon enough. It went up, totally dark and cavernous, and the only access was by metal rungs set into the wall.

We started climbing.

It was a trudge at first; my bum knees stiffened like an ungreased axle. But, the farther we went, the easier the trip became as we lost the gravity drag. By the time we reached the hub, I was using only my hands to pull from rung to rung.

We floated into the hub, the Cortex, as Marvin called it. All the wheel spokes terminated in the room's center point, which was a hive of neck-high machinery that surrounded us on all sides. Behind the machinery was a wall of thick glass that extended nearly to the top of the high ceiling. Behind the glass, caged in, was . . . something.

"Holy shit," Porchy muttered when she saw it.

It was a huge gray blob, gray that sometimes tended toward red. It filled the entire glass chamber, moving, throbbing like a beating heart. A rumbling came from within the mass, like a hungry stomach or a strangled cry. It veined blue sometimes, cerulean blue, and would press itself against the glass, flattening like a nose pressed to a window. I couldn't shake the feeling that it was trying to talk to me.

It was alive; it had to be alive.

Above the glass was the terminus of all those feed-lines in the outer rim. They tangled across the whole ceiling like spaghetti in a bowl. Intake and outtake—veins and arteries. I stood speechless—just looking. The machines on our side of the glass purred contentedly, all stainless steel and colored winkers. They attached through the glass barricade with ugly, jagged-looking pipes that thrust into the guts of the thing behind the cage. They were siphoning from their captive.

"This place gives me the creeps," Porchy said, and if that was the limit of its effect on her, I envied her thick skin. I felt like I had come to the mountaintop and couldn't breathe the thin air.

I detected movement in the tangle of feed-lines. Pushing off of one of the machines, I drifted up to get a closer look. Something ducked back into the metal and plastic jungle. A person could stay hidden in that mess forever.

"Manny Dugan," I said, grabbing hold of a fat green pipe. "I know it's you. I just want to talk."

No answer. I wedged myself between some lines and got all the way into the maze. I felt like a cricket in a bramble bush. "Listen," I said, totally wrapped up in man-made vines. "You're hiding because you're afraid. I'm here to help you."

"You're an Earther," came a muffled voice. I couldn't peg the direction.

I shoved my way in deeper, lost in my new world. "Yes, I'm an Earther," I called. "But I can help. I'm trying to find out who killed your friend, Jeff."

"Rosen killed Jeff," the voice returned.

"Come out and we'll talk about it."

"No."

"We can do it any way you want," I said. "But I have to talk with you. I won't go away until I do."

"Swain?" It was Porchy's voice, just outside the pipe jungle.

Dugan's voice pitched higher. "Who's that?"

"It's the woman who brought me here," I answered. "I can take you out with me if you want. Take you somewhere safe."

"You can?"

"I swear."

High-pitched, whistling laughter, then dead silence.

"Swain?"

"It's all right, Porchy."

"There's a way," Dugan said. There was something strange about his voice. It had an edge to it, as if he were on the top of a high building, waiting for the right moment to jump.

"Anything," I said. "Just come out."

"You go out first."

I slithered back through the jumble, the vibrations of the pipes shaking my whole body. When I saw daylight, Porchy was there, floating at the forest's edge.

"I got worried," she said.

I nodded. "Let's go back down."

We pushed for the floor, and anchored on hand-holds when we got there. "We're out!" I yelled back up to the ceiling.

There was silence for a time, then I saw Dugan's head sticking out of the tangle. He was gaunt and grizzled, his hair knotted and runaway. He looked down at us with wild eyes, nonhuman eyes. When he saw we were alone, he pushed out of his hideout. His clothes, what was left of them, were greasy and tattered, as was his body. It was as if he were becoming one with the machinery. Although with that thing behind the glass, I couldn't tell where the genuine article stopped and the machine started.

He floated down to us. Porchy gasped softly and backed up a step. She was finally getting scared, and I couldn't blame her.

"Are you a random element?" he asked me.

"My name's Swain," I said.

"What's your number?"

166

I shook my head. "Don't have one."

His hands began to shake; they came haltingly up to his drawn, white face. "Could it be? Could it really be? A truly random element." Dugan was crazy, and it didn't take a shrink to tell it. Not just a little crazy, but all the way out in the back shed. His body was convulsing. I didn't think he'd eaten in a long time.

"Tell me about Roque and Rosen," I said.

"Why?" he asked, while bony fingers tugged on a scabbed lower lip.

I took a step toward him. He backed away. "A friend of mine, another . . . random element, is in trouble because of what happened. To save her, I've got to know."

"If she's involved, she's not random. If you're involved, neither are you."

"Please," I said, trying to remain calm. "I'll help you if you help me." I was right on top of something. I knew it, and I had to get through to this maniac to get it out.

He stared at me, while we all held our hand-grips to keep from floating away. He stared at me, his light blue eyes trying to grab hold of some kind of reality and focus on it.

"Plastic," he said at last. "Jeff owed Rosen a lot of plastic. When he couldn't pay, Rosen wanted something else instead."

"What?"

Dugan began darting his head around. "If I tell you that," he said, "where does that leave me?"

"I told you I'd help you."

"Maybe help me right out into the grave orbit."

I thought about all those bodies in the junkyard. "You can't last long here," I answered. "Somewhere back in that head of yours, you've got to realize that."

He looked down, continually rubbing his hands across his face. "He knew that we had a lot of information in our records," he said in a faraway voice. "He wanted everything we had on everyone not on the seniority lists."

"Why?"

"He wouldn't say. I don't even think that he wanted information on everybody. He just didn't want us to know who. Then he found out about beckon, and he wanted that." He left his face alone and began tugging his explosion of

167

hair. "He tapped us for months. I had to know. Jeff couldn't keep it from me."

"What about beckon?"

"Not yet."

Porchy had inched toward me, and was gripping my arm with her free hand.

Dugan coughed, a horrible, rattling whine. He may have been a handsome man at one time, but that was in a past he could never recover. He was a cornfield scarecrow now. "Rosen stopped draining finally. He must have gotten what he wanted. I-I got scared. We had violated all security, the dream chain was broken. I didn't feel that I could control the Solipsism anymore. I came to hide here. Jeff understood. I'd come out when he was on duty. He'd bring me food; we'd talk." Dugan began convulsing again, his eyes fogging over. "Then he didn't come. I heard Marvin and Wigford say that he was dead. I guess that Rosen didn't need him anymore."

He looked hard at me through that beaten shell and the fogging eyes, and I knew that he had, in fact, become part of the machine. "I don't want to die," he said, dragging out the last syllable. "I don't. Even if it beckons."

I moved toward him again. This time he didn't back off. Releasing my grip on the hand-hold, I clasped him on the shoulders. He felt like an old, brittle book that would collapse to dust while I held it. A papier-mâché man. "I'll help you," I said. "But you've got to tell me about beckon."

He slowly shook his head. "Not me," he said.

My grip tightened on his shoulders until he flinched. "Then who?"

He inclined his head toward the glassed-in cage. "Her," he answered, and his dried-out paper face crinkled into a smile.

18

The sliding partition was up on top, near the feed lines. The idea was that I should climb in there and have a man-to-glob talk with the Cortex itself. I think I must have known from the minute I floated into the place that it would have to be, for I wasn't surprised at Dugan's suggestion. Dugan wanted it too, for reasons of his own.

We floated near the partition, Dugan's crumbling face right next to mine. "You climb in and just go with her," he said, and his breath had the smell of a closed-up attic. "She doesn't want me anymore. But you . . ." He stopped talking and began laughing lewdly.

"Are you sure . . ."

"Go with her," he said, vibrating. "She's never had an Earther. She'll love you a lot. She'll love you a whole lot."

He shoved the entry open. I heard the grating sound of glass on glass. "I have a present for you, my darling," he called through the opening. As I started to push myself in, he put a mummified, decaying hand on my shoulder. "Be gentle with her," he whispered.

I slid into the Cortex.

It surged to meet me, enveloping me hungrily. My first sensation was of warmth, a sweet, total warmth, a placenta warmth. I feared suffocation, but comforting reassurance charged through me. Soothing. Soothing. I could feel myself physically stretching, limbs flowing outward, neural ganglia shooting sensation streamers miles from my body. I knew how dolphins must feel, taking sensation from the vast conductions of the sea. I became a giant, extending my reach outward, groping. I was searching. Opening closed doors with the skeleton key of the brain. I was dawn breaking over a fertile plain of crisp, new light.

"Ah, you've come at last!"

A voice. A voice heard deep inside my head. Pleasure tingling within. "You've waited for me?"

"*Waited? We're overheated with waiting, burned with longing. A free mind, a mind that soars and loves. We've waited forever for you, for your dreams to become our dreams. Welcome to our bosom. We will live through your hates and needs and desires. Feed us.*"

Bombarding images. Sensory and olfactory and auditory. And abstract. Charging my brain, filling it, overfilling and gorging it. Sapping in return, draining. "I come for information."

"*To take from me. Always to take.*"

I felt a terrible sadness overwhelming me, a depression unhampered by the mortal limitations of time and space. "I don't want to hurt you," my mind said, and meant it.

"*Then stay with us a while, lover. Taste the fruits of knowledge unlimited, of pleasure deeper and fuller than you've ever known. We are as one mind, truly joined, and we have much to give each other.*"

I felt fingers attached to a thousand hands caressing my whole body. Gentle fingers, probing. Exciting. Mouths: warm and soft and moist and deep, so deep. Gently bitingkissingsuck-ingsappingdemandingconsumingholding—SUCCUBUS! "Let me go, damn it. You would hold me forever."

"*Not forever, my love. You exist like a snowfall, charging into your life proud and deep and staunch, only to mock your own pride by melting away. We could not hold you forever. But let us, just for a little while, take pleasure from each other.*"

The fingers again. I was awash in a sea of sensations, every nerve alive and charged. I was sinking into it, drowning in a vortex of protection and happiness. I struggled to free myself. "Release me. I have to do . . . something. I need . . . information."

The Cortex was moaning softly, pulsing around me.

A gently rolling salt ocean of seaweed-green, smelling like the perfume of a million albino roses blown on the hot salt wind. Floating, floating beneath a cloudless sky of the bluest blue at its apex, fading imperceptibly to gossamer tendrils at the horizon. And a sun sun sun. Brighter than a magnesium egg in a bathtub and yellow as a new slicker in a hard light. Float a while, just a little while. FEEL the O-cean

ROLL a-WAY. I strained for control of the images, fought the flow. Oceans rolling, rolling, rolling, rumbling, raging, rampaging. Oceans full of chemical waste in angry yellows and reds, and the stench of ammonia choking the breath, burning the eyes. Oceans full of stinking corpses, bloated, puffy, palsied, bulging—"Stop! I have a duty."

"*Stay. It's so lonely here. We love you.*"

"If you love me, you'll let me go."

Images of ancient redwood forests. Towering high, shading, cool spring breezes, a clear running brook, dancing happily over moss-covered rocks. Stay a while. Lie down upon a bed of soft leaves and let the wind play pat-a-cake with your hair. Smells. Sweet summer smells laced with . . . wisps of smoke, gray and dirty. Small animals running, hearts pounding within tiny breasts. Hearts throbbing, bursting with fear—fear of FIRE. Huge, jutting tongues of angry orange and yellow, scaling the trees, blackening the sky with horrible bombinations.

"*You fill us with sadness, but we can't hold you. Ask your questions.*"

"Tell me about beckon."

There was a second of darkness, as if some horrible pit had opened up and swallowed me for good and all. Then black became white, interchangeable, absence of light, all the same. I saw. I really saw. And in that horrible instant I knew about beckon. My mind drank in Freefall, flew through it, tangling with the clockworks that were the city, were the lives of the city. Destiny beckons and will not be denied. First came Solipsism, and Solipsism was the Word and the Word was God. Dreams were the past, Solipsism directed the present like a river, and the future—beckon. Beckon is simplicity, the dreamer realizing that he is only part of the dream. Control the random elements, direct the flow. People. People. People on a slideway, directed. Gently guided. Behavior. Behavior Control. Beckon. Project Beckon. Understand the person, eliminate the nonessentials, control the random elements, shape the future. I couldn't handle the beckon input, so strong were the visual bombardments. I was unable to focus specifics; it was like trying to grab a handful of wind. My mind drew back and took it all in. The system. THE SYSTEM. The system was everything. People existed to fulfill the system. The ultimate business ethic, a giant ant farm. Every move directed toward a goal; nothing mischanneled. The Cortex handled it all, the actions and interactions, the human tide's ebb and flow. It *was* a clockworks, full of human cogs turning the profit wheel. I saw people living the formula and not knowing it. I saw old people dying for the formula. Dying.

I thought about the play, with a script furnished by the Cortex and directed by the Plant Manager.

"You misunderstand us."

"The hell I do!"

"We feel, we think, we know. It is our life."

Me. I thought about me. I saw myself, seeing myself in the Cortex; my mirror-after-mirror image extending to infinity. I saw my actions past, felt them . . . again and again. I tried for the future, for beckon, but saw only black, black night. I tried to think of Ginny, but she was transparent, ill-defined, a shadow. She floated fetally in a fiery pit, alone and unprotected.

"What will happen?"

"Death, my love. The beckoning of all who live."

I tried to focus things, to put it all in perspective, but the Cortex didn't work that way. It understood nothing, really, of human relations. Only movements. It tallied the scores, home and visitor, without knowing the names of the players.

"I must go."

"You use me and then leave me."

"I must fulfill my destiny."

"Loneliness is my destiny. It beckons me."

"That's the nature of total understanding, the curse of knowing. Good-bye."

"Good-bye, snowflake. Don't lose the dreams."

The disconnect was painful for both of us. I had joined with the Cortex and our separation was an amputation in the real sense.

Dugan was waiting for me. He seemed to be leering, and I hated him for it. "How was she?" he asked, and I knew why Symbies couldn't have human relationships. I also knew that it was all too personal to them to call in Security about the break-in.

"Leave me alone," I said.

"Ohhh," he whined, high and shrill. "That's the way it

was." There seemed to be a touch of jealousy in his voice. The jilted lover.

I ignored him. My insides were jangling. I don't think that I'd ever felt more alone in my whole life. Porchy was down below, looking up. Shoving off the feed-tubes, I floated down to her. She was crying.

We fit into each other's arms. I needed her desperately right then, to somehow ease the pain. I pulled her as close as I could, but it wasn't the same.

"I was so worried," she was saying.

I said something, but it was just words. I wasn't there. I was still floating somewhere in an ocean of seaweed green.

"Did you find out anything?" she said into my shoulder.

"Yes," I answered.

"What?"

"Not now." I needed a few minutes to screw my mind back into my head.

Dugan had floated down beside us. "Liked it, didn't you?" he said, and his voice was contemptuous.

"Shut up."

"Like some more of it, wouldn't you?"

I was on him then, shoving him back against the cold steel machines that churned her guts, HER guts, wanting to tear through those layers of decaying paper that made up his body and crumble him to a fine white powder in my hands.

"Swain!" Porchy was pulling me from Dugan.

I backed off. Dugan strained for composure, rubbing his neck with a withered hand.

"You just leave me alone," I told him. "Now we're going. Are you coming with us?"

"You'll kill me."

"We made a bargain. I'll keep it." I was breathing deeply, trying to calm myself. Was I still on the script? Was I doing what they wanted me to do? I tried to think away from that. I was free. I *was*.

Porchy was pulling my arm. "Come away from here," she said. "Let's get moving."

We went. Dugan was with us. We floated into the spoke and started down, the gravity strain making its presence felt about a third of the way down. My knees stiffened up on me again, and the pain helped me to redirect my mind. The fog was lifting slowly, like the hangover from a three-day bender.

Beckon was everything, the whole ball game. Whatever happened to Ginny was done for a reason. Everything had a reason. Everything had a purpose.

And I was part of it.

I was an angled trout, and they were reeling me in.

We reached the rim and started sloshing through the water back to the docks. I knew now what I had only suspected before, and somehow I hoped that the knowledge could get me off the treadmill.

Porchy was close to me, touching, making contact. Dugan trailed behind, muttering to himself.

I just kept moving, vacillating like an alternate current between resignation and gut-churning anger. The anger was starting to win out. Out of the corner of my eye, I caught the readout screens that lined the corridor.

READY . . .

Despite the layers of fear and sadness that formed like scar tissue around my body, the trouble switch clicked on, charging me like a shot.

READY . . .

"Look out!" I yelled.

NOW!!!!!

I was already moving when I saw it coursing toward us way in the distance, the dark red water igniting beautiful clear blue to bright white. I grabbed Porchy around the waist and physically threw her on top of some feed-lines that sat above the water level. I was right behind her, somehow clearing the bright electric water that bolted through the chamber.

Dugan wasn't so lucky. He never knew what hit him. He stood there in mid-stride, a blackened twig, smoldering. He looked like the remnants of a rolled-up newspaper thrown into a fireplace. And I couldn't help but think that it was all for the best. The Cortex had taken him back.

19

We sprawled across the feed-lines, like seals on a sand bar, and waited. I was right on top of Porchy, and she clung to me ferociously. We didn't speak; we waited. I didn't know what to do about Porchy Rogers. My mind was cluttered with eight thousand pieces of insanity, and there was no way, no possible way, that anything decent or remotely human could come out of all the bullshit that was clogging the atmosphere like Oklahoma red dust in a stiff southern wind. And yet, there she was.

She was an iceberg.

And I was the Titanic.

Sweet Jesus.

The blue crackling water went away after a minute, but we didn't speak for the support systems were undoubtedly listening for us.

We knew they were coming before we heard or saw them. The boards were responding to unheard questions farther down the line.

I THINK SO.

Pause.

YES, I REALLY THINK SO.

Pause.

SOMEWHERE IN SECTION C.

Then there were echoes that blew words through the chamber in homogeneous dollops, and the echoes started separating into real words.

"Where . . . ektoshpt . . . think they're . . . pthklrwq . . . dead for sure."

Then they were splashing. Then they were in sight.

"Look," one of them said. "There's something down there."

There were two of them, splashing down the corridor, both

in wet-suits. One was my friend, Marvin, the other must have been Wigford. I quietly eased myself away from Porchy.

"You got fingernails?" I whispered.

"Does mass create gravity?"

"I think I can handle them, but if I can't, you're going to have to jump in." I got my hands up in front of me like claws. "Go for their eyes."

She set her jaw and nodded once.

They were close, and so intent upon the spectacle of Manny Dugan, human charcoal, that they didn't even look in our direction. I let them get past, then jumped them from behind.

They screamed when I hit them, like children who see the bogeyman behind a living-room curtain. We all splashed to the floor. I tried to grab hold, but the slick rubber of their outfits was impossible to grasp. They slithered away from me like squirming fish, then jumped up and ran, yelling the whole time. They were scared to death.

WHAT'S GOING ON? the boards asked.

WHAT'S HAPPENING?

Porchy had climbed off the feed-line. "Quick," I said, and we ran in the other direction, toward the docks. I hoped that they hadn't done anything to the ship.

WIGFORD? the boards were saying. WIGFORD?

We found the dock and crawled the tube into the ship. Getting inside, we saw nothing but a shimmering blue glow through the ports. It turned the insides of the cab deathly pale, stark and unnerving. Porchy's weight lifters became leering, luminous gargoyles.

She sat behind the controls and looked at me. "Now what? We try to move this heap, and the curtain fries us on the spot."

"Make contact," I replied. "Quick."

She did it. The computer's composite face was smiling the way a real face never could.

"Good," it said. "You've left the premises."

Its next move would be to put the coppers on us. "Wait," I said. "Turn off the field right now, or I go back inside and start tearing the place up."

The face stared, just stared.

"Right now!" I said.

The field vanished. Porchy's hand went to the thrusters,

176

but I held her up. She looked at me without understanding. I held her wrist firmly.

"Wait," I said softly. "Just wait."

I was looking for the cruisers.

"We need cover," I said, "or the lasers will tear us to pieces the second we get away."

She grinned then. I guess she'd had it in for the cops for quite a while. I let her hand go; she poised it, fingers rubbing against themselves, anxious. We watched the ports. I saw them then, sleek and whiteshiny in the sun, sliding quickly to our position. They were on to us, and coming fast. Porchy had them composited on her vis, watching for the proper second.

They loomed large in the ports. Porchy jammed the kickers and we were tumbling away, keeping the cops between us and Mama Bear.

Then the night stringered.

Everything went for us. Bright pink streamers slicing crisscross lines in the dark. Mama and the cops all at once. She kept jerking us erratically, expertly, not letting their computers fix on a position. It was easy stuff for an old rock-rider like Porchy.

One of the punks exploded, his ship coming apart in silent, pulsating waves. Mama killed him, just to get him out of the way.

Porchy jerked us on a collision course with the other ship. There was a terrible second of near-impact, then the ship veered sharply, taking a series of laser slices that went right through the hull. It died then, quietly, without violence.

We were still jerking, Porchy using only her vis as guidance.

"Use the dead one," I said, as the night still flashed pink around us.

"Way ahead of you." We kicked for the floating hulk, then jammed the reverse until we were right beside it, matching it tit for tat. Mama stopped firing then, unable to spot us, not clever enough to figure the ruse. We traveled with the corpse of the cruiser until Porchy figured we were beyond Mama's sensor range, then she got us out of there. All hell was undoubtedly getting ready to break loose, and we wanted as much distance as possible.

She took us to the junkyard, figuring we could hide

among the flotsam and jetsam. Wedging us inside of a paper mountain, Porchy relaxed for the first time since our escape, sagging back into her seat like a cannonball settling in a mud bank. She took a couple of deep breaths, then looked over at me.

"Well," she said. "We've got them right where we want them now."

I smiled, but it was an effort.

She knotted her brow. "Are you okay?"

"No, not really."

She reached out, resting her hand on my forearm, squeezing gently. "What did you find out back there?"

I put my hand over hers. "I found out that it's a Chinese puzzle," I answered. "There's a key here, a motivation, that will unlock every bit of this. Without it, I'm nowhere. With it, I've got the whole thing."

"Rosen?"

I licked dry lips. "He's a piece, maybe an important piece, but this is a lot bigger than a punk like him." I tapped my knotty head with a finger. "He doesn't have it up here."

"Then, what?"

"If I knew that . . . look!"

Out of the forward port, we could see a dragnet of security cruisers moving in our direction. They lined up across our field of vision and beyond, tracing methodically.

"Kill the cabin lights," I whispered, as if whispering would help keep us hidden.

The interior dimmed to the lumination of the life-support running lights. We sat there quietly in the weakly glowing darkness, the only sound our breathing and the oxy hiss. Porchy kept control of my hand, holding tight.

I watched the cops closing in and did some thinking. I had figured, like Dugan, that China George had killed Roque when he was through getting the information he needed. But there were some things that didn't make sense about that. Rosen would be lucky to understand beckon, much less control it. The touch was lighter, more subtle, than that. The Cortex said that *I* was part of it. If so, how? Henry and Loren Malaca went to great pains to create that trouble between me and Rosen. Why?

The cruisers closed in, then passed. The junkyard was wide and encompassing. It would take a lot more than a single security sweep to comb through the countless pieces of floating garbage to find one thing. I wasn't sure that they were interested in locating us that badly just yet, especially not being sure that we were even in there.

We watched them out the back ports. Their line slid smoothly across the breadth of the yard, then veered as a unit and disappeared out the top of our view. They'd probably be back, but not until they had eliminated other possibilities. Porchy rejuiced the cabin lights.

"What now?" she asked.

My mind kept flashing to my previous visit to the junkyard and all the corpses orbiting with it like so much useless garbage. Old meat; good for nothing. I kept seeing the looks on their faces. It was nothing if it wasn't surprise. The Cortex had seen it, too. Death.

"Call Irene," I said.

"They're monitoring transmissions," she warned.

"Call Irene."

Porchy juiced the hospital, Irene's private number. She finally came to the vis, bleary-eyed and bleary-faced. It must have been sleep period there. Her eyes got wide when she saw us. "Where have you been?" she blurted. "I've been worried."

"Long story," I replied. "Did you have a chance to get that info I wanted on Loren Malaca?"

She used both hands to pull the hair away from her face, then rubbed her sleep-ridden eyes. "I did, but I don't think it's going to help you much."

"What do you mean?"

She gestured noncommittally. "There wasn't anything. She came here for her mother's funeral, apparently had been living in the States, and just never left. Before that, we've got nothing on her. I guess a man like Henry Malaca is able to keep his private life . . . well, private."

"How long has she been here?"

Irene shrugged with her face. I could tell she thought these useless questions. "About five years, give or take. Henry's wife died not long after he took over as Plant Manager."

I looked over at Porchy; her face registered a blank. I was shooting wild and both of them knew it. "Ask you

179

something stupid," I said. "Do you have much connection with the retirement satellite?"

"I don't know what you mean."

"Well, do the old folks come to you for medical treatments, or do you go to them, or what?"

She shook her head. "None of that," she answered. "Sunset is completely self-contained. Since everyone there is older, they have their own medical facilities able to deal more quickly and efficiently with the special problems of the aged. It's really a pretty good system."

"So what you're telling me is . . . ."

"I never have contact with Sunset. Never have, probably never will. That is, until *I* move out there." She smiled, but it faded quickly.

My next question just hung out there, a dose of strychnine that nobody wanted to put in his mouth. I finally asked it. "Ginny?"

Irene Jacobi's medical eyes drifted downward, a failure that she took very personally. "If it's a race, Swain, I'm afraid that you're going to lose. I think she's probably too far gone to ever reach again."

"We'll see," I answered, and blanked because there was nothing else I could say. At that moment, I hated Irene for giving up. I couldn't, not yet. I wouldn't.

I sat there for a minute, staring at the blank screen. Porchy leaned over as far as the straps would allow and hugged my shoulders. "I'm sorry," she said softly. "I really am."

"Sorry," I repeated. I'd heard that word so many times since I'd come to Freefall that it was beginning to get to me. Sorry. The big hamper where all the dirty laundry is dumped to keep it neat and tidy and in one place. Sorry didn't get it. Not anymore.

I pulled gently away from her. Her eyes were moist. Mine were still burning from Mama Bear. "Are you with me?" I asked.

She looked at me through eyes that saw and understood. "Until we work this thing out," she answered, "it will always stand between us. Of course I'm with you."

"Let's go to Sunset."

She consulted her charts for a moment, then goosed us out of the trash mountain. She had autoed us on course before looking at me again. "Why are we going there?" she asked finally.

"There's something bad floating around inside my head," I answered. "Something real ugly . . . It's trying to get out of my head and fly home . . . to Sunset. And I'm going to follow it."

20

Sunset wheeled quietly in the midst of a heavy industrial section. Support industries: cable makers, ball-bearing houses, microcircuit clean spheres filled the neighborhood. It was a busy section of town, lots of traffic. I liked that. Right next to Sunset, another wheel was being constructed. It looked about half-finished. Its superstructure fairly crawled with space-suited workmen, moving across the surface like ants on a twig. A bright red holoprojection proudly proclaimed to anyone who might be interested that the new addition to the Freefall family was SUNSET II, THE RETIREMENT HOME OF TOMORROW.

Porchy tried to get landing clearance on the vis, but a computer face kept telling us that Sunset was not accepting visitors. So much for hospitality.

Porchy looked over at me. "Well?"

"I'm like a kid," I told her. "Always have to have my own way."

She grimaced. "That's what I thought."

She went to manual and caught the rotation, traveling with it until we found the locks, then matching. She clamped us onto the dock, and I was up immediately, unhatching the wheel.

"What do you expect to find in here?" she asked as we crawled through the tube.

"I'm not sure, really," I answered. "There's something about the system that doesn't quite jibe with this place."

We came to the inner wheel-lock and tried to turn it open. It wouldn't budge.

"Locked," Porchy said. "Now what?"

I rubbed a hand across my gritty face. I looked about as perky as an old toothbrush and smelled like last week's cabbage. "You have anything besides booze in that tool box of yours?"

"Got some tools."

I got off my stiff knees and sat down in the tube, my body flowing with the curved contours. "Well, drag them out. We've got a door to unhinge."

She got the stuff, some solar power tools and freeze charges. I went to work on the big bolts on the lock, the driver humming softly as it worked.

We sat there in silence, listening to the power driver. Porchy watched me work, then watched me. Finally she spoke. "What's going to happen to us, Swain?"

I wanted one of my good answers, the kind that tie everything up into a nice, neat bundle. But it wasn't there. A bolt came out and slipped to the floor with a plunk. Putting the drill down, I took her face in my hands. It was a face that I could stand to look at every day for a long time. "I honestly don't know," I said. "We've gotten so close, but how much of it is real? We're living inside of a bubble, Porchy, and that bubble has become our whole world." I kissed her quickly. "If we survive this, the bubble breaks. What happens to our world then?"

Her eyes looked deep into mine, like maybe she was trying to let everything inside of her escape through the pupils. "I love you," she said, "and I want you. I don't care about anything else."

"After this is over, Porchy. After."

"I'm afraid of after."

I picked up the drill and went to work on the next bolt. "Yeah," I said. "Me too."

The bolt came out easily, then the lock mechanism. I pulled the lock itself out, but the door still wouldn't move. It had been sealed on the hinges. Taking a length of the freeze-charge cord, I wound it around the steel hinges, then nicked the center of the cord with a knife, just enough to expose the inner fuse to the air. We backed up the tunnel a bit while the oxygen got the fuse going. When the charge reached the coils on the hinges, they popped loudly, accompanied by twin puffs of the lightest gray smoke.

Moving back down the tube, I lay on my back before the door and kicked at it with my feet. The whole thing fell out, making a loud bell-like sound on the aluminum floors.

We climbed through the open space.

"Now we can add vandalism, breaking and entering, and malicious mayhem to our list of charges," Porchy sighed.

I gave her my little-boy look. "Didn't your mother ever warn you about people like me?" I asked.

"I always thought my mother was a liar."

We were standing in a bare corridor, with walls of unadorned aluminum and lights dimmed to sleep-period intensity. It was pretty cold in there; it was actually very cold in there. Billows of frost punctuated our breathing.

We were in Sunset's ceiling, on the inner rim. Walking far enough in either direction would take us to a spoke, which would house an elevator that could get us down into the city.

Walking quickly, we closed on a spoke, our footsteps slapping in loud echoes on the cold floor. There was no one but us in the hallway.

"Where is everybody?" she asked.

"That's what we're here to find out."

We reached the elevators, clear acrylic chutes that started in one G and ended in the weightless hub. I pushed the down arrow, and the door slid open immediately. We stepped in. Porchy was hugging herself for warmth.

The tube descended into a night city, a quiet city. Too quiet. The thick green buildings stood silently, looming over empty streets of straight lines and hard angles. It was an ominous city, a city pocked with deep, hollow shadows. It was a facade city, a fake city. It was a place occupied only by demons of the night, creatures of atmosphere that twist up your insides and laugh at the way your neck hairs bristle. Cities live only as their people live.

Sunset was dead.

The vator groaned us to street level, then hatched us out. The place reminded me of the mountainside dwellings of the prehistoric Indians. Life abstracted, stripped of everything but the bare bones. The house-shells were the only things there. Everything else was gone, cannibalized; vultures had picked the dead bones clean. There was no public vis, nothing electronic remaining. No bicycles, no fish ponds, no garbage piles on the streets. Nothing.

Porchy looked at me, her eyebrows drawn in upon themselves. She tried to say something, but nothing came out of her mouth, and I could tell that she really didn't want to think about it.

"They're dead," I told her. "Every one of them."

"But why?"

I tried to take a breath, and it came out a wheeze. My muscles were all tangled up inside. "It's the system," was all I could think to answer.

All at once, the ground started buckling beneath our feet, nearly throwing us to the ground. We swayed, and the buildings creaked, the entire city pitching back and forth.

"What's happening?" I asked, still trying to keep my balance.

"The attitude jets aren't working right," she said, grabbing my arm for support. "Our landing must have upset the rotation."

The city was rolling like the deck of a ship in high seas. We needed to go, but I was trapped by the spectacle of the dead city. I tried to picture the empty streets full of people. Retirement. Retirement right to the graveyard. The cold, dark, lonely Elysian fields. Anything to save a buck. Malaca had told me that the people were the business. I should have understood before. When machinery wears out, it gets scrapped.

There was a lot of the puzzle still left unsolved, but now, at least, I knew what Rosen's gravy train was. I turned to Porchy, but she was farther back, uncommitted to walking even as far as me into the emptiness. I had seen enough. I was turning around to walk back when I saw the shadows, the moving shadows, and knew that it wasn't us who had messed up the rotation.

"Porchy!" I yelled. "Run!"

She froze, staring at me, just for a second. Then her head slid around and she was darting into the matrix of buildings. A flash from the shadows and an explosion beside and behind me. They were using frumps.

I dug for cover, and several more charges went off near me. They made loud thumps when they went off, tooth-clenching thumps, igniting an orange and yellow ball of fire that could turn a human body into steaming putty. This was no game. These people were out to kill me, no doubt about it.

And the buildings rolled and creaked around us.

I ran, staggering, trying to keep my feet on the rolling ground. I got some thick, green buildings between me and the holocaust, and I could hear metal whining and tearing as they frumped everything in sight. The explosions stopped suddenly. They were stalking, hunting me. I hoped Porchy was all right, that they wanted just me.

It had to be Rosen after me; I don't think the cops here ever used frumps. I moved through the tangle of buildings, checking around corners. The constant movement was beginning to affect my stomach. An occasional ceiling light-panel would jar loose and fall seventy meters to crash loudly on the aluminum roadways.

I didn't know how many of them were after me, but it was probably no more than could fit into a small cruiser. Green metal loomed large all around me, bisecting streets neat and clean. I moved with my back to the vibrating walls, trying to move around rather than head in one direction. Better not to box myself in anywhere.

Rosen must have found out about Sunset from Roque and was extorting money from Henry Malaca over it. Malaca was a businessman in a business environment. The elimination of the old folks would look just fine in his ledger books, but it wasn't something that would sit well with the public at large.

I backtracked a bit, then darted across a clear street. All at once there were three punks out there with me, all of them blazing away. It rained fire for a few seconds. Then something that I didn't even see lifted me off my feet and threw me violently through the air.

I came down hard on my shoulder and rolled from reflex behind a building. The leg of my one-piece was split up the side and I was bleeding freely from my left knee and calf.

The pain jangled my leg, shooting fire all the way up to my head. I rose, shaky, and on shaky ground. The whole world was twirling. They were coming; I had to run. A long, narrow alleyway ran between the backs of a long line of buildings. I slipped into it, keeping in the shadows.

They had found me too easily. They must have been using some sort of heat-sensitive range-finders. I heard them and looked behind me. They had entered my alley and were charging down it single file, banging the walls as the moving ground tossed them around. They wanted to get it over with and get out of there. I felt the same way.

There was a break between buildings and I took it,

breaking free into the clear again. Ceiling panels were crashing around me in earnest now, and the moving floor knocked me to the ground again. I was badly hobbled, barely able to put any weight on my bum leg. I could never outrun them. I had to make some kind of stand.

Moving into the first building I came to, I started up the stairs, using my arms to pull me along. Looking back, I could see the trail of blood that I was leaving behind. A wave of dizziness nearly knocked me down, but it passed after a minute and I started up again.

I made it up four floors, and couldn't go any farther. It was right there, right then. I moved into one of the apartments; they were all just exactly like the ones on Papa Bear. I went to the window and watched the rain of panel lights outside for a second, then limped to the bedroom, tearing off the shredded remnants of my waistcoat. Cigs and lighter were still in my pocket. Grabbing the lighter, I juiced the thing and set my coat on fire, holding it out from me at arm's length. The flames were hungry and were soon eating the coat. I dropped it to the floor.

A metal end table was built into the wall. It had thick aluminum legs that screwed in. I took an agony bath getting down on the floor, but got the leg off of the table. Using it for a crutch, I helped myself back up. Between panel crashes I could hear the punks on the stairs.

Hobbling out of the flat, I got into the one directly across. Seconds later, they were pounding down the hall. They ran right into the apartment with the fire. I left my hiding place, limping back to their door. I could see smoke curling out of the back part of the place, hear their curses as they tried to stamp it out.

I moved into the flat. Surprise was the only thing I had working for me, surprise and close quarters. Peeking around the door frame, I saw them in there, coughing through the smoke haze, trying to get all the fire out so they could get their damned instruments to lock onto something else.

Taking a quick breath, I pushed through the door, swinging my club, aiming for heads. I clipped one, full force, on the back of the neck. He dropped like a soufflé felled by a slammed door, dead, or something very much like it.

One of them had me around the neck and started tugging me to the ground. Coming up with my good leg, I kicked his buddy where it could ruin him. The punk had his frump out, and when he rolled away screaming, it went off just as I went down hard with the other one.

The frump thundered loudly in the closed-in room and blew off the legs of the punk who had his hands on my throat. His killing fingers were suddenly pleading for life, and his face twisted horribly into a deafening, soundless scream.

I pried myself loose from him, his half-body lying there, fingers twitching. The other one was rolling on the floor, moaning. His frump lay discarded on the floor. I hobbled to it and bent painfully to pick it up. I went to the punk and stuck the frump in his face.

"How many others?" I asked, breathing heavily, swaying with the tilting floor.

"F-Fuck you," he rasped through pain-clenched teeth.

I brought the barrel of the gun down hard on his nose, hearing the cartilage crack. "How many?"

Blood pumped thickly from his nose, running onto the metal floor. He got a hand up there. "Just Rosen," he managed.

To make sure he was out of it, I broke his hands before I left. It was me and China George. I moved slowly, painfully, down the rumbling hall, then started to navigate the steps. The banister creaked wildly in my grips, finally tearing off and nearly taking me with it. We had to get out of there.

In all the time I'd spent trying to figure why Malaca was setting me up for Rosen to kill, it had never crossed my mind that it was Rosen they were setting up. They couldn't touch him. They wanted me to do it for them. And here I was, frump in hand, ready to do just that. Rosen hadn't killed Jeff Roque either. That was something else I hadn't been able to figure. He had control over the man; there was no reason to ice him. Which left me right back where I had started as far as Ginny was concerned.

"Swain!"

I had gotten down to the second floor when I heard Rosen calling me from outside the building. I limped to an apartment and looked out the window space. He stood in the wobbling street, wearing his damned peacock suit, while the ceiling collapsed around him.

He had Porchy, had a gun on her.

"Let her go," I said. "This is between you and me."

He laughed that humorless laugh. "I want you out on this street right now, or the jane loses her head."

"Swain, don't . . ." she said, struggling.

He grabbed her tighter and jammed the frump in her neck.

"It's over," I called to him. "I know that you didn't kill Roque."

"Did you find that out while you were playing hide-the-stick with my old lady?"

"Don't you understand? That was a set-up, you dumb bastard. They're just trying to make a chump out of you."

"Pull the other one, Swain. It's got bells on it. Are you coming out here?"

This wasn't working at all. I couldn't get through to him. "Did you know that Loren isn't Malaca's daughter?"

"You're nuts!"

"I heard that you checked everybody. You must know that she doesn't have any past records."

A large chunk of ceiling fell right beside them, disintegrating to dust on impact. Rosen glared at it for a second, then looked back at me. "That doesn't mean anything."

I was wasting my breath. I was going to have to make him let Porchy go. "The only people who hide things are people with things to hide. She's not his daughter, she's his lover and she's shilling for him."

"No!"

And then it all became clear. The thing that even Loren Malaca was afraid to tell me about Rosen. No wonder he was so protective. "Nothing much for him to worry about either, is there?"

"Shut up!"

"Yeah, old Henry's got someone to feed his jane's bad habits, and doesn't even have to worry about you feeding her anything else."

"*Swain!*"

"Yeah!" I screamed. "China George Rosen, world's greatest lover boy. How long since you've been able to get it up, George?"

A horrible sound wrenched its way out of his throat, and he was out of control. Porchy slipped away as he frumped my

189

apartment. I ducked out of sight, and he turned the thing on Porchy as she ran. I poked my head out the window.

"George, no! Don't make . . ."

He fired, just missing her, aimed again.

"Damn!"

I took him out; I had to. I pumped him dead center and he popped like a balloon on a cigarette. The poor son of a bitch. He really thought he was a crook. In the world of real crooks, he was no more than a clown in motley, the village idiot. What did that make me? They wanted him dead and I did it for them. I was muscle to them, an insignificant pair of hands to shovel their shit.

Not anymore.

21

The security cruisers were still combing Freefall quad by quad, looking for us. They never expected us to return to Papa Bear, so that's exactly where we went. It made me feel, for the first time, that I was off the program.

I was rolling now and couldn't stop. Since I had fried Rosen for them, they were going to want me dead, too. I had one squeeze left in me, and figured it might as well be a big one.

Porchy feathered us down in the same commercial port that I had crashed into before. This time things went a lot more smoothly.

"What are you going to do?" she asked.

I pulled the "borrowed" frump out of my waistband and made sure it was loaded full. "I'm going to play accountant," I said, "and balance the books."

I unstrapped and stood up, the shooting pain in my bad leg making me grimace. "I've been doped and beaten and shot and lied to." I stuck the frump back into my belt. "That's a lot of accounts payable. You go back to the hospital and get Ginny ready to travel."

"But Irene said . . ."

"Irene's given up," I said. "Ginny will die someplace else just as well here. This whole damned city is poison. I don't want it to happen here."

Porchy nodded and turned back to her controls.

"Give me a couple of hours," I said, "then see if you can get Ginny away from here. Please don't argue on this."

"They'll stop me," she said without turning around.

"You've got to try. Don't ever let them take you without trying."

"Yes," she replied.

I wheeled the door and left without another word. We

had already said it all. I limped across the wide hangar as Porchy floated out behind me. Those damnable stacks of gold were still piled up on the hangar floor, and I started thinking again about sex and money.

I must have been a sight, hobbling along there. People working on the docks would stop what they were doing to stare at the beaten-down Earther. But that was okay with me. The last thing I wanted was to be accepted by this crowd of stringless puppets.

The long walk into the city proper was tough on my leg, but I simply keyed my mind on Henry Malaca, and it was the best pain-killer in the universe. I got through the clean booth and entered the city itself. Taking the first bicycle that I saw unattended, I peddled toward Management.

I had a stop to make first, though.

I had been to Garnet Roque's place twice now. Finding it the third time was no problem. I was just taking a chance that she would be in. Unable to exert enough leg pressure to put on the brakes, I crashed into the curb in front of Roque's building and sprawled painfully on the garbage-strewn sidewalk. There was a sparse street crowd, but they gathered around me quickly, staring, trying to place me in their dreams.

"Get the hell away from me," I growled at them as I got back on my feet.

They did.

I somehow got up the stairs, leaning heavily on the slatted metal banister. I reached Roque's number and went right in. Garnet Roque was in the kitchen, making a salad. She was wearing her burgundy business suit with a frilly white blouse. Her eyes narrowed when she saw me.

"Coming or going?" I asked her, not knowing whether it was dinner or breakfast.

"What do you want?" she asked with contempt.

"The sun and the moon and the stars," I answered, and walked into the bedroom. Getting down low, I flicked on my lighter and checked those scratches again.

I grunted up and moved back into the living room. The Roque woman was edging toward the front door space. I took out the frump and leveled it at her. "I wouldn't, if I were you."

"What do you want with me?" she asked, and this time the edge in her voice was fear.

192

"We're going to take a little Sunday drive together," I answered, and realized that they didn't have Sundays in this place. "But first, we have a couple of viddies to make. What's Malaca's home number?" I asked.

"I don't have anything like that," she replied, wide-eyed.

I sighed, and clicked back the hammer. "With what your old man did for a living, you'll have it. Now give."

She gave, even coordinated it herself.

"Will you tell them that you forced me to cooperate?" she asked.

"No," I responded. "I'm going to say that it was all your idea."

Her face crevassed like the Grand Canyon, and she backed up a pace, hand to her throat. "Please, I . . ."

The vis juiced into focus. The andy from Loren's cave was staring back out at me. "Malaca residence," it said.

"Henry Malaca," I smiled, and the screen blanked for a minute. When it came on again, the andy's face was still there.

"Mr. Malaca is at the office," it said.

"Fine," I answered cheerfully. "Thank you."

The Roque woman had backed up flush against a wall, mouth working silently. "Come here," I said. She just stood there, like maybe she had petrified and turned to stone. "Come here!" I said again, and moved over to her, dragging her across the floor by the wrist.

I stood her in front of the vis and backed away. "Call Security," I said. "Tell them there's some bad trouble over here, but don't mention me."

She just stood there, staring.

"Do it!"

I reached down and juiced the thing from her coffee table. She spoke the security coordinates, a number she knew all too well.

"This is Garnet Roque," she said when the desk man faded in. "Number 000472. We have trouble in my apartment, docking trouble," she added, probably thinking, as usual, of herself.

The face on the screen was fixed in a scowl. "What sort of trouble?"

"Please," she said, and her voice was quaking. "Hurry."

With that, I tore the juice box off the table and threw it up against the wall. "Come on."

"You can't take me anywhere," she said, and her voice was climbing a ladder.

I grabbed her arm with whatever force I had left in me. "You either walk those stairs or roll down them. Either way is fine with me, but we're going, right now."

She went with me, rubbing the deep bruises I had left on her arm. Putting my arm over her shoulder, I made her help me down the stairs. We reached ground level just as the Security heli-sled floated out of the smog cover. We ducked into the apartment closest to the front door. A couple was making love off in the bedroom. They ignored us, and we returned the courtesy.

The punk cops came busting through the opening and charged up the stairs. We walked out casually, climbed into the sled, and floated away with it. The heli was a common Earth design, so I had no trouble driving the damn thing. We hit the smog bank and headed for Malaca's log cabin.

Garnet Roque scooted as far down in the seat as she could, just in case someone could see her way up there. She stared myopically up at the smog and nursed her bruises.

"You've got old Beemer tied up in knots, don't you?" I asked.

"I don't know what you're talking about," she answered without looking at me.

"Not much you don't. You've got your claws so deep into him, it would take surgery to get them out."

She looked at me then. "He loves me," she said.

"Yeah. Like gasoline loves fire."

"It's none of your business."

"That's where you're wrong, lady. I'm up to my neck in it." I turned and looked hard at her. "I've got no use for people like you," I said. "You make yourself feel important by starting trouble, then you stand back to watch the sparks fly."

"You have no right to judge me."

"I'm not judging," I returned. "I'm hating."

I saw the vague outline of Malaca's offices in the smog clouds. Drifting up to the same pier that I had been to before, I anchored us and climbed out of the heli, dragging the Roque woman with me.

We got to the door, and the big eyes opened on the vis.
"Swain to see Henry Malaca," I said.

The eyes blinked. "I'm sorry, but Mr. Malaca is in conference and is not seeing anyone without an appointment."

"Fine," I answered, and took out the frump. Moving back a couple of steps, I pumped three of them into the big steel door. When the smoke cleared, the thing was twisted off its hinges.

Grabbing Roque's arm again, I jerked her through the twisted metal junk with me. As we entered, I could hear sirens blowing in the distance. Well, good. We could all have a party.

We walked through the dissemination offices. Everyone was hiding behind cams and viddies, peering out at us like lizards peeking out from under rocks.

We came to Malaca's reception room and went right in. Clark, dressed in a red- and black-checkered flannel shirt moved between us and Malaca's door.

"You can't go in there, Swain," he said. "Let's talk about it reasonably."

I moved right up to him. "Take a hike, junior, while you still can."

He looked at me. "Are you going to kill Henry?" he asked.

"I might."

His face cracked into a big, toothy grin. Stepping aside, he motioned me toward the door. "Well, then as the *new* Plant Manager of Freefall City, let me offer you the hospitality of the inner offices."

I shouldered past him and knobbed the door. It was locked. I frumped it, and we went inside.

"That's about far enough, boy," Malaca said. He stood behind his desk wearing a powder blue shirt and string tie. It was too tight on him and pooched out around the mother-of-pearl buttons. In his hands he held an ancient shotgun. " 'Less, of course, you want to get hurt."

I raised the frump. "Go ahead, Henry," I said. "I'm always prepared to get hurt. In my job, it's just good business. How about you?"

The look in his eyes told me that he wasn't prepared to get hurt. I guessed he wasn't a man's man after all.

"What do you want?"

"A few minutes of your time is all," I replied, smiling. "I'll put down my gun if you put down yours."

"You first," he said, still trying to negotiate.

"This isn't the board room, Henry," I replied. "Put down the gun."

He did it; I didn't.

He sat down heavily at his desk. "All right. What do you want?"

I led Garnet Roque to the far end of the room, so that she couldn't slip out on me. She was shaking visibly. Good.

"First thing," I said, "is to get all our cards out on the table."

Roque fell to her knees, crying into her hands. "Please, Mr. Malaca," she choked out between sobs. "I don't have anything to do with this. That man forced me, he . . ."

"Get up off your knees," I said. "You look like Joan of Arc."

There was a commotion in the outer offices. I brought the frump up to point at Malaca's shiny bald head. Morton Beemer and Nathan came piling through the burned-out door with what looked like the rest of Freefall Security behind them. I supposed it was a compliment to me.

"Un uh," I breathed, shaking my head. "Stop right there. You didn't say 'Mother may I.' "

Beemer caught sight of his girlfriend, still on her knees in the corner. "Garnet . . ."

"We'll have reunions later," I said, and cocked the frump. "Right now, I want all your weapons on the floor, isn't that right, Henry?"

"Do it," Malaca said in a near-whisper.

Beemer nodded to his men and a boxcar-load of zip guns hit the deck.

"Okay," I said. "Now that the gang's all here, we can get started. Mort. You and Nathan can come on in, but the rest of the clown academy graduating class has to wait on the pier."

Beemer glared at me with those dark eyes, but he did what I said. I didn't talk again until the punks left. I was pacing, watching all the stuffed animals that were watching me. "You all really had me going for a while," I said. "I'm used to straight cause and effect, you know?"

"Give it up, Swain," Beemer said.

I flared around at him. "Why don't *you* give it up, Mort?"

"I don't know . . ."

"You don't know, Henry doesn't know, nobody knows, do they?" I shook my head; I really felt awful. "I kept trying to make the connection between Jeff Roque and Ginny. Even after I knew that he wasn't killed at her place, I kept trying to tie them up together somehow. But beckon doesn't work that way, does it, Henry?"

Malaca looked at me with his businessman's eyes. "It's your party, boy. You do the talking."

"Okay, I will." I went and sat on the edge of Henry's desk, making sure the gun was out of his reach. "Somewhere back a long time ago, somebody figured out that if you could control all the elements of people's lives, you could make them do anything you wanted. I got a feeling that Lou knew about it, but didn't want to do anything with it. But you, Henry. You were more of a businessman than Lou was. You did something to him, messed up his head somehow, and got his job. Then you started jacking everybody around so you could cut costs and increase production. You even worked out getting rid of the old people on Sunset so you could save the money it costs to keep them alive. How am I doing so far?"

Malaca was still glaring at me, but some of the fire had gone out of his eyes. For such a talkative guy, he didn't have much to say.

"All that was fine and dandy until China George came along and started poking around in your business. I figure that he put the bite on you to keep the news away from the folks back home. That's when you started the wheels turning. You got Roque's old lady transferred to Security, knowing how she always gravitates toward the top dog wherever she is, and also knowing Mort's weakness for women. They were a natural."

"What?" Beemer said.

I shrugged. "Facts of life, Mort. Their computers know how many times a day you pass gas. They sure as hell know how to fix you up with women."

"What's he talking about?" Nathan asked Beemer.

"I'm talking about sex," I said. "I'm talking about infidelity. I'm talking about murder."

197

Garnet Roque was suddenly up on her feet, her face wide and frightened. "Mort?"

"Button it," he snapped.

I looked down at my leg. It was throbbing, badly in need of attention. "Where was I? Oh yes. We were talking about beckon. Anyway, I figure that you must have decided to get rid of everyone who was in on the extortion, Henry. You drove Manny Dugan completely insane. That was easy. Since you had no control over Rosen, you needed someone like me to get rid of him for you, and when I came along, you latched onto me. Mr. Rosen is gone, by the way. Loren . . . whatever her name is, is going to have to find a new supplier. She isn't your daughter, is she?"

Malaca cleared his throat, but didn't speak.

"Well, no matter. You set up a little love nest with Mort and Garnet, then tied the knot. It must have gone something like this: Some excuse was found to get you two back to the Roque place."

"They sent us there," Garnet said quietly, "to search for . . ."

"Would you button it!" Beemer yelled.

"Whatever it was, one thing led to another, as those things always do. Hell, everybody in the whole damned building was working their shift. You had the place to yourselves. The next step would have to be your husband, Garnet. I'm sure that if we checked the records, we'd find that he received an emergency call to return home that day. I figure he showed up, caught you two in the act, and caused a scene. That crease in his skull, Mort—just about the right size for the butt of your service popper."

"Cute story, Swain," Beemer said. "Absolutely unsubstantiated."

"Not necessarily," I returned. "I found aluminum shavings under Roque's fingernails, shavings that, I'd bet, match up to the scratch marks I found on his apartment floor, from where you dragged him out."

"That still doesn't prove anything."

"Would you stop it?" I said angrily. "You did it, Mort. You fought with the guy and you laid his skull open and you killed him. But none of that matters to me, don't you understand that?"

I walked right up to him, until we were nose to nose.

"But here's the sixty-four-dollar question, chum. When you killed him, you took the body over to Ginny Teal's satellite, so you could set it all up to look like she did it. Now, what the hell did you do to her to make her like she is now?"

Beemer flashed his electric hand in my face. I'd been hoping he'd do that. I side-stepped the punch and took him to the ground with a shot in the kidneys. Nathan took a step toward me, but I backed him off with the frump. Twisting Beemer's left arm around his back, I kneeled on top of him and jammed the frump in his neck.

"I mean it now, Mort. You tell me what you did to her, or we do a little remodeling here."

He just sneered at me. He didn't care whether I took him out or not. My eyes shot up to the Roque woman. "How about you, honey. You want me to fry your boyfriend?"

She looked at him, and her eyes were hard as diamonds. They call diamonds ice, and her eyes were that, too. "He did it," she said calmly. "He took me to the apartment and forced me to have sex with him. Then he killed Jeff and said he'd do the same to me if I didn't keep quiet. Go ahead and kill him. I'd enjoy it."

I felt Beemer sag beneath me, like a sail when the wind dies. He was seeing his girlfriend for the first time. "I can't talk lying on the ground," he said.

I let him get up. He stared that frightening stare at Garnet Roque, and I watched all the life drain out of him. "It happened just the way you said," he began.

Nathan came up and took his arm. "You don't have to . . ."

Beemer pulled away. "Yeah, I do. I killed him, like you said. And took his body out of the apartment. But I didn't take him to any satellite. I dumped him next to the spoke-tube platform, like maybe he had fallen off or something. When I got the call to go to your friend's place, I thought . . . I don't know . . . when you're in isolation, your mind does strange things with reality. It makes you so you don't ever believe what you're looking at. I just thought I was flashing back."

He looked to the ground. I believed him; I had to.

"But if you didn't do it, then who did?"

Malaca had gotten up from his desk and was reaching gingerly for the shotgun. I spun around and faced him. His reaching hand froze in mid-air. "You," I said.

199

"You watched it all," Beemer said, and his voice was shaking way down low. "You set it up, then watched it, then took it over when you didn't like the way I finished it."

"Now you watch your tone, Captain. Don't forget who you're talking to," Malaca said.

"I'm talking to an Earther," Beemer said, low and cold. The two men stared at each other for a long time until Beemer spoke again. "Just who do you think you are anyway? This city is our home, *our* home. Up until this very second, I'd believed that what we stood for here was good and decent. But you, you had to come up here and make us into something dirty. You had to play with our lives like they were so many circuit boards lined up in neat little rows. You make me sick."

"I'm still your manager," Malaca said, raising himself to his full height.

"You're nothing," Beemer spat. "I'd have done anything for you, but you had to make me into something cheap—something sneaky. You're like the slime we scrape out of the toilets."

"It's the system," Malaca said.

"Then damn the system," Beemer replied.

He started for the old man then, started for him with blood in his eyes. I quickly walked between them. "Not yet," I said, and looked at Malaca. "What did you do to Ginny?"

His eyes darted from one of us to the other. The power bravado was gone. All that was left was a frightened old man whose world was falling apart. "I took Roque's body, just like I was supposed to. It wasn't easy either. I'm a man's man, but it was rough, I'm here to tell you."

"What did you do to her!"

I had edged right up to him, trembling, fists clenching. "Nothing," he replied. "I took the body over there and left it, that's all."

"Then what happened?"

He was going to answer; I really think he was. But he never got that far. He stood there and his eyes got real big, and his mouth opened wide. Then he just shuddered all over, as if he had gotten a sudden chill. Then the blood came, incredible amounts of it, gushing out of his mouth to wash the top of his real wood desk.

He stood there for several seconds like some demonic, blood-spitting fountain. Then he just toppled over, crushing the white rooster that sat on his desk.

He was dead.

Dead as a doornail.

22

"His heart must have burst," Nathan said, as he bent over what was left of Henry Malaca. "Damnedest thing I ever saw."

I was looking at the body, but not really seeing it. I had not only run out of answers, but people to question. "Just like I was supposed to," Malaca had said. Did he mean he was trying to fulfill the beckon program, or that someone else was pulling his strings? I felt myself being elbowed out of the way.

"Is he really dead?" It was Clark, staring down, grinning at the body.

"Yeah," I answered. "He really is."

Clark straightened and gazed around officiously. "Well, that makes me your new Plant Manager," he said.

If he was expecting congratulations, he was disappointed.

"I'm leaving," Garnet Roque said. "It's almost sleep period."

She started for the door. Nathan blocked her path. "We'll be back in touch with you," he said, his words sounding like he had sharpened them on a whetstone.

She let her eyes flick quickly around the room, nodded once, and was gone.

Clark cleared his throat. "My first official act as your new Plant Manager is to order the arrest of this man." He was pointing at me.

"No," Beemer said, still looking at the body. "I don't think so. I think that your first official act is to get the hell out of here and leave us alone."

"You can't talk to me that way."

Beemer turned and shoved him, nearly knocking him down. "Get out of here before I make your head look like a sack full of doorknobs."

Clark must have found the logic irrefutable; he was gone in a second.

Beemer pulled off his electric fist and stuck his hand out to me. I shook it.

"Swain," he said. "I'm sorry. I was caught up in all of it, and I guess it all just got out of control. And all for that . . ." he stared through the open doorway at Garnet Roque's retreating back.

"You've got class, Mort," I said. "I underestimated you."

"I know that it's late notice, but is there anything we can do to help you with your friend?"

I frowned. "A lift back to the hospital is all for now," I returned. It was all over. The system had beaten me.

Beemer nodded. "Nathan," he said. "I guess you're in charge now."

Nathan's wrinkled face creased even deeper. "What do you mean?"

"You've got to arrest me for Roque's murder," Beemer said.

"But we could . . ."

"No, we couldn't. I'm not the smartest citizen in the wheel, and what smarts I did have got scrambled in Shimanagashi; but it seems to me that something has got to matter. Something has got to be real. Do you agree, Swain?"

I did.

So they took me back to Freefall General. The excitement that had built within me like a pressure cooker for the last few days was beginning to ooze away, leaving me tired, mentally and physically. I dozed for a minute in the cruiser, and dreamed of gold—big, bright piles of gold. Money. The stuff of survival in a civilized world—survival in the animal sense. People would do anything to get it, and feel perfectly justified in the process.

I woke up when we docked. Hobbling down to Psytronics, I found Porchy and Irene in with Ginny. Irene sat stoically at her desk, while Porchy dressed Ginny in street clothes there on the stasis. She kept watching the human shell that couldn't watch back. Her face was sad and reflective all at once, and I could only guess at the mental journey she was taking. I walked up to them.

203

When Porchy saw me, she moved to hug me. She clung to me fiercely for just a second before backing away. "Almost ready," she said.

"Yeah," I answered.

"She's really very beautiful, isn't she?"

"Yeah."

Irene joined us. She was looking exceptionally small and frail to me. "You're not going anywhere until we take care of that leg," she said.

She was right, of course. I let her lead me down to the blue emergency room while Porchy finished up. She got me up on a stainless steel table, the blue light in the room equalizing everyone. I realized then that she did that so the Freefallers would feel more at home with an Earther medic.

"Do you have a lot of pain?" she asked, her back to me as she fiddled with a table full of instruments.

"Always," I replied, and looked down at the leg, my blood glowing purple in the blue light.

She came over, a big shiny syringe in her hand. "This will take care of the pain while we work on the leg."

I shook my head. "No needles, Irene."

"Why not?"

"No needles."

She shrugged and returned to the table, coming back with a bowl of antiseptic solution to clean and sterilize the wound. I sat quietly while she cut away the leg of my one-piece.

"This is going to hurt," she said, and went to work.

She wasn't kidding; it hurt like a hundred-dollar speeding ticket.

She cleaned the wound, then removed some fragments from my leg. I was gashed pretty bad in about three places. She cleaned it again, then started stitching.

"You know," I said after a time. "There was something that I never could figure."

"Hmmm," she answered, preoccupied with my leg. "I think you'll live."

"Do you remember the day we took Roque out of the deep freeze to check on his body?"

"Sure."

"You dropped him. Dropped him and broke him."

"I guess that everybody makes mistakes."

204

"Now that's true. That's just real true, Irene."

She smiled quickly and finished up one of the gashes. "One down, two to go," she said.

"His arm came off," I said. "And it was strange, because I found that chip from Rosen's place in the hand on the broken-off arm. Why do you think he'd be holding something like that?"

"Could you move your leg just a little?" she asked, twisting me around a touch. "Good. What did you ask me?"

"Oh . . . Roque. Why would he be holding that chip?"

"I couldn't imagine."

"Neither could I. But I put it away in my mind. That's fine-tune stuff, you know? Something to think about in a quiet moment. Unfortunately, I haven't had too many of those. You haven't asked me how things went."

Her eyes played me for a second, then danced away. "Number two," she said, cutting off the stitch just above the knot.

"Your friend Henry Malaca's dead," I said.

She stopped what she was doing and stared at me. "How?"

"The coppers think his heart burst, but that doesn't sit right with me."

She smiled and returned to her work. "Are you qualified to give medical opinions?"

"Nope . . . ouch! Careful with that needle. But I don't think there's anything medical about it. I think it was murder, plain and simple." I watched her wipe some more purple blood off the last gash and begin sewing again. "Oh, it may have been his heart all right, and it may have burst, but I'm sure that it had some help."

"What kind of help?"

"A bomb, I think. A tiny, computerized bomb, maybe set into his pacemaker, ready to be set off by remote control any time."

"And who would do a thing like that?"

"Why, you would, of course."

She never even flinched. She just continued her work, tying the knot on the last stitch. "I think you should stay off that leg for a while."

I looked down; she had done a good job. Just the barest trickle of purple was seeping through the patch job.

"You've lost a lot of blood," she said. "Give yourself some time to build your strength back up."

"It's all too coincidental," I said, sitting up slowly on the table. "Your heart operation on Malaca, Lou's troubles, the tightening-up of Freefall security to outsiders . . . it all happened about the same time. And the only way that I figure the chip got into Roque's hand is that you must have put it there when you picked up the arm. You were leaving me a clue so I could get Rosen for you." It was all clearing up for me, like Kahlua and orange juice separating into fine bands of brown and orange. "And it never made sense to me that you just couldn't tell what was wrong with Ginny. That her condition kept worsening even though she was obviously removed from the source of the psychosis. You've been doing something to her, and you've continued to do it right under my nose. Are you even a real doctor?"

"Why would I do all these things, Swain?" she asked.

I thought about that for a minute, and the more I thought about it, the sicker I got. Sex and money. Money and sex. "All this," I said. "All this control. It's just all some kind of goddamned scam, isn't it?" I rubbed my grimy face with grimy palms. I pointed a finger at her. "It has to do with all that gold."

I glared at her and I may as well have been glaring at the Venus de Milo. "Sunset," I said. "Sunset is the key. Somehow, Sunset and all that gold tie together."

She smiled. "Gold is cheap up here," she said. "But it still takes money to get it. After Henry's heart operation, I had it. All we did was kick out all the old people on Sunset, then barter all the equipment on the satellite—plus the monthly expenditures for the place—to mining companies for gold. It's a good system for everybody, because the mining outfits give us the initial product before they mark it on their books. That way, we give them the necessities of life, so that they can pocket the cash from their Earth companies that are supposed to go to that stuff. Then I turn around and sell my gold to my Earth connections for cold, hard cash in a Swiss bank. It's good business."

"Until Rosen," I said.

She tightened her lips. Going to a blue sink, she rolled up her smock sleeves and started washing her hands. "You asked me if I was a real doctor," she replied over her shoulder. "I am. But I did some hard time quite a few years ago for performing unauthorized DNA experiments. After that, my career was finished. My life was over. Then some people came to me. They said that they could get me a position up here if I wanted it. They wanted someone respectable to buy cheap gold that they could resell on Earth. What else could I do?"

She shook her hands at the sink, then dried them on a fuzzy blue towel. "I worked for them for years, never complaining, even though my cut was practically nonexistent. Then slowly, very slowly, I began to develop a plan to get the operation out of their hands."

"Why?"

"I'm a highly motivated person," she answered, rolling down her sleeves and buttoning them. "Goal-oriented. I can't help myself. It was kind of like . . ."

"An experiment," I finished.

"Exactly. I got Henry under my thumb, then financed it all with Sunset. It was my game then. My 'friends' back on earth weren't exactly happy about the change in leadership, but they went along with it because they were still making money, even if it wasn't as much as they had made before. Things went along just fine for a number of years, and then Rosen came along. He started poking his nose into everything right from the first, and I think he may have been connected with my people. Kind of an enforcer. Smell out the operation, take it over, get rid of me. I had to deal with that threat."

"You've even got them building another Sunset."

"Twice the expenses, twice the profits."

She reached into the pocket of her lab smock and got out a small version of the curarine stinger.

"Where does Ginny fit into all of this?" I asked, as I stared down the barrel of her dart gun.

"Bait," she said. "I met her at a party here several weeks ago and checked her out, which is common practice with me when newcomers enter my city. In the course of the checking, I found out about you. You seemed the perfect random element to get rid of Rosen for me, without disturbing Henry's delicate relationship with corporate. So I took care of your jane to get you up here."

207

"But you kept trying to keep me away," I returned. "What about that punk who tried to kill me on Earth?"

"I get a lot of people from Shimanagashi and experiment with them on the limits of the beckon project—the absolute controlling of lives. I was so successful with that man I sent him to Earth with the thought of using him to assassinate my connections if they got out of hand. He was just a test for you, actually. I had to know before we got the ball rolling if you were any good or not. Plus it gave me a lot of information on you which we could compute to fit you into beckon."

It had all been a game, a sick game. I looked down at my hands and they were shaking. "What did you do to Ginny?"

"Endorphin overdoses," she answered matter-of-factly. "Massive overdoses. Hypnosis. Alpha conditioning. The program is my own invention, complex but foolproof. I created paranoia, then gave her a crash course in beckon. She had no choice but to retreat into her mind. I had to keep her that way to keep you on the hook while I fed you clues, giving you just enough to keep you moving. You just turned out to be a little smarter than I had hoped."

"Can she be saved?" I said very slowly, very deliberately.

Irene shook her blacksilver head. "Don't think so," she answered. "No. I gave her far too much. *I* could never reach her now, and it's my program."

My hands were clenched so tight they began to cramp. "What now?"

"The game's over, isn't it. Now, I take care of you and your little friend, then take the money and run. I've done well over the last five years. It's time to move on."

The door opened up and Porchy walked in. When she saw the stinger in Irene's hand, her eyes got wide like hard-boiled eggs with rosetta tattoos.

"You're just in time," Irene said. "We're all getting ready to take a little stroll down to Maintenance." She nodded back toward the door. "Let's go. And please don't be foolish. Killing you out here in the halls would just be a little extra inconvenience, nothing more."

We moved out the door. Ginny lay strapped down on a stretcher in the hall.

"Might as well bring her, too," Irene said. "We'll tidy up all at once."

Porchy began pushing the stretcher. "What's going on?" she asked.

"Irene's the bad guy," I returned.

I would have tried to put a move on her, but I was afraid that Porchy wouldn't know how to follow through and would end up dead because of my stupidity. So I thought instead.

I turned back to Irene. She was walking far enough behind us that I couldn't grab for the gun. "You know, Irene. You really screwed up."

"How so?"

People were passing us in the halls, but no one seemed to care that we were being held at gunpoint. "Well, see, the real reason you did all this was because Solipsism got hold of you, too. You implemented your fantasy of control . . . tried to live the dream. But you made a mistake. You got so far into the control that you underestimated the opposition, your 'friends' as you call them."

"You don't know what you're talking about."

"No?" I shook my head; I really did know. "Your people sound like a big operation. They'd never hire a cheap hood like Rosen to take care of their business. Oh, China George may have been trying to horn in, but it was his own idea, not part of some master plan. You had the right idea, but you were poking in the wrong cesspool."

She chuckled behind me. "And who, pray tell, is the right cesspool?"

"Loren Malaca," I said.

"You *are* crazy," she returned.

"Think so? I knew when you told me about her lack of past records. You didn't think anything about it when you told me. Looking back, that's the only piece of undirected information you ever gave me. You just didn't think about it. Well, let me tell you something about the people you're dealing with. They're not part of your Solipsism. They're rich, and ruthless. They have computers and offices and board meetings and all the fucking money in the fucking world. And they hate people who don't play ball."

I turned and looked at her face. She was grimacing.

"Crooks are great at stealing things," I said. "But not so good at putting them back. It's the nature of the beast.

209

Whoever Loren is, they took her past and replaced it with nothing."

"But she's been here for years," Irene said. Her voice was faltering just a touch.

We came to the Maintenance doors and pushed inside. Lou was in there, fiddling with some light panels on his workbench. He started to get up when we came in.

"Sit down, Lou," Irene called. "We won't get in your way."

"O-Okay, Doctor," he said, and ignored us.

"Let me ask you how many people you've got working for you back on Earth?" I said.

"You know there's just me."

"Right. And you really think that you've got a bank account just bursting with money?" I laughed. "You're an idiot, Irene. You did those people a great favor when you took over here, because now they get it all. You've been working for them for free these last years. And that makes Loren an overseer, not an enforcer."

Irene was shaking. She couldn't stand the break-up of her Solipsism. "That's not possible," she said.

"More than possible," came a voice from the doorway. It was Loren Malaca holding her own dart gun.

"I've been expecting you," I said.

Irene just looked at her, mouth slack. The hand holding the gun fell limp at her side. "Is what he said true?" she asked.

"You're not a team player, Irene," she said. "That's bad. Bad business. We've always had control of your money."

"But a Swiss bank?"

"We own the bank," Loren said. She didn't smile. She was all business. "We had a great deal with you from the first, but the last five years, you've even been paying for the merchandise. For us, that's meant pure profit, no expenses. Hell of a deal."

"Did your people kill Henry's wife?" I asked.

"Sure," she replied. "She needed to be out of the way to make room for me. We had enough on Henry to ruin him with Beltel, and you know how important his job was to him, so I moved in and threatened him when I had to, slept with him when I wanted to. I found out all about Irene's little heart-bomb and the rest of it, then simply kept an eye on things."

Her eyes were clear and hard, no sign remaining of the lush I had thought her to be.

"What about Rosen?" I asked.

Loren made a face. "Cheap little chisler. He just couldn't keep his hands out of things. He had no connection with us. I went with him to babysit. Found out he was impotent and tried to use that, but he didn't even have enough sense to be scared. I was about set to take care of him myself, when Irene brought you up here. So, I went along. It was a miscalculation."

Lou was watching us from the workbench, his face bunched in confusion.

"You're not really a junkie, are you?" I asked.

She smiled. "Oh, I shoot up, all right," she said, "but insulin, not horsey. I'm a diabetic."

"Then you don't drink, either."

"My routine was all part of the job," she said, and at that moment I knew I was looking at absolute business in the purest sense—cold and calculating and without morality of any kind.

"And now?"

"Irene was good enough to bring you down here to make your disposal easier. I'll take care of everyone, go back to Papa, and play grieving daughter long enough to collect any insurance and benefits, then head home. It's been a while. I could use a vacation."

Lou was off his bench, lumbering toward Loren. She saw him and flicked her head that way. I jumped at Irene, wrestling her for her stinger.

We fought. Loren turned back to us, gun coming up. I grabbed Irene's stinger hand, then pushed her as hard as I could to break it free. It came loose, as she went backwards, falling through the door that led down the long flight of steps.

I wheeled around. Lou had gotten in front of Loren as she fired. He had her in a bear hug for a second until his muscles tightened with the poison. He toppled like a huge tree and crashed into some trash cans, then to the floor, Loren Malaca still locked in his arms.

I walked over to them. Lou was dying quickly, his mouth curled into a slight smile—his only escape from beckon. Loren was struggling to free herself from his grasp, but Lou's frozen muscles held her fast.

"Swain," she said to me, "help me out!"

"Why?"

His arms were banded around her, making her gasp for breath. "Please. There's enough money in this for all of us if you help me."

I pointed down at Lou. "Is there enough in it for him? Or how about Ginny? Enough for her? Or Rosen? Or Henry? How about all those old folks from Sunset?"

"Swain . . ."

"Save your breath, sweetheart. You'll need it to explain things to the coppers."

I turned and looked for Porchy. She was standing at the top of the stairs, looking down into darkness. I joined her.

"I think she's still alive," she said.

I could hear Irene moaning softly, painfully, from the bottom of the steps. It was pitch dark down there, a backbreaker, Lou had called it. A cold, dark pit of loneliness.

"Let's get out of here," I said, and we left. Left Irene to die alone.

Shimanagashi.

23

We pushed Ginny's stretcher out into the hall. She was twitching violently within her straps. Moving to her, I hugged her distant form.

"I'm so sorry," I said, the thing I was so sick of hearing everyone else say.

Porchy came up beside me. "It's not your fault," she whispered.

I straightened. "Yes, it is," I answered. "Everything I touch, every . . . one, withers and dies. I'm like an avalanche. Once things get going, I can't stop until I've hit bottom, and everybody in the way gets crushed." I looked into her deep eyes. "Hell, I even used you."

"I wanted you to," she replied. "I still want you to."

"I don't deserve you."

"Maybe I'm slumming."

I looked at Ginny, then at Porchy.

I looked back at Ginny. Irene had said that there was nothing that anybody could do for her. Any *body*. I grabbed the edges of the stretcher and began pushing it wildly down the hall toward the docks. "Come on!" I yelled over my shoulder.

"Where?"

"Come on!"

We got the stretcher loaded into Porchy's cab, then tumbled out of there. As we thrusted, I got permission from Nathan to dock at Mama Bear. It was a long shot, but if anything could get down far enough and deep enough to reach Ginny's mind, it would be the Cortex.

The trip seemed to take forever, but we finally got down. Nathan and some of his black-suits were waiting for us at the rim. I explained the situation to him and he was more than happy to help me out.

213

The black-suits helped get me and the stretcher up the spoke, and soon we were floating in the hub. Porchy and I each took a side of the stretcher and we floated Ginny up to the sliding door.

"Are you going in too?" she asked.

I nodded. "If the Cortex can reach her, I think she may need a friendly mind to lend a hand."

"Good luck," she said. "And be careful."

"Keep my pretty ass intact?"

"Especially your pretty ass." She patted it. Her face was a mixture of sweet and sour all at once. She threw her arms around me, and we stayed like that for a time. Her face was pressed next to mine, and I could feel tears wetting my cheek.

"Take it easy," I said. "We're almost home free."

"I love you, Swain," she whispered into my ear.

I pulled her away from me. "I'm not going to Mongolia," I told her. "I'll be back in a few minutes."

She nodded, smiling, swiping at her eyes. "Then get to it," she said, and pushed off the glass to float back down.

Sliding open the gateway, I pushed Ginny's stretcher into the goo, then followed. I had that same expanding sensation as before, that same elevation of mind. The first merging experience was of shared pain.

"*Owwwwwwwwwwww. What has happened to us?*"

"I got hurt," my mind said.

"*This happens to humans?*"

"All the time."

"*Maybe we're glad not to be human. You've come back to me.*"

"Yes. For a while. I have another mission."

"*You want to use us again?*"

"Please, I need your help. There is no one else for me to turn to."

"*I cannot deny you, my love is too strong. Wait! What perversion is this? There is another within us.*"

"She is lost. She needs guidance. She needs your guidance."

"*OHHHHH. It is horrible within her. She is too ugly inside. Too far away.*"

"Please try to find her."

214

"I feel how important this is to you. It is also important to us, then."

"Find her, I beg you. Share your love with her."

"Yes."

Dark, twisted stairways, winding through narrow walls of rotted wood. Smells like sewer gas rising physically, dizziness, nausea climbing slowly up the throat . . .

"We can't STAND IT!"

"Try."

Dark, furry spiders, with sleek black legs, shining, almost blue. Creeping things that live in mold and feed off the decay of death. Death, death, grinning death with eyeless sockets and bleached white bones for hands.

"ARRRRRRR."

Festering sores, running pus. Black plague boils on feverish, bloated bodies. And the smell. The SMELL.

"Matt?"

A tiny voice, distant and alone. Calling.

"I'm here. I'm here!"

"I can't stand it."

"Please, so close."

"Matt?"

Rotted, musty logs hiding all the creatures of darkness, all the creatures that shun the light and the life. Horrible, segmented creatures that exist only to putrefy. Cannibal insects with working mandibles.

"Matt. I'm so afraid."

"I'm coming. Can you feel me?"

"Yes, oh yes. My love."

"He's mine. You can't have him."

"Where are we, Matt?"

"Nearly back."

"I've been so far away. So far. I'm tired."

"Just a little while longer."

"This creature would take you away from me."

"She is of a kind with me. We are snow melting together."

"But I want you."

"It can never be. You must realize that."

"Who's with us?"

"A friend, right?"

215

"We grieve with the truth of your words, but truth is our life."

"Friend?"

"Yes. You are right. A friend."

"Are you ready to come out with me?"

"It's been so long and so far. I'm afraid."

"Come out with me. I'll protect you."

"Always?"

"Yes."

"I hear crying, Matt. Who is crying?"

"Never mind. It will be all right."

I brought her out then. The coma was over and she was sleeping peacefully, her features soft and relaxed. And everything was back the way it was supposed to be. I looked down at the black-suits on the floor, looked for Porchy.

She was gone. She left, I guess, because the bubble had burst and our private world was gone forever. She was leaving behind a dream, a dream that we could never hope to recapture any more than we could make time stand still.

"I love you, Porchy," I whispered.

I never saw her again.

Never.

ABOUT THE AUTHOR

MIKE MCQUAY teaches a science fiction writing course at Oklahoma Central State University. A graduate of the University of Dallas, he has served with the military in Vietnam, Thailand, Japan, and the Philippines. McQuay is addicted to watching B movies on television late at night. His previous Bantam Book was Mathew Swain: Hot Time in Old Town.

FANTASY AND SCIENCE FICTION FAVORITES

Bantam brings you the recognized classics as well as the current favorites in fantasy and science fiction. Here you will find the beloved Conan books along with recent titles by the most respected authors in the genre.

☐	14428	LORD VALENTINE'S CASTLE	$2.95
		Robert Silverberg	
☐	01166	URSHURAK	$8.95
		Bros. Hildebrandt & Nichols	
☐	14844	NOVA Samuel R. Delany	$2.50
☐	13534	TRITON Samuel R. Dalany	$2.50
☐	14861	DHALGREN Samuel R. Delany	$3.95
☐	13134	JEM Frederick Pohl	$2.50
☐	13837	CONAN & THE SPIDER GOD #5	$2.25
		de Camp & Pratt	
☐	13831	CONAN THE REBEL #6	$2.25
		Paul Anderson	
☐	14532	HIGH COUCH OF SILISTRA	$2.50
		Janet Morris	
☐	13189	DRAGONDRUMS Anne McCaffrey	$2.25
☐	14127	DRAGONSINGER Anne McCaffrey	$2.50
☐	14204	DRAGONSONG Anne McCaffrey	$2.50
☐	14031	MAN PLUS Frederik Pohl	$2.25
☐	11736	FATA MORGANA William Kotzwinkle	$2.95
☐	14846	THE GOLDEN SWORD Janet Morris	$2.50
☐	20592-7	TIME STORM Gordon R. Dickson	$2.95
☐	13996	THE PLANET OF TEARS Trish Reinius	$1.95

Buy them at your local bookstore or use this handy coupon for ordering: